People of the Storm

People of the Storm

HRB Collotzi

People of the Storm
Text copyright © 2022 HRB Collotzi
All rights reserved.

Published March 2022
Cover designed by Getcovers
Copyright © 2022 HRB Collotzi
All rights reserved.

ISBN: 978-1-962628-00-6
Library of Congress Control Number: 2019909507
Published by HRB Collotzi
Rosemount, Minnesota

www.peopleofthestorm.com

For Jason

Thank you for inspiring me, encouraging me and never
giving up on me!

People of the Storm

HRB Collotzi

Chapter One

"Get outside!" they said. "Have some fun!" they said. I wouldn't agree until they tried, "Maybe it'll be relaxing?" Aunt Daisy and my cousin frequently told me they hated seeing me sit at home by myself day after day. Not even the warm days, beaches and palm trees of Florida could coax me outside more often than absolutely necessary. I eventually caved to go golfing with my cousin Missy and a small group of her friends. Hopefully, it might be something calming that I wouldn't have to think too much about. Stupid. The last thing I remember was teeing off with storm clouds overhead. I had been raised knowing the game should have ended then, but no one listened to the depressed girl. They probably thought I just wanted to go home and hibernate…again. Maybe after this, they'll leave me alone.

When my brain started up again, a brilliant white light swallowed me, assaulting me from every angle until it seeped into my soul. I tried to close my eyes against its intensity, but it didn't work as the light burrowed deeper into my mind. There was no escape. Finally, when the burning threatened to make me burst into flames, it began to subside.

As it trickled away, I heard slow, steady beeping. Strange, given what I'd just been through, but the sound irritated my senses, and I wished it would just stop. A clicking followed by a rush of air, like someone blowing in a tube, echoed in the background. Feet shuffled on a hard floor and I heard muffled voices I didn't recognize.

The bright light dimmed then gradually disappeared. It was then I realized my eyes were closed. At least I had a body again. I was alive! As if I needed confirmation, a stabbing pain ripped through my head, feeling like someone had taken a baseball bat to my skull.

I became aware of something strange stuck to my forehead from a distinctly separate pinch at the source of my pain. I tried to move my hand to feel whatever it was, but I couldn't lift my arm. I tried the other hand, but it wouldn't move either. Then the thing on my forehead moved. What a strange sensation! What was that? Wait...as I thought of lifting my hands again it moved toward my hands as if trying to help me. I could control it! How was it doing that? What *was* it? What was happening?!!

Panicked, I could feel my heart pounding and every muscle in my body tensing. I struggled to move my hands and cracked open my eyes ever so slightly. A bright light stung my vision again. Little by little, I pried my lashes apart against the blinding light. At least this light didn't sink into my mind, and my eyes gradually adjusted. It was a simple florescent light, like the ones in office buildings. It couldn't possibly be the light that made my insides feel like they were boiling.

The thing on my forehead moved outward again, almost like it was shielding my eyes because my hands couldn't at the moment. Then the thing on my forehead bumped into something, but the obstacle didn't slow it down…whatever "it" was. Whatever they both were! That's when I heard it. Just a voice, but it reminded me of an echo, like someone talking in a tunnel.

Holy crap, she's waking up already… 96 over 48. Low, but it should get better. It was a woman's voice, but I didn't recognize the sound of it. *I'll let the doctor know in a few minutes,* the voice continued. *He'll release her. I'll go tell the family first…. She's going to need a new dressing on that burn before she goes… What did I do with my pen? Oh yeah, Doctor What's-His-Face took it…*

The voice kept going; a constant stream of thoughts, one leading to the next. I heard a few other sounds—laughing, crying, yelling and a few unfamiliar pictures flashed in my mind in conjunction with the strange voice. The extra sights and sounds grew overwhelming, so, since I could control it, I tugged the thing on my forehead away from whatever obstacle had slowed it down. Gratefully, the confusing flood of information ceased.

I could open my eyes more as they got accustomed to the irritating, flickering light. I tried to find my voice.

"Where am I?" I croaked, but it sounded like, "wuummaahhh." I licked my lips trying to wet my mouth, but my tongue felt like cotton. "What are you talking about? What happened?" I said, a little louder.

The voice came back, more distinct, "It's okay, honey. You were struck by lightning, but you're going to be fine. You're lucky to be alive."

"What? What are you talking about?" I said, confusion rapidly shifting to panic. What had happened? Was she telling the truth? How could this happen? I thought you couldn't live through being struck by lightning! Again, I tried to reach out with my hands trying to grab at… what? Reality? Something that made a little more sense? But I could only wiggle my shoulders.

"What's on my forehead?" I asked, not sure if I wanted to hear the answer.

"It's just a burn," the woman said. She leaned over me a moment and gently touched around the area where I sensed the little thing moving. But she never touched it. "I gave you some pain meds, so it shouldn't hurt much. If it bothers you, just let me know and I'll get you something else."

Great, I thought, drugs. That'll help. Hopefully this was all just some opioid-induced hallucination.

I noticed my surroundings for the first time as I blinked to clear my vision. Sure enough, I was stretched out on a hospital bed in a tiny room with two doors on opposite sides. My normal clothes had been replaced with a scratchy hospital gown. Where were my clothes? Noisy machines crowded the small space around the bed. That explained the beeping, but the swooshing noise had stopped. The smell of industrial strength cleaners and starch on the crisp sheets overpowered everything except the noise. This place reeked of cleanliness. A blood pressure cuff squeezed my left arm, an oversized, plastic, white clothespin pinched my finger and an IV tube protruded from my right hand. Good thing needles don't bother me.

The thing on my forehead moved again, reaching out like I had tried to with my hands. It could move more than my hands because my arms had blankets, wires and tubes draped all over them. That, added to the fact that every inch of my body ached, made it hard for me to move at all. Like I'd been hit by a truck. No, worse than that. Like the truck had hit me, run over me, backed up over me and run over me again. I couldn't even move a blanket.

As I tried to disentangle myself, the nurse asked me a few weird questions without looking at me. I wanted to scream, "Who cares if I know who the president is, just tell me what's going on!" but I didn't.

As my thoughts raced, the thing moved, but I knew I had moved it on purpose. I had willed it to move. Maybe I could get her to shut up by waving it in front of her face. I tried, but nothing appeared in front of her. I waved it in front of my own face. Nothing. Okay, so I could feel it, move it, but not see it, though I always knew where it was. I had an invisible new appendage. Super weird. Maybe I should go back to sleep until somebody woke me up for real. Maybe I should say something about it? Sure, and get admitted to the psych-ward too? No thanks.

The nurse, a maternal, kind woman whose name badge read, "Denise" looked over at me. "Don't worry, dear. I'll go get your aunt. She's waiting just outside." She bustled out the door.

Daisy, yes, I could remember Aunt Daisy, Crazy Daisy, me and my mom had called her, and my cousin Missy. I could remember who I was too—Ella Hemlock, sixteen years old. A student at the local high school here in Jacksonville, Florida. Practically an orphan. I could do without remembering that.

Aunt Daisy had insisted I go out with my cousin Missy and her friends. This meant I didn't have any brain damage, right? Or at least no amnesia. I took a few calming breaths relaxing back on the pillows. I'd worry about the thing on my forehead later. The nurse certainly seemed to think I was fine. It must be some new-fangled medical machinery. Sure.

Daisy was great. A little eccentric, a little odd, but a perfect aunt because of it. After my mom died, two years ago, she took me in. She'd been divorced a couple times and Missy was from one of the earlier marriages. Even though Daisy was younger than my mom, she looked much older. Maybe that's why she never visited us. Her short brown hair only just turning gray, but she acted like a teenager sometimes. Daisy wasn't strict. She trusted us to come home at a decent time and get our homework done. Living with Daisy and Missy was what I imagine living at a sorority house must be like.

While waiting to see my aunt, I examined the thing on my forehead. It seemed like it was attached on the left side of my forehead closer to my hairline than I thought. It snaked out in a long cord at a single thought. I wondered how far it could go. It seemed to have no limit. When I wasn't doing anything with it, it coiled back up a little bigger than a quarter. My head hurt the most right at the point where it nestled on my head. I wish I had a mirror. My strength began to return so I continued trying to get my arms out of the blankets.

Just as I knocked the blanket off to uncover the myriad of wires underneath, Daisy and Missy came through one of the doors. "Ella!" Missy burst out as she swept into the room. "Oh, my goodness, sweetie. I'm so sorry I made you go!"

"Don't worry about it," I lied to her, "I'm fine." Daisy sat in the small chair next to my bed, throwing me the "poor baby" look again. She often gave me that look when I turned down another chance to venture out with Missy and her friends. Sometimes I wanted to smack that bottom lip of hers.

Missy perched on the end of my bed looking like she was afraid to touch any part of me.

The nurse came in behind them to give everyone the run down. My vitals were fine. I was stable enough to go home if I wanted. Daisy had already filled in all the pertinent insurance information.

"You'll have to take it easy for a few days," the nurse said. She turned to Daisy and Missy. "You'll be able to keep someone with her for at least 24 hours?"

"Sure," Daisy nodded, then threw a look at Missy. "I have to work, but Missy can stay home with her tomorrow, right?"

Missy slightly paled. She hated missing school and not because she was a straight-A student. She hated going more than a few hours at a time without seeing her friends or hanging out with whomever her current boyfriend was at the time. I guess she would have to settle with texting.

I thought about what my loving cousin might really think of being forced to stay home with me. I wanted to reach out and rub her shoulder and tell her that it was okay if she didn't want to stay home with me. I wanted to tell them both that I would be fine without them and they shouldn't stop their lives for me. Almost instantly the little, invisible thing on my forehead stretched out like it had been waiting for the chance. But instead of gently touching her shoulder like I tried, the little appendage flopped like a half-asleep limb and sunk into her head instead.

Oh my gosh! I heard Missy exclaim in that weird echo voice, but her lips didn't move. *I'm sorry I made her go golfing already. Do I have to be on nurse duty for it? This isn't fair!*

A little shocked at her anger, I yanked back on the little serpentine appendage. Did I really just hear that? It sounded like Missy's voice. It sounded like something she might think or say. But how in the world did I hear it? Did I just read Missy's mind? My mind churned with confusion, shock and maybe, just maybe a little excitement, as the nurse cleared away the tubes and wires so I could move. I had to be imagining this. This had to be some kind of dream.

"I'll get the discharge papers," the nurse said, addressing Daisy, "But I'll need a parent to sign them."

"I'm her guardian," Daisy said, the same sad expression entered her eyes as I had seen so many times. "Both Ella's parents are gone."

It's true. My dad disappeared when I was little. Neither Daisy nor I knew much about him. My mom had worked at a water treatment plant in Pennsylvania where we had lived. She had worked there all my life, day by day making her way up the ranks over twenty some-odd years. So much perseverance literally washed away when she fell into a large vat of water to be treated. There wasn't even enough of her left to cremate. After that, I came to live with Daisy and Missy, my only family left.

"Oh, I'm sorry," Nurse Denise said as she stood to leave. "I'll get the doctor to talk with you and come back to take out the I.V. I'll need to um…" her voice trailed off as she tapped a few things into the tablet in her hand. "To uh…" she stuttered again distracted.

"Change the dressing on my burn?" I said, hoping what I had heard earlier was wrong.

"Yes," she nodded absentmindedly, then swiveled toward the door.

After she left, I turned to Missy. I kept the thing tightly coiled on my forehead. "So, what happened, anyway?" I asked.

"Oh, my goodness," Missy exclaimed, "it was so scary!"

Animated, she proceeded to tell us the whole story. She recalled the smell of burnt hair and burnt meat. She told me how everyone in the group had been far enough away that they only got a little shock. She said it felt like an earthquake and sounded like standing in a thundercloud. She told me how her amazing boyfriend had tried to take my pulse, but everyone was afraid to do anything until the ambulance arrived. Then she launched into exactly what the "gorgeous EMTs" looked like.

"Hailey got sick at the sight of you unconscious and burned," Missy said. "I guess no medical field for that little daffodil."

"Both of you just promise me you will never golf with a single cloud in the sky *ever again*," Daisy ordered.

I nodded. How about, just *never* again? Missy continued with her narrative as I rested against the pillows. She told me my doctor was pretty good looking but married. Leave it to Missy to be checking out the men. Before she finished her narrative, the doctor came in, but that's not saying much because Missy never completely finishes anything.

"Miss Hemlock," Doctor No-Name-Badge addressed me. "All your tests are normal. Unless there are any effects you need to tell me about, you should be able to go home." He looked at me, hesitating for a moment. "The only problem I can foresee is the fact that you have no exit wound from the strike. I'm not positive what it might mean for you in the future, but if you have any problems, call the hospital and talk to a nurse. The nurse will bring in your discharge papers."

I noticed he didn't say to call him or talk to a doctor. Nice. He scooted out of the small room before I had time to ask anything. Daisy muttered something about him being unhelpful. Giving him the benefit of the doubt,

I assumed he had more urgent patients to attend to. An idea flashed in my mind, but I didn't want to think about it. My little forehead problem stayed there.

Once he left, the nurse came in. She had a pile of gauze and rolls of tape and a plastic bag. She set everything down on the bedside table then set to work. She gently peeled away tape, pulling strands of hair with it. When she moved to place the new gauze over the wound, I stopped her.

"Wait," I said, "can you get me a mirror so I can see it?"

"I have one," Missy offered. Of course Missy had a mirror. She slipped me the small round compact.

Popping it open, I angled it in front of my forehead. The burn spot was exactly where I thought, the left side of my forehead at the top, next to where my hairline normally was. I don't know what I expected, but it looked just like an ordinary wound, if any wound is ordinary, with some black, peeling skin around the edges. My hair was fried and melted in a large radius from the burn. There was nothing to indicate I had an appendage sprouting from it though. The burn had an interesting shape to it at least. It looked kind of like the branch of a fern. The burn marks stretched across my forehead, into my hair, above my left ear and even trickled onto my cheek. Maybe the thing I'd felt was a trick of the nerves or something. Like a phantom limb? Yeah, sure. We'll go with that.

After I put the mirror down, Denise covered the worst of the wound, which was centered above my eye, with a slimy ointment and new gauze, securing it all with new tape. In the background I could hear her explaining to Daisy how to take care of the burn, but my mind wandered. I wondered when someone would explain what was really going on here. When the nurse took a breath, I kept my eyes on the blanket in front of me and asked, "How long will it take to heal?"

"It shouldn't hurt or bother you after a few days."

"Yeah, but how long until it goes away?" I asked again, trying to be more specific. When I realized the nurse wasn't answering me, I looked over at her to see her avoiding my gaze.

"Well dear," she said. "It might take a long time. It won't be noticeable way up there. If you hang your hair just right no one will see it at all."

I knew she was trying to make me feel better, but I didn't care what I looked like. I gave up caring about it a long time ago, which drove Missy nuts. No, I wanted to know how soon this thing on my head would go away. But I couldn't ask them about it. That would sound crazy. Then I wouldn't go home at all. Locked up in the cuckoo unit for a lightning strike? No, thanks. I'd just wait for it to heal and see what happened. Who knew how long this intriguing little side-effect would last?

Chapter TWO

Daisy drove us home that evening with her mouth going as fast as her lead foot would move her little Camry. She talked so much she didn't see a man stepping off the curb as she spun around the corner into our apartment complex. I don't know how she missed him; he almost seemed to be reaching for the car. I caught a glance of his face and he didn't look afraid, so I figured he would be fine. Ironic that I might have survived a lightning strike only to end up as roadkill.

The next day was Monday. As I woke, my hand drifted immediately to my forehead. I gingerly touched the gauze taped there. The invisible appendage wriggled and seemed to wake as well. Still there. Interesting.

I should have had school, but Daisy agreed I should stay home. Didn't have to tell me twice. I had taken a couple of pain killers the night before, but I woke up feeling fine. I assured both Daisy and Missy I could manage without them. Daisy left for work, but she insisted Missy stay with me a little longer. I finally convinced Missy it would be fine for her to go to school. I knew she would love to be the center of attention and tell everyone who would listen the entire saga. She was politely hesitant, but eventually jumped in the shower.

What I needed was some time alone to figure out this new appendage. So, with a mug of scalding tea, I plopped on the sofa. Now what?

Before I could come up with a test or a plan of any sort, I was saved the trouble with a knock at the door.

Where Missy would have thrown the door wide to see who had "come to call," I tried to be a little more cautious. Peeking through the peephole, I saw a tall younger man in a suit accompanied by an older woman. The man was good looking, couldn't be more than nineteen or twenty, if anything, with a round face and dark, almost black, hair. He wore a simple suit off the rack, but he wore it well over obvious broad shoulders. I knew if Missy saw him, she would pounce.

The woman, who looked to be in her early 50's, had blonde hair piled in a loose bun on her head. She had a bag like an old-fashioned doctor's bag. I figured there was no way the doc at the hospital could be concerned enough about me to send a house call.

I had no idea who they were, so my first impulse was to pretend I wasn't home. Then I started to wonder if my new appendage could go through objects. Like, say…a door. After all, how would I try this thing out today if I was stuck at home with no one around? I uncoiled the little thing and pushed it against the door. The door put up more resistance than Missy's head had, but the thing still easily pushed through.

Seeing as a larger, stronger man is more of a threat, I touched his head first. I could hear as he ran over similar confrontations he had had with other people in my same situation. I saw him sitting down with several different people. He wondered how opposed I would be to this new information. Would I question him? Believe him? Above all, if I had any, what were my new powers?

POWERS?! Of course! I snatched my mind back through the door. So that's what this was! Not only were these people safe, but they had answers! I fumbled with the lock before I ripped open the door.

I'm not sure what my face looked like, but the pair seemed a little taken aback when I greeted them wide-eyed.

"Miss Hemlock?" the man spoke first. When I nodded, he continued. "My name is William McCurdy. This is my associate Gretchen Callister. We're here to talk to you about—"

"Yes, come in." I interrupted him. I moved away from the entry way to let them into our small living room.

As they crossed the threshold, Missy came into the room as well. She held a small mirror up in front of her face. Without looking at me, she asked, "Did I hear the door?"

"Yeah…" I started to answer her, but her breathing had already stopped at the sight of the tantalizing man I had just invited in.

She snapped her compact shut, a wide grin spreading over her face. With the look of a child who just got delivered an early Christmas present she held out her hand to the gentleman. "Hello," she said with the ease of a practiced artist. "I'm Missy." Leave it to Missy to completely ignore the older woman standing next to him.

"Missy," I tried to get her attention in vain, "this is…" I struggled to remember their names.

"William McCurdy," he helped me, while offering his hand to Missy. Glancing back to me, he added, "You can call me Liam. And this is my associate, Gretchen Callister." He indicated Gretchen standing next to him, who held out her hand to Missy.

After shaking Liam's hand, Missy absent mindedly stuck her hand out in Gretchen's general direction. But Missy didn't even glimpse at Gretchen, hence missing her minute eye roll. "How do you do?" Missy muttered, breathless. I wondered how long a person could go without blinking.

After a short awkward silence and Gretchen straining to keep a straight face, Liam said, "We were just here to visit Miss Hemlock, actually." He turned to look at me with anticipation.

"Yes," I said. "Have a seat." I indicated our old, overused couch.

As they stepped past Missy, she seemed to come to a decision. "Um, you know, Ella," she tore her eyes from Liam in order to try to look at me intently. "I've been thinking." Never a good thing. "I should probably stay home with you today. That nurse yesterday at the hospital did say I should keep an eye on you." The look of supplication made her intentions so apparent I didn't need an extra appendage to know what she wanted.

However, I did need to know what the other two thought, so I tried dipping back into Liam's head.

Not good. How can we get rid of her? She probably won't trust us enough to leave Ella alone with us. Maybe Gretchen will invite Ella to her "office" so we can talk to her alone later. Maybe I can just ask her out to coffee or something. For once, I might not mind taking that route. Whatever we do, we need to keep an eye on her since Jack is out there somewhere.

When he thought about asking me out, an idea struck me. "Oh, it's all right, Missy." I said, putting on a big smile. "I'm fine. Someone from the hospital told me to expect a visit today. I feel pretty good, so it won't take long." I lied, then stepped a little closer to her. "Besides, shouldn't you let your boyfriend know we're okay?"

She narrowed her eyes ever so slightly.

I watched rather than listened as the gears in her mind turned at an alarming rate. She deliberated between someone she had been with for a few weeks and someone she had just met. Granted, William McCurdy towered over Thomas in the looks and maturity departments, but she already had Thomas. With a brief grimace, she caved.

"You sure you'll be okay?" she asked. She had to make sure not to ruin her chances with Liam.

"I'm positive," I said. "Thanks anyway."

Once Missy had checked the time, she had to rush out the door. I sat down facing Gretchen and Liam. After the door shut behind her, I said, "Sorry about her," directing the apology at both of them. "She's a little…friendly." That was the nicest way I could think to put it.

"Don't worry," Gretchen grinned, "I'm used to it."

Liam squirmed uncomfortably for a moment then said, "We really just needed to talk with you."

The dirt-covered peephole hadn't done Liam justice. He had a round face, but with chiseled features. Heavy dark eyebrows threw shadows over his eyes but served to give him a more mysterious look. His eyes were a dark green one might mistake as foreboding, but expressed immeasurable kindness when combined with his smile. I was suddenly hyper-aware that I hadn't showered since yesterday morning. My hair probably looked like brown seaweed.

The pair seemed out of place in our apartment, like I was talking to a couple of cops. They were sophisticated and confident. Our home was haphazard and eclectic. However, neither of them looked like it bothered them. They acted as if they were used to these kinds of surroundings.

Powers, he had been thinking. Remembering the word, I began to probe their minds to find all the answers I could. Then maybe I wouldn't have to talk to them for very long.

At first, I just lingered, listening to Liam's forethoughts. He thought I was pretty, but very young. He also wondered about how I would take the information they were about to throw at me, but he wasn't focusing on the details. He liked how I got Missy out of the apartment and viewed me as a 'quick thinker'. I almost laughed at that thought, but I got distracted when I realized my little powers could dive deeper to look at things he wasn't even thinking about at the moment.

His mind (holy crap, was I seriously rifling through someone else's mind? Guess so.) was organized like a filing system with varying degrees of light sporadically dispersed throughout. Some images shone so bright I could hardly make them out. Others were dark, but I could still see them. I dove so deeply into his mind that I wandered into his subconscious. It was kind of creepy. So many different strange emotions intermingled to misconstrue memories. I could discern the basic meaning of what happened in them, but obviously his mind didn't see these thoughts the same way. It would be fascinating to study it in a psychological situation, but for now I didn't like how these emotions clawed at me in the darkness. As I pulled out, the emotions tried to follow me, but released as I left the recesses of his subconscious. It was a place I would probably stay away from for the most part.

Being surrounded by his normal memories again, I soon became overwhelmed with all the information. Certain things popped out to me because they repeated so many times. "People of the Storm", "Storm People" and "People of the Shadow", "Shadow" were prominent titles in most of his thoughts. Different names, faces and powers were there too, attached to the titles. I couldn't make heads or tails of any of it and got frustrated by the overload. I pulled back out to the front of his mind to eavesdrop while he began his spiel again.

"We thought we should talk with you because we're very much aware of what you might be going through right now." *We're People of the Storm,* he thought. *We all know how confusing everything is for you right now.* "Gretchen and I have both been struck by lightning. We know you might be having some interesting side effects." He recalled to his mind the moment he got struck. I could feel the horror that overcame him when he learned of his powers. He could bend light making anything he wanted invisible. I saw him in an open field, covered in dirt trying to make an odd farming tool disappear.

I snapped out of his mind when I noticed a woman he had strong feelings for. I realized I shouldn't be intruding. I caught myself staring at him, although I don't think it was as long as it seemed to me. I must have looked like a crazy person to him nonetheless. He looked at me cautiously then glanced at Gretchen who returned his glance. Could they read minds too? Did all People of the Storm do this? Maybe they were reading my mind right now!

Gretchen reached out, putting a calm hand on top of mine. She gave me a big sister-type smile saying, "It's okay, Ella. We're here to help." She left her hand there for just a second, seeming to focus on something far away. Then, moving her hand away, her warm smile lifted again. As she leaned back, she gave Liam a casual nod. Suspicions blossomed in my mind of the seemingly harmless woman, so I whipped my mind's attention to her.

Her mind could've been in Greek, Chinese or Dutch. I would've been just as lost. Everything centered around the human body. I mean, like, INSIDE the body. She had tons of diagrams of the muscles, bones, blood, brain, tendons, you name it. Pieces of bodies swirled around like a horror movie. Charts churned in her mind of all the major organs. Everything connected with cords of energy. Her mind was a veritable web of information on the human body. Unfortunately, I was the fly. I couldn't make sense of any of it, so I scrambled back out. In the few memories I could decipher, I caught the name *The People of the Storm* a lot.

I mustered my courage blurting out, "Who are the 'People of the Storm'?"

Liam and Gretchen again shared a glance, but this time wide-eyed. Liam leaned toward me asking gently, "How do you know that name?"

I hesitated. I knew they wouldn't be shocked. I knew I wasn't in any danger from them, but I hadn't said anything about this ability or appendage out loud yet. It would be like admitting something was wrong with me. I pulled myself together long enough to answer. "I heard it in your mind."

"Oh," he said. He sighed with relief then started to laugh. Gretchen matched him and they sat chuckling for a second, thinking back on my strange behavior. I even relaxed a little at the sound of it. "A mind-reader?" he commented.

"We haven't had one of those in quite a few centuries," Gretchen put in.

The chuckling subsided, and Liam leaned back on the sofa. "So, how much have you been able to learn?" he asked.

I followed his lead relaxing into my chair. "Not much." I answered. "I know you both have powers, but I'm not sure what Gretchen's are. I heard the name Storm People a lot, but I'm still not sure who or what they are."

Liam pointed to his head, "Would you like to do this yourself," he asked, "or should I just tell you everything out right? Apparently, you're going to believe us either way."

"I'd rather you tell me," I answered, "It's still a little confusing." Just saying it out loud helped me feel a lot better. I already realized there's a lot in others' minds that I didn't want to know. "Don't worry," I reassured them. "I won't enter your minds again unless you want me to. I can't figure out Gretchen's mind anyways."

"Ha!" Gretchen burst out. "You're not the only one. It's still confusing for me. And I've been doing this a very long time!"

Liam grinned at me. "Well, to start, Gretchen is able to understand the human body on a very detailed level. That's her power. She can communicate with a body to find out anything that might be wrong with it. She can also help it heal at an accelerated rate. Do you mind if she works with you while I explain everything else?"

"Of course not," I answered. "What do I need to do?" I sat up, hoping I didn't have to get undressed or anything. Maybe Liam could make me invisible while I did it, but it would still make me uncomfortable.

"Nothing at all," Gretchen responded, alleviating my fears. "All I have to do is be in contact with your skin. I'll just put my hand on yours again. That's what I did last time. I just gave your body a quick check to make sure everything was okay for the moment. But this time I'll dive a little deeper to see if there are any viruses or infections your body is fighting. I'll be zoned out for a little bit." She placed her hand on mine again. Her eyes immediately glazed over, trance-like.

While she sat there, I looked back at Liam wondering where to start. A wave of bashfulness washed over me as I suddenly felt like we were alone together.

But my shyness was replaced with all my questions bubbling to the surface. I knew it was safe to ask, but I didn't know where to start. Immediately, confusion clouded all thought. The tears didn't quite spill over, but my vision blurred as my eyes welled. I decided in an instant to keep it simple. I almost whispered, "What's happened to me?" Until this moment I had been harboring a hope that this would all end eventually. The visit from this pair revealed the situation to be more permanent than I realized.

I swallowed hard then forced a few slow breaths. Answers would be coming. He regarded me kindly, but through narrowed eyes. "We've been called many things over the years. Demons, sorcerers, monsters, mutants, aliens…well," he shrugged, "Roswell *was* sort of my fault—"

"—Roswell?—"

"But," he continued, ignoring my question, "it's a lot more complex than anyone knows. "You see, humans only use a small percentage of their brains. What percentage is under constant debate, but the fact remains they don't use anywhere near all of it. Even some other parts of their bodies are never used or seem to have no purpose. Have you ever wondered why? What could people do with that extra part of their brains they never use? The answer lies within us. Within you. That's what has happened to you, Ella. You've been touched by a non-telestial force and it has brought your mind and your body one step closer to reaching your full potential.

"So," he continued, relaxing again, as did I, "You asked who the People of the Storm are. Well, simply put, *we* are The People of the Storm. You, me, Gretchen, and many others. We've called ourselves different things in different cultures, but the basics of how we're created has remained the same over time. The People of the Storm, or Storm People, are people who have been struck by lightning. Those of us who survive a lightning strike are occasionally endowed with different powers. We're able to use more of our brains. Like I said, Gretchen has power over the body. I have power over light."

He paused, I guess wondering if I already knew what he meant or maybe waiting for a shocked response on my end. I nodded, "You can make things disappear."

His eyes lit with recognition. He knew I must have pulled it out of his mind earlier. He must have been used to that being the climax to his little speech. "Yes, well, usually I have to prove what I'm capable of for others to believe me." He tapped his temple, giving me a knowing look. I just nodded in response, a little embarrassed I hadn't thought of etiquette sooner. "So, we're kind of a secret society, so to speak. Above all else, we try to hide who we are and, most of all, what we can do. No one wants to be a science experiment.

"Most of our people try to fit into a regular life again. There are a few whose powers are, um, somewhat hard to control. They usually withdraw from all society. There's one man who attracts more lightning, but never gets struck. People around him get struck often so he's become something of a hermit." He was lost in deep thought for a second, but shook it off. "Your powers should be easy to keep hidden though.

"There are also those of us who help our people whenever the need arises." He paused again while I processed what he said.

"What do you mean 'help our people'?"

He shifted a little on the couch, folding his hands together. "Well, for the most part, it's usually helping them find work or relocation. But recently we've discovered an organization we call the Shadow. As technologies have advanced, others who know about our people have tried to gain these powers for themselves. Lightning is extremely dangerous to attempt to harness. There are a few of those so called 'storm chasers' that have these ulterior motives. Back when electricity was booming, relay stations and massive generators were being put into production, and a handful of people realized they could risk their lives trying to yoke considerable amounts of electricity into themselves to simulate a lightning strike. Some of them survived to gain powers very similar to ours. While the People of the Storm have been around as long as the world has existed, this new group, the Shadow, have been growing over the past century. They feel as if we, the Storm People, are being selfish in keeping these gifts to ourselves. They think, however twisted it might sound, that we're trying to take over the world. Make everyone else our slaves or some such nonsense. In recent months, they've been surfacing, causing problems for us. We've been trying to figure out ways to deal with them."

"Why do you call them the Shadow?" I asked.

Liam grimaced. "Because they live in shadow and create it. When the Shadow shock themselves to try to gain powers, they sap all the power from large areas. That, plus the fact they don't like the sun because it's too bright for their eyes. Ironically," he shrugged with a smirk, "they're kind of pale."

As I processed everything he told me, I noticed my fingernails digging into my palms. I tried to relax my fist without losing contact with Gretchen's hand. I took a few deep breaths trying to think, then settled on a question whose answer I thought I could handle. "So what do I do now?"

"That's up to you, Ella." Liam seemed sincere in his concern. I sensed he had my best interests in mind. He opened his mouth a little then closed it again. I wondered if I should probe his mind again, but I decided if he didn't want it said then I shouldn't pry. I would have to remember that etiquette thing.

I just wanted my quiet, boring, sad little life back. I didn't know how much interest these people had in a newbie like me. Like he said, I could hide my powers. I would probably try it.

At that moment Gretchen decided to come out of her stupor. She blinked a few times and removed her hand from mine. "You're all set. There were a couple of infections, but those are gone now. I also healed up your scar for you. All Storm People have fern-like scars. It's how we identify each other, although sometimes they're hard to see." She turned her face away from me lifting her bun that hung over the top of her neck. "See," she said exposing her own fern-like scar. Her own scar shone a silvery-white at the nape of her neck. "I tried to make it as unnoticeable as possible, but I can't get rid of these entirely on any of our people." She replaced her hair, turning to face me again. "At least the burnt part won't bother you anymore."

I did my own mental check noticing my burn didn't hurt anymore, but my little tether was still firmly attached. "Thanks" I mumbled, peeling off the dressing. There went my last hope of getting rid of the little sucker.

"Sure," she replied with a wide smile.

I looked over at Liam and noticed I didn't see any scar at all. "Where's your scar?" I blurted out before I realized it might be in a place he couldn't share in polite company.

My cheeks started to flush, but he saved me from my embarrassment when he said, "It's in my hair, over my left ear. All of our people have our scars on our head or neck. The Shadow have scars on their hands, arms and sometimes other body parts because that's where the shock enters them. And their scars don't look as much like a plant as ours do." He turned to Gretchen, flashing a glance as if passing her the baton.

Her smile wavered as she said, "I heard a little of what you guys were talking about, although not all." She looked back at Liam, "Did you go over our life spans with her?"

Life spans?!

"Not yet," he answered. "I thought I'd wait for you to get to that little detail. You explain these things so well."

"Uh, huh," she narrowed her eyes giving him a sarcastic tight smirk that shifted to more of a grimace. I half expected her to stick her tongue out at him. "Well," she turned back to me, "after a mortal is shocked, whether by lightning or by man-made electricity, we're altered at the cellular level.

"Liam explained how the human body is capable of so much more than it's used for. When touched by lightning we gain more use of our brains accounting for the powers we're given. We can see in the dark better than mortals, but our eyes are also a little more sensitive to the light. It's different for everyone, just like our powers are different for everyone. The long and short of it is, our bodies' age differently after we're struck as well. Some of us age close to the same as we did before we were struck, but slower. I, for instance am 97 years old."

My eyebrows popped up to my forehead. Sure, she looked good for early 50's or maybe late 40's, but I never expected 97! I stared at her dumbfounded.

Gretchen nodded at my speechlessness. "I would guess I'll live to be about 200 or so. If something else doesn't kill me." She threw a quick glance at Liam, who nodded at his shoes.

"So," I asked when the obvious question occurred to me, "do you know how fast I'll age?" This would have serious implications for my future.

"I checked that just now." She paused, pursing her lips. I thought she was hesitant to answer me, but then she touched the tips of her fingers in sequence. She counted to herself then answered. "You're using more of your brain, but we never quite use it to full capacity. Your metabolism rate is severely decreased. Cellular decay has been fractionalized. Hormonal flow was like molasses in winter, but your energy connections were brighter than I've ever seen. Your blood process—"

"Spit it out, Gretchen." Liam interrupted her.

Gretchen sighed, with an apologetic look she said, "Generally, the more potent the powers, means the longer you'll live. Like Liam for instance. He's probably the most powerful Storm Person I've ever seen. Liam, you got struck at what age?"

"Seventeen," he answered her.

"And his body has only aged the equivalent of maybe a couple of years in…"

"Too long," he interjected.

Gretchen gave him an exasperated look. "Why are you shy about your age now?"

With a quick glance to me, Liam cleared his throat, then said, "Over a hundred years."

My eyebrows must have disappeared into my hair. "Wow," I said, to cover the shock, "you must be pretty powerful."

Gretchen shrugged. "You are too Ella. In fact, you must be only scratching the surface with your new powers, because I'm guessing you'll have a similar lifespan to Liam and a very long time to explore them."

My shoulders dropped with the weight of it. I wasn't sure how long I wanted to live this crappy life missing my mother, now the sentence was a million times worse.

Chapter THREE

After leaving a contact number and promising they would be in touch soon, my new acquaintances left me to my thoughts. I said I would let them know if things became difficult for me or if I had any issues they could help me with. Gretchen encouraged me to practice my new talents and try to discover as much as I could about them.

For the next couple of hours, I pushed my mind through walls, doors and anything else to ferret out minds. I tried not to pry into anyone's thoughts too much, but I had to figure out how this thing worked. Once I found the mind of a woman sleeping a few apartments away. It was surreal to watch her dream. Even with her in a state of oblivion I realized I could still rummage around in her unconscious thoughts. Although much more disorganized than Liam's, her relationships, hopes, worries, crazy dreams, regrets, and loves were all like an open book to me.

I got bored after examining the tenth man waiting at a bus stop nearby our apartments. He was late for an interview but his thoughts wandered from his anxiety to attempting to distract himself by wondering about another man who stood nearby in the shade of a tree. I eventually came to the understanding that most mortal minds repeated the same boring crap, so I took a nap.

When I woke up, the rest of my day was quite productive. I caught up on homework, cleaned my room, our bathroom and even made dinner.

I woke up the next morning bewildered for a moment, wondering if everything that had happened had been some long, drawn-out nightmare. Maybe the thing on my head had gone away. I held my breath as I did a mental check of my new appendage. Sure enough, it flew out from my head, sweeping around the room at a single thought. I sighed into my pillow remembering my dream from the last night.

It was nothing too distinct, but somehow, in dream fashion, I knew my outward appearance hadn't changed. I sat in a booth with Missy's current boyfriend, Thomas, (eww) at the Hot Cookie Café where I worked, but he was, like, a hundred years old. He leaned over meaning to kiss me, but I backed away when I noticed long white hairs growing out of his nose. I almost lost my lunch even in my dream.

I didn't know if I would be able to be with anyone "mortal" ever again. Would I want to leave them as soon as they got old? The thought introduced a whole new set of questions for this new life of mine. Could I ever trust anyone with this secret? Of course, I could just read their mind to see if I could trust them, but what normal, sane person would take that kind of news well? I could see it now, "Well dear, now that we're married I have something to tell you…" It would be like a nightmarish case of Bewitched. Better to stay away.

Tuesday morning, I was planning on going to school. All lingering aches, pains or even fatigue had been cleared up by Gretchen, not to mention, a good night's sleep. But Daisy insisted I take another day off from school. She claimed the doctor had told her it was important for me to rest, but I figured the real reason was the note and instructions Gretchen left for Daisy along with her number if we had any questions. After reading it, Daisy seemed pretty set on me not doing anything.

However, I was scheduled to work that afternoon. Okay, it's true, I hated hanging out with happy people, especially all the cute little families, but I was bored. I had to almost beg to go to work. I insisted that I wouldn't do much work. It was usually pretty slow on a Tuesday afternoon anyway. Finally, Daisy caved.

I got a quick shower, getting ready for work like usual. I pulled my long, straight brown hair into the accustomed waitress ponytail and put on my uniform. Looking in the mirror, I studied the silvery-white fern pattern on my forehead. On a tip from Gretchen, I had covered my scar with a fake gauze bandage after they left yesterday. We didn't want any "How did your burn heal so fast?" questions. I donned a fresh gauze patch before coming out of the bathroom.

I don't spend as much time on my looks as Missy does, so I got out the door in plenty of time, like always. As I pulled my apartment door closed, I noticed movement in my peripheral vision. I could've sworn I saw a man next to the neighbors' door. I almost reached my mind out to the area, but I decided I was being stupid. It must have just been the light. Gretchen was right, the bright sun overhead dazzled my eyes, but I could tolerate it with some cheap sunglasses.

Work was just a couple of blocks away, so I always walked. That was one of the things I appreciated about this job. The little mom-and-pop café where I worked depended on reliable employees and I would hate ditching them.

These thoughts dominated my mind until I turned a corner and noticed a man standing across the street looking at me. The warm day did nothing to quell the goosebumps that prickled up my neck. I had seen him somewhere before. He stood with his back against the tree lounging in the shade. One would assume he was waiting for a bus, but it wasn't a bus stop. He had on a dark baseball cap, long sleeves and jeans. A little warm for spring in the South.

I started to reach my mind in his direction, but he turned his attention to something small in his hands. I realized he could be just any guy checking his cell phone. So I recalled my mind, wondering why I was getting so jumpy. I decided it wasn't worth standing there staring into space just to probe some random guy's mind.

My shift was pretty uneventful until the end. After a boring day yesterday of reading people's minds without any of them aware of it, I decided I would try it out on the customers. No one would know. I justified myself by thinking I could find it useful in some way. So, I tried to figure out what patrons wanted to order. It would be rude to read my co-workers' minds.

Most of the time, I would get distracted trying to dig around in their head, ending up missing what they said out loud. Then I tried it from a distance, to see if I could tell if they were leaning one way or the other in their ordering. Although easier, I often got caught staring at people, and they thought I was weird or creepy. I stifled my laughter; they had no idea how close they were. After a while I could project my mind out through the door, not even having to look at the person whose mind I entered.

Playing around with my newfound power proved interesting, but tiring. My mind wore down toward the end of my shift. For the last hour or so I stopped using my new appendage altogether. I got so tired I didn't even recognize the man from the street when he came in to order coffee.

When I finished pouring his coffee, his face clicked in my head. A cold chill crept over my skin. He had been standing under the same tree for the past couple days. On top of that, he was also the man Daisy almost hit with her car coming home from the hospital Sunday night. To confirm my suspicions, I asked, "Didn't I see you earlier? Outside?"

"Oh yeah," he mumbled not meeting my eyes. "I was waiting for someone. I saw you come in here, so I figured it might be a good place to wait." He scraped the table at an invisible piece of dirt.

"Oh," I answered trying to hide my anxiety. "Glad to know I'm drummin' up business. Let me know if you need anything else."

"Thanks, Ella." I almost turned around to question him, but I stopped myself, glancing down at my own name badge.

I stumbled back into the kitchen. Gripping the counter, I took a deep breath to calm myself. He's just a harmless guy, I told myself. No need to freak out.

I looked up to notice the door to the alley in back open the tiniest bit. I figured one of the cooks must have left it unlocked when they took out the garbage. They had a habit of doing that several times a day. I stepped over and peeked outside to make sure I wouldn't close anyone out. I about jumped out of my shoes when I heard my name whispered right behind me!

"Ella." I braced myself against the door while inspecting the kitchen for the voice. The cook was on a break, the kitchen was empty, and only a handful of customers were sitting in the dining area. As quick as a striking viper, my little serpent struck out in the area I thought the voice came from. At first it didn't hit anything, but I swung it around in the area until it hit something substantial. A flood of information poured into my head. Although still a little rattled, I sorted through the information much easier than ever before. My practice the last couple days paid off. I slowed the flow of information while picking through names and places. I scanned the memories to find something familiar before diving in further. I recognized one of the faces. Gretchen. Then I recognized the scene from the day before when I learned of the People of the Storm. But I saw it from someone else's point of view.

I sucked air back into my lungs. "William?" I whispered.

"Please," he said as he became visible, "I told you to call me Liam. I'm sorry if I frightened you."

"It's okay," I answered as my pulse decelerated, "it's not your fault. I'm a little jumpy right now."

"Why?" he asked. His eyebrows pressed together as he reached out to touch my arm. "What's happened?"

"There's a man in the dining room. I think I've seen him before. His face seems to keep resurfacing the past couple days." I shook my head trying to dispel the growing suspicion.

"Did you check him?" It seemed very logical when Liam mentioned it so casually. I wondered why I hadn't thought about it sooner.

"No, actually, I hadn't thought about it, yet." I felt a little stupid admitting it. I also couldn't admit that I was afraid of what I might find.

We turned when we heard the waitress for the next shift and the cook coming through the door to clock in. Only employees were allowed in the kitchen area. I turned to tell Liam this, but he was gone. Well, not really gone, probably just invisible. I said hello to Candy, the middle-aged blonde who would take over for me in a half an hour and scampered out front to get my stuff together.

I went over to the cash register, pretending to be interested in the stack of flatware wrapped in paper napkins. While shuffling them, I reached out to the mind of the man in the booth sipping on his coffee. I held in a gasp as I realized his thoughts centered on me. He planned to wait for me to leave; then he would follow me. Someone named Devin, or Mr. Ross if you were one of the lesser thugs, had sent him to find out about me. His name was Jackson Samuel Portman, but few people knew it. Almost everyone knew him as Jack. Just Jack. His instructions were to bring me back to their base, willing or not. He had a gun he could use to scare me. He figured it would be all he'd need. But it depended on my powers, if he could figure them out. I might not even be the one they wanted. I jerked out of his head when someone tapped my shoulder. I didn't see anyone so I figured it was Liam. I turned to the shoulder he tapped, whispering, "He's here to kidnap me." Silence followed, then I added, "He has a gun."

Candy came out of the kitchen to take over the front desk for me. Without looking at me, she said, "You can take off, Ella."

"Oh, okay. Thanks." I picked at the knot in my apron trying to give myself time to think. As the ribbons fell away from each other, Liam brushed against my ear.

"I'll meet you by the back door." He said it no louder than a breath of air.

"Okay." I couldn't whisper as quietly as he could so Candy heard me.

"What'd you say, honey?"

"I didn't say anything." I tried my best to hide the fear in my voice. I didn't want the man in the booth to notice I would be leaving any minute. That wouldn't happen.

I tried not to purse my lips as Candy practically yelled, "Well, have a good night." She said it loud enough I knew Jack heard it. He would get up to leave as soon as I left. Once the kitchen door closed behind me, I sprinted for the back door. It would be a race to see who could get out first.

I almost forgot to clock out, momentarily wondering if I should even bother. I fumbled with the timecard, but finally swung the back door open. At first, I just stood looking around for Liam. Although the sun had gone down, I could see even the smallest details.

The alley behind the café consisted of a brick wall running the length of the building but circled back around to dead-end one side. The other side opened to the street where employees would come and go. Four metal garbage cans lined up next to the door. A lone dumpster hunkered at the cut-off end and the alley itself was just wide enough for a garbage truck to get in. The smell of rotten food always made me lose my appetite when I came out here. This time, I was nauseous for a whole different reason.

I knew Liam would be invisible, but it took me a second to remember to reach out with my mind to find his. I whispered his name as loud as I dared before I heard noise around the corner out of the alley. My mind got there before I could blink. Jack.

"Hold still." Liam whispered in my ear. I felt his hands on my arms and watched as the light distorted around me. It was something out of a nightmare except this time I knew he was hiding me. The distortion stopped just as Jack appeared. I turned to see Liam at my side. I opened my mouth to ask him what we could do when he motioned for me to be silent with his finger. I assumed that meant I could see him, but Jack could not see us. Jack stood at the end of the alley blocking our path, but there would be enough room for us to squeeze past him if we were careful.

We eased our way toward him. Before I had gone more than a couple steps Liam tapped my arm to get my attention. He pointed at the ground. I had almost stepped in some ketchup splattered on the ground. It would have led Jack right to us or at least me. Then Liam pointed to my head then to his head. I nodded and reached out to his mind. I made sure to just skim the surface of his thoughts. I heard him addressing me.

Can you hear me? He asked. I nodded. *Good. Let's take this slow. Is it okay if I help guide you?*

He held out his hand to me and I nodded and slipped my hand into his. His hand was soft and warm. He held my fingers firmly but gently. He wore a light t-shirt in contrast to the sleek suit from yesterday. I only noticed because I could see the curvature of his bulging arms.

I kept in contact with Liam's mind enough to hear any instructions he had to give me. We went a few more steps when Liam stopped. Jack lifted his gun. He raised it to point into the dark alley.

A grin slowly spread across Jack's face. "It's you, isn't it, Liam?" Jack said it barely above a whisper, but it echoed in the silence. This must be the "Jack" Liam had been thinking about being around when they visited previously. "I don't want to hurt anyone," he continued as he pointed the gun to the sides of the alley. "Let me talk to the girl. She doesn't know everything she should yet…does she?" He stood silent for a moment squinting in the dark, probably trying to discern any fluctuation in the light. "I know you're here, Liam. Give me the girl." He paused again, then sighed. "Fine. If that's how you want it, we'll do it my way."

He lowered his gun, but just enough to push up his sleeves. That's when I noticed the scar on his right forearm. Serrated like a real lightning bolt, it almost seemed darker than it should be, as if drinking in the darkness. A Shadow. The name seemed fitting.

Get down! Fast! But as quiet as you can! Liam's voice yelled in my head. As I crouched down I couldn't see Jack, but I saw the garbage can on my left float up beside me then crumple like a soda can crushed by a giant hand. After a second, the metal screeched as it blasted apart, treacherous pieces shooting throughout the alley. I stifled a scream as shrapnel flew past me at breakneck speeds. It dawned on me, Jack didn't need a gun.

Crawl for the end of the alley as fast as you can!

The barrage of metal pieces flew around the alley. It was a matter of time before a couple found their marks. One caught Liam in the lower back; another sliced my leg. Liam contained his pain, although I heard him curse in his mind. However, I wasn't as well disciplined. Jack took full advantage. He pointed his gun in the vague direction of the noise, but didn't use it. Probably too loud. Instead, he directed more chucks of mutilated garbage cans toward me. Liam yanked me out of the way as bullets ricocheted off the spot I had just been.

Get up! Move! Zigzag down the alley as best you can! I'll head off Jack!

I don't know if I stepped in something or maybe I just made too much noise, but Jack raised his gun as I ran a serpentine path across the alley. I had to fight the urge to run *away* from a gun, because in this case the only escape would be toward it. I remained in Liam's mind when he tackled Jack, surprised at how easy I stayed with him as we separated.

He had a myriad of martial arts training running through his head. I couldn't follow any of it. A few more steps would take me past the two men when I heard in Liam's mind he would have to submit so I could get away. Jack was tough. Although he had the element of surprise, Liam wasn't as well trained. He kept himself invisible the entire time to try to give himself the advantage, but Jack fought for blood. You always have the upper hand if you're not trying to be nice.

I paused a moment. I couldn't just leave him. I knew I should run, and part of me, well, okay, most of me, definitely wanted to. I swung around with a sharp kick at Jack's head. The kick did its job. It gave Liam leverage again. He got an elbow into Jack's face. Jack's head hit the asphalt as we heard another garbage can explode. New shrapnel screamed at us. I raised my hands to shield my face from the onslaught, but it never came. The metal rained to the ground. Liam had knocked Jack unconscious.

Liam produced a cell phone from his pocket. While he dialed, he asked me to get something to tie up Jack. I slipped back into the café to get some heavy-duty string we used to tie up meat. Rather poetic. I brought it out just in time to hear Liam finishing his call.

"What?" he almost yelled into the phone. "What? Ow!" he yelped as a spark of electricity zapped his ear. "Just come get him," he said holding the phone an inch from his ear so he wouldn't get zapped again. "I'll get Ella back the old-fashioned way."

He hung up the phone with a grunt and rubbed his ear. The phone smoked as he muttered about "stupid phones" and tossed it next to the garbage bags. Using the string, Liam tied knots around Jack's wrists and legs, pinning them behind his back. We hid him behind a few bags of garbage left over from the attack, then we ran out into the street.

"Are you all right?" Liam said.

"Yes," I answered, surprised my voice didn't shake. I definitely wasn't all right. I expected to go into shock any moment.

We stopped at Liam's car. I thought he was reaching for his keys, but instead he pulled out a smooth stone that fit in the palm of his hand. He looked down at my leg, "Let me see that cut."

I showed him the slice in my pant leg about two inches long just above my knee. He held the rock against it for a moment saying, "This shouldn't hurt at all." After just a few seconds, the cut tingled. Liam pulled the stone away to show unscathed skin. The pain had gone although I hadn't noticed it much before. Liam said, "That should be better. Now would you mind putting this on my back?"

"Of course," I said. I took the stone from him as he turned his back to me. The cut on his back pulsed trickles of blood because of its depth. Guilt washed over me. What if it didn't work again or work as well? With a little bit of worry I pressed the stone to the long deep gash in Liam's back. He only flinched a little.

After another few seconds the muscles in his back relaxed. "That should be good. Thanks."

I pulled the stone away to reveal the skin on his back looking as if nothing had happened to it at all. I couldn't help but ask, "How does it work?" as I passed the stone back to him.

"The stone is saturated with Gretchen's powers. If she had been here she could have done it herself, but I always carry one of these with me when she's not. I'll have to get her to refill it for me." He tucked the rock away while leading me to the passenger side of the car.

The car sat on the side of the road situated with a view of my apartment as well as the Hot Cookie Café. "Have you been watching me?" I asked Liam. I knew it sounded crazy, but I couldn't see another explanation.

"I'll explain in the car." He didn't sound sorry or even embarrassed as he opened the door on the passenger side for me.

Chapter FOUR

The first thirty seconds in the car I saw my apartment fly past. "Where are we going?"

"I have to get you somewhere safe," Liam said.

"My home isn't safe?"

"Not right now," he said. "Can you call your aunt and tell her you'll be home late? I need you to talk to the other people I work with. The People of the Storm."

My own phone had been fried in the lightning strike, so Daisy had given me a cheap throw-away phone until she could get me a new one. I had yet to use it. As I typed a quick text, the numbers and letters flickered on the screen and even shocked my finger once, but I eventually got the message to her that I was going to a friend's house to help her with homework.

"I'm sorry for watching you, but you must understand we were worried about you," Liam said after a few minutes in the car together.

"I'm assuming by 'we' you mean the storm people. But why are you worried about me? My life is boring. And, if you don't mind, I'd like to keep it that way."

Liam sighed. "We've been hearing things from The Shadow. Their movements suggest they have plans. We've been trying to find out what those include. The latest chatter we've heard is something about a young woman. When we heard you had been hit, we had to come and meet you as soon as possible. I saw Jack in the area recently, then again today. That's why I showed up at the diner," he said.

"So you think this 'chatter' you heard was about me?" I still couldn't imagine why any of this had anything to do with me.

"Well, with your abilities, it seems even more likely."

I remembered, "Someone named Ross sent him to kidnap me. I don't even know a Devin Ross."

Liam's face turned brittle. That name definitely meant something to him, but he didn't say anything. He sat in stony silence for a few more minutes then said, "We'll have to talk to the others."

I didn't ask any more questions. We drove in silence for a while longer until Liam said, "You might have to make some difficult choices in the next few days."

"Like what?"

"Like where to go from here," he said. "The best idea right now might be to lay low for a while. You'll be safe at the base until we can figure out what the Shadow wants with you."

"I can't just stay home? Claim the strike hurt more than expected?" I could do that. That would make sense and it would be my ideal situation anyway.

Liam shook his head. With a glance at me from the corner of his eye he said, "Jack found you at work. He probably followed you."

So, I couldn't just go about my business while I had dangerous people after me. I guess that made sense. I knew the Storm People could help me. I also knew these powers could help me, but practice time was over. Wonderful. Liam and whoever he worked with thought I should just "lay low" until this gets figured out. That was fine with me. I like to lay as low as I can, but Daisy and Missy wouldn't let me. What would happen with school, my job, and my family?

"What about Daisy and Missy?" I asked.

Liam sighed. "We'll discuss that with the others." He paused for a moment then added, "This type of stuff happens a lot with our people."

"So, what's your role in all this?" I wanted to learn more but not intrude on his thoughts.

"I help take care of my people," he said seriously. "Which now includes you." He flipped his eyes to me with a soft smile. From a single look I could tell he really meant it. He wanted me to be safe. I didn't even need to be in his mind. When I had been in it before I could tell he was a very caring person. He wanted everyone around him to be happy.

I looked out the window not really seeing the landscape. After another few minutes I said, "How can you afford to focus on our people? Don't you have a job or something?"

"We have some very powerful people who back us. You would even know a few if I told you, but they like their privacy. They live all around the world. One man in Africa can manipulate rocks. He mines all kinds of jewels and precious metals. The excess profit alone can finance us for quite a while."

"Wow. When do I get my People of the Storm diamond necklace?" I asked jokingly.

"Well, you have to get more seniority," he grinned back.

As we flew north along the freeway, I wondered where we were going. But I had been so distracted thinking about what happened in that last few days, that I was shocked when we passed the state line into Georgia. I realized I had no idea what the future might hold.

After about an hour, we arrived in the middle of nowhere. Liam suddenly pulled off the highway onto a little dirt road I hadn't even seen before we skittered across it. If I hadn't been able to read his mind, I might have been afraid of ending up as an amber alert.

The road dipped down out of sight. A few cars appeared in front of us huddled together. Some were new and expensive, some old and beat up. They were perfectly placed to be hidden from the highway and parked under overhanging trees to hide them from the air.

"Where are we?" I asked as Liam pulled the car up next to a Lexus.

"Inside the border of Georgia. This is the rendezvous to enter our base here in the South. Wiki should be here any minute." We got out of the car just in time to see a guy about my age rambling up to us. I had no idea where he came from. He had bright blonde hair stuck up in all directions. A half-smile danced on his playful, elfish face, and I noticed his eyes perused me as he approached.

He stopped in front of me nose to nose because he didn't stand much taller than me. I pulled my chin back for a moment in surprise at his brusqueness but stood my ground. He invaded my space long enough to let his eyes drift up to the scar on my forehead. Then he backed up as his smile spread. "What's a pretty girl like you doing with this loser?" He indicated Liam with a jerk of his head, who must have been used to this.

"Ella, this is Cole Wickludi. We call him Wiki because—"

"'Cause I'm wicked fast!" Wiki interrupted. With that he disappeared.

"—because his last name is a mouthful," Liam finished.

I thought for a moment that Wiki could also manipulate light, but he appeared again before I could say anything. "My favorite flower from Hawaii," he said holding up a beautiful hibiscus. He gave it to me with a slight bow.

I thanked him, but a question creased my brow. He clarified for me saying, "I'm a transporter. I can go anywhere in the world I have seen or been to before. I've been just about everywhere and I can take passengers." He lifted one eyebrow to me adding, "I've shown you mine."

Realization dawned on me so I reached out to his mind as I tucked the flower behind my ear. I tried to stay near the front of his thoughts so I didn't get too personal with him. Then I asked him, "How old do you think I am?"

His thoughts flew by quiet and rapid, but I heard what he thought about answering before he said it. I repeated it out loud. "Twenty, easy. But you're always supposed to guess low for a woman. Minus five would be fifteen, but that's way too young. But don't younger women want to seem older? Maybe I should just stick with twenty. Minus two to be safe. Eighteen. Yeah, eighteen." I stopped and we stared at each other for a moment. I echoed his grin saying, "Is eighteen your final answer? Apparently, I come off older because I'm only sixteen."

At first, he looked a little surprised, then fear flickered in his eye. I almost investigated but decided it would probably scare me too if I met someone who could read my mind.

"Mind reading, huh? Nice. That could come in handy." He looked over at Liam who silently watched our little show. "Is that why you had me bring Jack back here?"

"We need to discuss this below." Liam didn't exactly answer, but Wiki obviously figured it out.

Both men walked over to a tall tree with thick branches overhead, essentially hiding them from all prying eyes, whether on the road or in the air. Liam motioned for me to join them. Wiki faced us and placed a hand on each of our shoulders. Immediately everything around me began to swirl together. I tried to gasp in surprise, but I couldn't find my breath or my voice. I didn't have time to worry about it before everything began to solidify around us again.

Even in the low lighting, I immediately got the sensation of being underground. It wasn't a dirty, dank cave you might go spelunking in. It resembled a modern building, but for the noticeably solid, rock walls. The smooth, flat floor had to be solid rock as well, but a thick rug covered most of it. Rich, contemporary furniture gave the atmosphere of a lawyers' office. Doors led off to other rooms, some with names on them, some without. Two gaping archways at opposite sides of the large room we stood in seemed to invite explorations. I took a deep breath hoping I wouldn't come to realize any claustrophobia. Although bland and slightly dusty, the smell of cool, fresh air filled my lungs dispelling any such fears.

Liam indicated the meager light fixtures hanging from the ceiling. "It's a little difficult to get electricity down here. Especially without everyone top-side noticing."

"Good thing we can all see in the dark, huh?" Wiki chimed in.

Liam led the way down a hall to the right with Wiki following close behind. "Does Jancarlo know we're here yet?" He asked Wiki without looking at him.

"I'm not that slow, Liam. He's waiting for you."

"Who's Jancarlo?" I asked.

"What? You don't already know?" Wiki piped up with a mock-shocked voice.

"It's a lot to sort through. Give me a minute to dig through your brain and I'll figure it out myself.," I shot back, then added with a shrug, "Or you can just tell me."

Wiki gave a loud guffaw. "I like this one!"

Liam gave a small chuckle himself then answered my question. "Jancarlo Mecina manages things around here. He also coordinates our efforts with the others around the world. He's been around a long time. His power is rock manipulation. He built this base and he's very protective of our people."

"Yeah, but he doesn't have a great sense of humor, like me." Wiki added.

"He's got a lot on his plate. He does a great job handling a lot of stress." Liam said it with awe in his voice.

As we continued down the hall, I saw a kitchen with an eating area attached. I think that's when Wiki disappeared. When we passed an office door that said, "Doctor Gretchen Callister" I wondered how often I would run into her here.

We finally entered a door off a hallway to the left. Inside, a large office greeted us with stone shelves filled to overflowing. I realized how hungry I was when I saw a bowl of fresh fruit sitting by a pitcher of water in the corner. Liam led me up to the desk, introducing me to Jancarlo who stood to shake my hand. The name on his door read "Jancarlo Mecina," but Liam pronounced his name "John Carlo."

Jancarlo was a tall, black man with broad shoulders who seemed coarse. I couldn't help but compare him to the rock around us. With his fern-shaped scar across his cheek he appeared very intimidating, but he welcomed me kindly. I could see how this man commanded allegiance.

Liam motioned for me to take a chair next to him in front of the desk. When I sat down, my eyelids immediately wanted to droop, but I had no idea how rest would happen now.

"Are you hungry, Ella?" Jancarlo said, motioning toward the food.

"Um," I hesitated not wanting to be rude, but Liam got up for me. He returned, offering me the bowl of fruit. I thanked him and pulled out a green apple while he took an orange for himself.

Jancarlo turned to Liam, "So tell me everything you can."

While Liam peeled his orange, he explained what happened with Jack in the alley. He didn't mention anything that happened before tonight so I assumed he had been in contact with Jancarlo recently. Over the past couple of hours since the attack, my adrenaline had decreased, leaving me free to look at the situation objectively.

Luckily, I had finished my apple when Jancarlo turned to me. "Can you add anything to what Liam has reported? You have a very unique insight that could shed more light on it for us," he said.

"Not really," I said. "I told Liam everything I could figure out. I'm still trying to get a handle on the whole mind reading thing." I squirmed a little saying it.

Jancarlo nodded. "Ok. For now, Ella, we could use your help with something. I won't make you stay or help us. No one will. If you want, we can just take you home right now. Wiki could get you there in a blink."

"Will it take long?" I asked.

Jancarlo shook his head. "No, we just need to find out what Jack wanted with you. Then, maybe we can get you home."

Chapter FIVE

Liam led the way down the hall, through the lobby, off another hallway. This place was a maze. We took the stairs down a couple levels. When we got there, I definitely got the impression of some kind of high-tech holding area.

Liam opened the door for me into an observation room. Another man I hadn't met yet glanced at us as we entered but turned his attention almost immediately back to a one-way glass window. Upon entering the room, I looked through the window to see Jack strapped to a wooden chair in a small room. He seemed in a daze but awake. Gretchen stood in the room with her hand on his neck. Her eyes drooped and her forehead glistened slightly with sweat.

Jancarlo introduced me to the other man in the room. His name was Kin Sitlaki. Although not much taller than me, Kin looked like his arm was as big as my waist. He couldn't be mistaken for anything but security. With his head shaved, I could clearly see his fern scar on the right side of his head where his hair should have been. According to Jancarlo, Kin and his twin sister were fire starters. He shook my hand with a firm, but not crushing, grip. "Nice to meet you, Ella. My sister is Kimi. If you need any hand-to-hand training, you'll probably work with her. She's a great fighter." He studied me for a moment then asked, "So you're a mind reader, huh? We could really use your help here." He motioned toward Jack. We all turned to inspect the pair.

"Gretchen has been keeping Jack's powers suppressed," Jancarlo said. "It's not easy work, but we can't get any answers out of him if he's unconscious."

"We haven't been able to get anything out of him anyway," Kin muttered.

Jancarlo turned to me, "So, what do you need? Do you need to be in the same room? Do you know how it works yet?"

"No," I stammered out, "I don't need to be in the same room. I don't think he even has to be conscious."

Kin perked up. "Brilliant," he exclaimed as he practically ran from the room. A couple of minutes later he burst into Jack's room with a syringe in his fist.

"Do you really think you can scare me with that?" Jack mumbled as if he were already on drugs.
Kin just snorted and stabbed the needle in his arm, pumping all the fluid into him. Curiosity seized me so I reached out to Jack's mind as the drug swept him into unconsciousness.

"Wow," I said out loud from the surprise of watching his consciousness slip away. Jancarlo and Liam turned to look at me. "The front of his mind is completely empty." I left them with that information as I dug through the rest of Jack's mind. His mind slowed. He wasn't pulling up memories or shuffling things around. It definitely made it easier to read someone's mind with them unconscious.

I took a deep breath, trying to find something relevant. I could get an idea of what the memories were before I dove into them. It was as if my little serpent could stick out his tongue to taste the memories before I had to experience them. In this way, I didn't have to see a lot of anything I didn't want to. I passed memories of women, parties and other unpleasant things. I saw the name of Devin Ross and zeroed in on it. A memory of The Boss's face came up with the name. He was tall with sandy brown, curly hair. He didn't seem intimidating the way Jancarlo and Kin did, but I could sense the fear he struck into others. He gave me the creeps. "I see Devin Ross," I said to my audience. "I'll follow these memories to see what I can find. Is there anything specific you need?"

"Why they wanted you. Also, the location of their base would be good," Jancarlo said. "Or what their plans are if Jack knows them."

With these instructions I dug through memories of discussions with The Boss. I hit on the instructions he had received to kidnap me.

Vincent says it will be a young woman. All he can say is she'll have dark brown hair, The Boss said.

I'll check out the café to see if anyone pops up. What should I do if Jancarlo's friends show up? Jack asked.

Boss answered grimly. *Find some metal.*

"Do you know who Vincent is?" I asked. I kept searching the memories to see if I could find instructions on how to get to their base while I waited for an answer. I figured I'd have to go pretty far back.

"I've heard the name before." It was Kin. I hadn't even realized he had come back into the room. "All I know is he's pretty close to Ross."

"Vincent knew about me before I was struck," I offered. "It sounds like he can tell the future or something. Jack doesn't like him so most of the time he avoids him. I can see conversations with other people where they're saying that Vincent doesn't make sense a lot of the time," I kept reporting as much as I could. Someone pushed a chair behind my legs and I sat. "The group as a whole doesn't know if they can make heads or tails of what Vincent says or does, but Ross seems to believe every word. So they try to follow through as much as they can."

I kept digging, mentioning other information I came across. "They have a transporter of their own. Samantha. She can only transport two people at a time at short distances. Wait!" I had found a memory of when Jack had first brought Samantha (or Sam as Jack called her) to their base. "They're located in Wyoming. Near somewhere called Cheyenne Peak. Uh," I wanted to roll my eyes, but they were focused on the images in Jack's head, "They like being near Casper. They think of themselves as ghosts." I heard a few snickers around me.

"Of the fifty states, Wyoming is at the top of the list for energy usage per capita," Kin pointed out. "I must be Ross using it to change people."

"But we've been looking there," Jancarlo voiced everyone's concerns. "They must be out in the middle of nowhere."

"Not just in the middle of nowhere, they're literally underground," I said. "Give me a minute. I think I'll be able to take you there." I tried to memorize the coordinates. "The real problem will be trying to get underground. They have a couple of ways, but they are a lot further underground than us, so it's difficult getting there. They know we're underground as well but only roughly where. Wait—"

"Ella?" Liam asked, kneeling next to me, I could see him in my peripheral vision, but my mind was focused on something else. "What is it? What's wrong?"

My heart stuck in my throat. I wanted to scream and cry at the same time, but I couldn't bring myself to do either. I took a gasping breath that sounded more like a sob as I watched the horrible scene play out in Jack's mind.

You want me to bring her here? Jack said as he shoved a gun into the back of his pants.

Ross nodded. *Hopefully, in one piece.*

If she fights?

Do what you have to, but don't hurt her. Ross said. *We want her for an ally if possible.*

And if it's not possible? Jack almost glared at Ross.

Ross shrugged. *You get to do what you want.*

Jack grinned. *What if she's with her family?*

Use them for leverage, Ross tapped thoughtfully on a desk. *Leave them be, as much as possible. We want to keep a low profile for the time being. But if they get in the way or seem like a problem at all…* Ross shrugged.

At that moment, being in Jack's mind, I saw the torturous possibilities flooding through Jack's thoughts. Past torments he had inflicted on others, flashing in succession as if he were choosing which to start with. He reveled in the thought of putting me, Missy and Daisy through so much pain. He knew us. He knew our habits, schools, workplaces, everything. He knew where we lived. He knew where Missy and I went to school. He knew the names of the people Ross would send after him if he failed.

"If I go back," my voice shook and I didn't even care. My stomach twisted and I had to force it to keep my apple down. "He'll hurt them. Ross will order men to hunt me down. They'll…they'll kill anyone who gets in the way. They'll kill anyone associated with me."

I jerked my mind out of Jack's head. Tears ran down my face as I turned to look at Liam. "I can't go back," I said, half-crazed with fright. "Because Jack is gone, Ross is probably already sending more people to watch for me. If I'm seen…" My entire body shook with the memory of the images of torture Jack had planned.

Lightheaded and nauseous, I allowed Liam to lead me away from the holding area. I hardly noticed as he helped me use a keypad to scan my fingerprint on a door. He guided me toward the only bed in the room. Once I was seated on the edge, he knelt in front of me.

"Ella," he said. His voice soft and soothing. "they'll be okay."

"How do you know?" I asked. The tears had stopped, but I still couldn't focus my mind on anything else.

Liam placed a warm hand on my knee. "I'll go check on them myself," he said. "We'll have someone watch them. As soon as it's safe, I'll take you to see them."

"No," I shook my head. I had seen it all. I knew what had to happen. "The only way to keep them safe is to make sure they never see me again. They'll be better off without me now, anyway."

"We'll figure it out," he said. "Try to get some sleep."

He left slowly, as if I was already asleep, pausing briefly before closing the door. I fell onto the pillow thinking of the only family I had left. I hadn't been unkind, but I'd been so ungrateful. I lost my mom so suddenly, now I would be losing Daisy and Missy just as suddenly. I cried myself to sleep.

When I woke up, I wasn't sure what time of day it was or how early everyone else got started around here. I rolled over to see a simple alarm clock on the nightstand next to a lamp. It said 8:35 A.M. I remembered the visions of terror from Jack's head and rolled over, not wanting to get up.

I finally decided that I couldn't lay in bed forever. Maybe Liam found a way for me to go say goodbye to Daisy and Missy. Maybe they would be willing to bring them down here. And what? Live with the People of the Storm forever?

I got up and wandered around the room, not really looking for anything. I switched on the single lamp to check out my new home. It gave the impression of a really nice hotel room. I guess the Storm People did well for themselves. The queen size bed had plush sheets and lots of squishy pillows. I wanted to curl back into them, but forced myself to move around the room. The stone walls didn't have any paint on them, but they remained inviting. I could certainly get used to it. I would have to.

On one wall, I saw a painting of a mountain view. I glanced at it briefly, but my eyes were quickly drawn back to it. Upon closer inspection, I realized it wasn't an ordinary painting of the scene, but it was a fully functional projected illusion of looking out a window onto such a landscape. I even saw a bird fly by and watched as some trees swayed in the breeze.

The lamp offered the only light in the room. In the corner sat a table and a couple chairs with stationery essentials. There was a large closet in the corner stocked with a few generic clothes that would make Missy's skin crawl. A robe hung on the door, so I decided it would be easier to keep myself out of bed if I took a shower.

The bathroom was well stocked with full sized bottles of shampoo. Under the sink were plenty of extras along with piles of large bars of soap. Four towels and washcloths hung on racks.

I took stock of my meager clothing supply. I still wore my clothes from work, tan pants with a tear on the leg and a plain black polo top with "Hot Cookie Café" stitched on the chest. I decided I would have to wear the pants and maybe a sweatshirt from the closet after the shower.

I wanted to stay in the shower. Melt down the drain along with the layers of dirt and grime from the alley. But I forced myself out. When I came back into my room in the robe, I heard a knock on the door. I clasped the robe together at my neck peeking around the door.

"Hey there," Liam greeted me with a careful half-smile. "Sorry to interrupt. We made sure your aunt and cousin are out of their house and safe. While there, we got some clothes for you." He held up a little stack proudly. I widened the door a bit to accept them gratefully. "Hope you don't mind me going through your stuff."

"That's fine," I said. "I'm just glad to have a change of clothes." He brought me mostly jeans and shirts. It was perfect.

Grateful for thoughtful people, I threw on some clean clothes. Clean and dressed, I figured I couldn't stay in my room forever. Or could I? No, I was hungry. I found the kitchen just in time to see Liam scooping eggs and bacon onto two plates.

"You're just in time. I made too much for one. You want some?" he asked, pointing to the eggs and bacon. This man was too good to be true. I resisted the temptation to dip into his mind to see how this coincidence happened but got distracted by the food. More bowls of fresh fruit adorned every table. It was the best I had ever tasted, even working at a restaurant. They had fresh orange juice, milk and everything else I might need. Someone obviously did take care of the kitchen at least a little bit. But all the flatware was plastic, I supposed to cut down on who had dishes duty. The tables were small but could be put together if there was a need. Liam led me to a table by the door.

I was afraid to ask it, but I had to know. "What happened?" I asked hesitantly between bites. "With Daisy and Missy?"

"Well," Liam squirmed, "we kind of…had to start a fire."

"What?"

He threw his hands up defensively. "We made sure everyone got out safe and Kimi put the fire out herself so there wasn't much damage or anyone put in danger."

I shook my head and turned back to the food.

"Daisy and Missy," Liam continued, "are staying at a nice hotel, all paid for by 'insurance'," he said adding air-quotes.

"What about me?" I asked. "What do they think about me not coming home last night?"

"Uh," Liam pushed the eggs around on his plate, "see, Jancarlo thought it might be best if you just kinda…disappeared."

I stared at him until he looked up and met my eyes.

"We kind of do this all the time…"

"Do what?"

"People disappear," he said, stabbing another chunk of eggs.

"Disappear?" I asked. "Why?"

He waved his fork at me. "We don't age properly. It raises questions. Although with the cosmetic surgery options these days we don't have to do it for a long time. We've gotten better at faking deaths."

"But they just don't know where I am?"

"Yeah," he said. "That way they don't know if you disappeared before or after the fire and we can take you back anytime. As soon as it's safe."

I thought about it for a moment then gazed down at my food. "You're right, it's best this way. The Shadow will leave them alone and I can stay here."

"Ella," Liam whispered. "We can always take you back later. Like I said, there's no conclusive evidence of your whereabouts."

"No," I said, "honestly, I don't care where I end up." What I didn't tell him was that I was miserable anywhere I went. Since the day my mother died. I would be just as miserable anywhere.

Liam spent the rest of the meal talking about the Storm People and how things worked. We were located some hundreds of feet underground, but hidden openings kept us well ventilated. A man named Adam manipulated clean water to flow through the cavern. A few farmers topside manipulated crops to grow faster and with better quality than any others. They sold some to restaurants for extra income after they sent the best down to us. We had everything we needed. We could live down here for years never having to come up. We had workout areas, living quarters, offices, doctors (Gretchen and others), a few holding cells along with everything else anyone could ever need.

Finally, I screwed up the courage to ask what I wanted to know. "What will be done with Jackson?"

Liam looked confused for a moment then asked, "You mean Jack?"

"Yeah, his name is Jackson Samuel Portman. I used to know a guy named Jackson, so I guess I just called him that," I tried to keep my voice indifferent, but I hated the man. I'd never hated anyone the way I hated the man in the holding cell. I was calling him something else so I didn't have to do what he wanted, calling him the name he preferred. After a few seconds I realized Liam was staring at me. "What's wrong?" I asked, feeling like maybe he heard the edge of hatred in my voice.

"You know his name? Of course, you know his name. Everyone else only knows him as Jack. That's all he's ever called himself. I don't think Devin Ross even knows his full name." He shook his head bringing himself back to the present. "To be honest, we don't even know what to do with him. He's locked up downstairs, so he can't hurt anyone." He pushed around the remains on his plate then dropped his fork. "But that's not what's important right now. Your family is fine, and Jancarlo would like to see you after breakfast. If that's all right?"

We cleaned up breakfast and walked back to Jancarlo's office. Instead of sitting next to me, Liam leaned against the wall behind me. I couldn't see his face, but he didn't seem very happy. Jancarlo also seemed hesitant.

"Ella," he said, "I need you to give Liam directions on how to get to the Shadow base."

"Sure," I said, but something nagged at the back of my mind. My mom. She would've wanted me to help. "But it might be easier if I just go along," I added. "There's tricks to getting in the door and I'm not sure if it's changed or if they added anything." Not that I wanted to do anything, but I certainly didn't want to be stuck down here with that maniac in a cell below my room.

"You'll be safer staying here," he said, with a glance at Liam. "We can take the risk."

"And do what?" I sounded snarkier than I meant to be. I wanted to be away from that horrible man. "Lift weights? Make sandwiches? What am I supposed to do?"

"You're still upset about last night," Jancarlo said.

"You're right," I nodded. I knew I didn't want to be anywhere near Jack, but somewhere deep inside of me, I wanted to help out as well. I liked working at the diner because I felt like I was helping people. Before she died my mom said that was my best quality, I always wanted to help. I couldn't let her down.

"You're not thinking straight," Jancarlo kept his voice even. He didn't seem like the type to get angry easily. "Last night was a huge ordeal for you and, although you could be a help, you being upset could also be a hinderance."

I certainly didn't want to be a burden. I didn't want to make matters worse by insisting on coming along. But there was something in Jancarlo's tone and Liam's stance. I decided to take matters into my own hands...or mind, or whatever. Something about it all bothered me. There was something going on, and I would find out what whether they wanted me to or not.

"It's me they're after," I said out loud to cover what I was doing silently. "I want to know why."

I knew I told him I wouldn't, but I couldn't help myself. I hate not knowing what's going on, and if they weren't willing to explain everything, I figured I had just cause. I slipped into Liam's mind first. Just a little.

She's still grieving, and she's been traumatized. He can't let her go. She shouldn't go. It's too dangerous. If we get caught...

Before I could blink, I slipped out of Liam's thoughts and into Jancarlo's.

I've never seen Liam like this. He's being protective, but that could be even more dangerous. If she's willing, it would be better for her to keep busy. Perhaps I should let her choose.

I jumped on it. "Look," I took a firm voice with them, like I used to with Missy when I really didn't want to hang out with her and her friends. "You said you wouldn't make me do anything." I tried to drill my eyes into Jancarlo's. "I want to leave, but I can't go home. Where better to go than with some of the Storm People to see if I can help?"

She's right. I can't force her to do anything. Including staying here.

"It's dangerous, Ella," Liam offered as he stepped forward. "If we take you there, we might be doing exactly what they want."

"If they catch us, at least we'll find out why they want me either way," I said. At this point I didn't care if they caught me. I'd get some answers and my family would be safe.

"We're just going to check it out first," Liam said with a shrug.

"But if I'm there, I can get more information than I did from Jack," I countered. "I want to know why they're willing to go to such lengths. I want to know why Devin Ross would be willing to allow such horrible things to happen just to get to me." Thinking of the danger my family and friends might be in, I looked back at Jancarlo, my eyes pleading.

To my relief, I heard his decision in his mind. *I'll have to talk to Liam more about this later.* He gave a defeated sigh. Nodding, he said, "You're right, Ella. You can go."

"You're going to send her to the people that are trying to kidnap her?" Liam said in unbelief.

"I'm sure you're perfectly capable of bringing her back safely, Liam," Jancarlo answered with a tone of authority.

I couldn't look Liam in the eye as we stood to leave so I slipped into his mind. Just a moment. Long enough to hear him think, *At least I can keep an eye on her this way.*

We were ready to leave shortly after my meeting with Jancarlo. While I went to join the group, I reminded myself that I needed to stay out of everyone's minds unless they gave me permission. They wouldn't know unless I told them, but I'm sure I would get caught eventually. I couldn't make it a habit.

The team consisted of me to lead the way; Liam to keep us hidden, also because he was the most experienced; Wiki to transport us to Cheyenne, he had never been to Casper; and Kimi, the fire starter, for added security. Apparently, Kin stayed pretty close to Jancarlo, almost like a personal bodyguard and personal assistant in one.

When we gathered together to leave in the lobby, I got to meet Kimi. She was nice, but she meant business. Although sleek, I could tell she was strong like her brother. She had straight black hair and a smooth pointed face like a cat. I couldn't tell how old she was. She seemed younger, but she acted so serious she could have been middle-aged. She and Kin punched each other in the arm a few times to say good-bye. She turned to examine me with a smile. "Well," she exclaimed, "maybe we'll have some time for some sparring on the way."

"My mom always wanted me to do some self-defense, but we couldn't afford it," I said.

"Every woman should know self-defense. I'll get you in shape." She smacked me on the arm with her fist then turned to heft her enormous pack on her back. Without anyone noticing, I tried to rub feeling back into my arm.

My tiny, little pack consisted of a change of clothes, a flashlight, some batteries and a few granola bars. Gretchen had given me a healing stone that now lay nestled next to my water bottle in a side pocket. We didn't plan on being gone long so we traveled light. All except Kimi. I guess she wanted to be prepared for anything.

The plan was for Wiki to get us there, get any information we could and get back here ASAP. If anything went wrong Wiki could get us all out with Liam's help making us disappear. Since Wiki could transport dozens of people along with himself, getting out should be no problem. Everything should go pretty smoothly, at least, that's what we all expected.

Chapter SIX

I expected it to be much more mountainous. There were some hills close by, but the trees were sparse. The sun glared at us from the right above a sprawling city I assumed to be Cheyenne. I took a deep breath. I had never been on the west side of the country. It smelled like sage and grass. The lack of saltwater is what threw me off the most. I guess I'd grown accustomed to it in Florida. The temperature jolted me as well. It was spring, late May, but it was still easily twenty degrees cooler here in Wyoming.

To our left, stretched mostly barren countryside. Further away to the north rose some dark mountains. I pointed to them, and our group kicked into gear.

"Jackson's memories said to go north on I-25 up to Casper," I told the others. "It's the only way I know to go."

"It's all good," Wiki said, "I'll get us there."

We held hands again, Liam's hand warm in mine, and jumped from hilltop to hilltop. It would have taken days to walk it otherwise. But once we got to a more forested area, Wiki had to call it quits since he couldn't see through the trees.

We walked for a few hours with rests here and there, but we only covered a portion of the remaining miles. Thanks to Gretchen, we were all in excellent health, so we moved at a brisk pace, making more progress than we would have otherwise. I was the slowest of the bunch, and I'm sure they waited on me, but no one complained.

"So how does it work?" Wiki asked with a nod toward my head.

I shrugged. "It's kinda like another appendage."

"Cool," he muttered.

"How far can it go?" Kimi asked. Probably wondering how much of a tactical advantage it was.

"I'm not sure," I said.

"Try it out," Kimi said, nodding toward a car driving in the distance.

As the car flew past, I reached out to find the mind of the driver. I found it faster than I expected. I held onto it as the man, on his way to get something in Casper, drove further and further away. I also practiced looking through the files in his mind without delving too deep. I skimmed through the memories trying to find out about him without getting too intimate. It took some practice, but I was getting better.

"Well?" Kimi asked after a while.

I shrugged. "Pretty far." I tried to make a mental note to test how far away I could be to hear someone's mind.

While we walked, I took the time to talk with each person. I learned a lot about how our people operate. I learned about someone named Kathryn who could manipulate the powers of others. She could store powers of others in inanimate objects. She was the one who helped put Gretchen's powers in the healing stones. In this way they also set up relay stations for transportation, but they didn't have many of those since they were difficult to coordinate. They opted instead to have Wiki take them wherever they wanted. It was faster.

As we walked, Wiki started to make small talk with Kimi, who didn't seem very inclined to hold a conversation with him. She seemed personable enough to me but somewhat aloof with Wiki.

Liam saw me notice the dynamics between Kimi and Wiki. He bumped me with his elbow to get my attention then pointedly tried to look at his own forehead. I took it as an invitation to enter his mind.

Drop back a little.

I slowed my pace and pulled out of his mind when we were out of the others hearing range. I nodded toward Kimi and Wiki, "Is there a story there?"

Liam grinned, "There's always a story. Wiki keeps trying with her, but she has no patience for him. She's all business. He's all fun. It would be hard for him to settle down with anyone I think, but he's had his sights on Kimi for a while. Usually having Kin around keeps Wiki at bay, but not today."

Kimi looked back at us for a moment. Although she narrowed her eyes a little bit, she did nothing. Liam didn't notice. He was busy watching his step.

I loped along next to him, longing to ask him about his history but not wanting to pry. When you have unlimited information about people, it makes you even more sensitive to what they might not want you to know.

That night we decided to camp in the area rather than return to the base. We rationalized the Shadow had no idea that we were in the area and it sounded better than being cooped up at the base. I certainly didn't want to go back knowing Jack was still there. Without checking in their minds, I got the feeling everyone wanted to allow me time to relax a little after dealing with Jack. I used to love camping with my mom, but I hadn't bothered with Daisy and Missy, even when they asked, which was rare. They weren't much for the outdoors unless they had on a skimpy bikini and cute guys were around.

We walked at least a mile from the road and behind some low hills to camp out under the stars. We ate a few rations Kimi had brought along with her. Wiki disappeared for a second to come back with some fresh fruit from the base, water to refill our bottles, and a few sleeping bags. We sat around our little campfire making plans for getting into the Shadow base. Then one by one, we fell asleep.

That night I dreamt of a woman who seemed only vaguely familiar, in a place I didn't know. She brushed her dark red hair while humming a tune I didn't recognize. I looked down to inspect the rough wooden table in front of her. When I focused back up at her, she stared back with curiosity. I looked down to see that the brush was actually in my own hand. I was looking in a mirror.

The next morning I woke feeling a little uneasy about the strange woman in the mirror. When I opened my eyes I saw Liam still sleeping on my right side with a troubled look on his face. Wiki snored on his other side. Kimi had been sleeping on my other side, but she was gone. I sat up to see Kimi sitting by our little fire pit. She stirred it around, covering the black marks with fresh dirt. When she finished, it looked as if no one had been there.

"I guess you're pretty good at covering your own fires, huh?" I joked as I sat down next to her.

She gave me half a grin. "How'd you sleep?"

"Fine," I answered casually. "I think the hard ground gave me weird dreams. I dreamt I was someone else, but I guess I kind of am now, aren't I?" It troubled me more than I wanted to let on.

"You'll always be the same person," she said, I guess trying to be comforting. "You define how you use your powers. No one else would use them the same." I could tell she had had these same thoughts, especially having a twin brother with the same power.

Kimi was very personable, even knowing she could kill me by pointing her finger. "We need to get going," she said. She stepped over to the boys and shoved her boot into their ribs to wake them up. "Come on, guys. Don't make me light you on fire to wake you up."

"I'm up," Wiki shouted as he bolted upright. He sounded almost scared. I wondered if he had been threatened with this before and maybe not believed her. As for me, I totally believed her.

Liam on the other hand was not afraid of her. He rolled over pulling his sleeping bag over his head, he and the bag disappeared at the same time. After Kimi scrambled around on the ground for a minute cursing him, he materialized next to her. He ruffled her hair like a little kid. "Stop fooling around on the ground Kimi. We gotta get going."

"Very funny," she muttered.

"What's the matter Kimi? Didn't you sleep well?" Wiki asked as he scooped all his stuff into his pack.

"I slept fine until this morning," Kimi said. "I had a rude awakening with a slap to the face." She looked at me pointedly. My eyes widened when I realized I had been the only one sleeping next to her.

"Oh," I said embarrassed, "sorry. I've been told I move a lot in my sleep."

"That's okay," Kimi smirked. "It'll be the only shot you get on me, though."

Kimi passed around hearty granola bars for breakfast. These things weren't the skimpy little things you buy at your local grocery store. You could tell in one bite they had all your nutrition in them and more. They were probably made by the same person that grew all the fruit and vegetables. I made a mental note to meet this person later.

We walked again for a long time that day, but this time we didn't walk alongside the road. I knew we would have to walk up into the mountains of this region to find the Shadow's base. We were on the east side of the mountains when we arrived. I knew from Jack's memories the Shadow trained on the west side of the mountains and underneath them. Really, really far underneath. They only came to the surface at night.

As we got closer, I started to go over the details with Kimi. "They'll have two sentries out, but they stay well hidden during the day. Night is the time we should worry, because there will be a lot more movement," I said.

"Ok," she said thoughtfully, "so we need to find a way in before nightfall. I think we can pull that off." She thought for a moment then looked like she had made a decision to ask me something. "Is it possible for you to… I don't know… maybe keep your mind out there to see if anyone sneaks up on us?"

I furrowed my brow. I hadn't really thought about it. The question made me think how much I needed to play with these new powers.

"I'll try," I answered. I reached my mind out for maybe one hundred feet, sweeping it in a circle around us. I couldn't tell if it worked because I wasn't running into any minds to probe until suddenly I ran into something very different. I stopped short in my tracks when I zeroed in on the mind.

"What is it?" Kimi asked urgently. "Is there someone out there?"

"No," I listened to the serene mind I had found. "It's a deer," I said. "I had never even thought to enter the mind of animals. It's so peaceful." I stayed with the deer for a few minutes as we all picked our pace back up, but I grudgingly left it in order to try to keep a look out for other human minds.

After a few minutes of sweeping my serpent in circles I decided if I could reach it out so far, maybe I could walk with it encircling us. I made the circle a lot smaller, only about ten feet or so then tried to push it out further from there. When I had it at nearly fifty feet around our group in every direction I told Kimi.

"Impressive," she said, "do you think you can keep it up while we hike?"

"Sure," I said, "but I might go a little slower."

"That's fine." She sounded sincere.

We continued our hike with me keeping an "ear" out for our group. I occasionally ran into more deer, but nothing else. It wasn't all that practical. I couldn't keep it at the same height for every person and I couldn't tell the difference when my appendage would go through a tree or a person, but it was interesting to try. After a while, I gave it up.

When we stopped for lunch, Wiki and Kimi went back to the base to grab some sandwiches along with yogurt and protein shakes. Kimi wanted to make sure we had all the energy we needed for anything that might come up. As I sat with Liam to wait, I got the same shy feeling I had the first time I met him. He broke the silence by asking how far away we were.

"It should only be another couple hours, as long as the terrain doesn't get any worse." I knew it wouldn't from Jack's memories, but I thought I would throw it out there anyway.

After a few more minutes, Liam asked softly, "Are you scared?"

I looked at the ground as I thought about it. "Oddly enough, not really," I said. "Maybe I just don't know enough, but it's just not affecting me. I'll be the first to know what is going on, so I'll be the first to get scared."

"Don't worry," he said, "we'll all be here with you. I want to know everything you know. Sometimes that makes it a little better."

"Do you ever get scared when you do stuff like this?" I asked.

"Sometimes," he said. "Of course, we've never had to do anything quite like this, before. We've been trying to find these people for a while now. We've only known of this group for a few decades or so. We still don't know much about them. They have eluded us and refused to contact us for so long that we got suspicious. This is a very important mission in order to try to find a way to co-exist or find some kind of peaceful solution if it's at all possible."

"Usually," I retorted, "when people are bent on destroying you, there's only one solution."

Liam looked into the trees for a second then asked, "Would you fight them, if you had to?"

I shrugged, "I guess. Maybe. If I had to."

"You know, you…" he stopped. His face fell and he continued to study the ground.

"What?" I asked.

"Nothing," he said, shaking his head as if to rid himself of the thought. But it didn't seem to go away.

After another minute I said slyly, "You know, I could just find out for myself." I tried to downplay just how tempting it really was. My powers uncoiled from my head inching toward Liam like a snake creeping up on its prey.

He looked up at me seriously. "You wouldn't."

"Don't worry," I said holding my hands up defensively. Silently I fought to pull my powers back toward me. He would never know, but what if I saw something I couldn't forget. Or forgive. "I promised you I wouldn't do that anymore, so I won't. Unless you want me to."

Lucky for us, our travel companions chose to come back at that moment. As they handed out food, Kimi seemed to pick up on the slightly tense atmosphere. Her eyes bounced between me and Liam. "Did we interrupt something?"

"No." Quick with an answer, Liam smiled at her, his face returning to normal. "Looks good." He took a big bite out of his sandwich, effectively ending the conversation.

Chapter SEVEN

We trudged through the hills for another hour and a half before I started to lead the way. As we closed in on the mountains, trees began to encroach on us from all sides. In the early afternoon we finally got to the point of entry for the Shadow base.

I pulled the group down behind some bushes, pointing out a large rock in the distance. It was about thirty yards in front of us around the gentle curve of the mountain. The trees encompassing the area hid it well, but the guards were even better concealed.

While we crouched, hidden, I searched for the sentries. "There are only two," I told the group. "Give me a minute to find more information." I searched their minds while the others stashed our packs. Luckily, the sentries' jobs were close to the front of their minds, so I didn't have to search long. "One is Frank. He's a fire manipulator, but he can't start it. He's limited. His job is to make a distraction if someone shows up. The other one," I continued, "is Douglas James. He goes by Jimmy. He's a rock thrower. His job is to open the stone door while

Frank makes a distraction. Then they both slip inside to trigger the alarm that's right inside the door. When the guard is changed, the alarm is tripped before they come out. If it's not turned back off in just a few seconds everyone in the base is alerted."

"So, when's the next guard change?" Kimi asked.

"In about a half an hour," I answered.

"That doesn't give us much time to come up with a solution," Liam said.

By curving my mind, kind of like I had in a circle as we walked, I could be in both of the guards' minds at the same time. Although it was a little confusing to pay attention to everyone at once, I wanted to stay with them in case the men were alerted to our presence.

"We'll have to try to slip in while they change the guard," Kimi said. "Obviously Wiki and Liam have to go. Then Wiki can come back for us."

We all nodded in agreement, but my heart rate started to accelerate at the idea. So many things could go wrong. I dug through Frank's mind to see if I could find out how big the opening was. Could it really fit three people at the same time? Then I found something. "Wait," I told the group as quietly as I could. "The new guards will be standing in the doorway for a moment while they make sure everything is okay. They check to make sure the other guards are able to switch before they set the trip, to make sure someone else can turn it off. You might be able to slip in then."

"All right," Liam said firmly looking at Wiki. "Let's go."

Afraid my nerves might show, I stared back at the guards. When I knew my face was composed, I looked back, just in time to meet Liam's green eyes as the two men disappeared.

Luckily, Kimi came up with a solution for my worry without me voicing it. "Keep in contact with Liam's mind. Let me know what's happening."

Oh crap, can't lose him now. I whipped my serpent out to where he had been before. Luckily, he hadn't started moving yet. I relaxed slightly when I heard him say in his mind:

Can you hear me? I nodded in response. *Good. Stay with me.*

I could hear what he wanted me to, but I could also see the images being passed from his eyes to his mind. My mind easily adjusted in his so I could see what he was seeing as well. I saw myself and Kimi crouched behind the bushes. I had a dazed look in my eyes just like Gretchen. Although seriously helpful, it made my skin crawl.

As the men transported from our hiding place, I reported to Kimi. "They're coming up on the entrance. They're going to sit as close to the door as possible but off to the side so they're out of the way." I sat back to force myself to relax. "All we can do is wait."

Kimi tried to relax next to me in the bushes, but she stayed facing the large rock and the Shadow guards. She tilted her head a few times until she finally had a good view of everything going on by the rock.

We waited for what seemed like forever. Liam tried desperately to keep his mind empty, but in vain. I tried to ignore things that popped into his head, especially when it was about me. Finally, Kimi checked her watch again. "Just a few more minutes," she muttered more to herself. But as she said it, the large rock right next to Liam, the entrance to the Shadow base, began to shudder.

This is it, He said to me in his mind.

"The rock is moving," I told Kimi.

She perked up, peering through the bushes again. She watched from the bushes as the huge rock moved out of the way of the entrance with a strong, low rumble. I watched from Liam's view as he saw the rock moving toward them.

"They're in the way of the rock," I whispered urgently to Kimi. "Wait, they're moving."

I watched as Liam and Wiki backed up enough to let the rock roll in front of them. As it came to a rest, they slipped around it. Liam glanced back at Wiki to see him attached to his back while they quickly circled the rock. When they got to the front, they could hear the guardsmen reporting. A very large man with bright red hair stood in the doorway almost entirely taking it up. Liam slid close to him brushing in the doorway right past him. The man stopped what he had been saying to look around warily.

"Liam's in," I told Kimi quietly.

"What is it, Eddie?" Frank asked him.

"You sure you haven't seen or heard anything today?" Eddie asked.

"We never see or hear anything out here. Nothing but sun and trees, and I'm sick of it," Frank retorted as Jimmy shook his head behind him. "You just don't want to come out in the sun. Now stop procrastinating and flip the switch so we can come in." Frank sounded bored and angry at the same time.

Eddie sighed, turning to the side to flip the switch. As he turned, he made enough room for Wiki to slide past him.

"Wiki's in," I sighed with relief. Kimi nodded while her shoulders dropped by a fraction to show her relief. I hadn't realized I was so anxious until I tried to relax my shoulders too.

"Good," Kimi breathed. "Stay with them if you can."

I nodded agreement, making sure I stayed in Liam's mind. I watched as the men found somewhere to hide until the former guards turned the switch off and replaced the plastic cover over it. Then they watched Frank and Jimmy walk away down the long hall, talking about what there might be to eat in the mess.

The new guard, Eddie, replaced the rock as his counterpart disappeared into the trees. They were both dressed in dirty green to blend in with the surroundings. Once they found a comfortable spot, they were trained to stay there, remaining alert, for hours.

I paid so close attention to the men, I missed the first nudge Kimi gave me. The second nudge was probably a little payback for the way I woke her up that morning because I definitely felt that one. I returned to watching Liam and Wiki as they left the wall and invisibly followed the off-duty guards down the long hall. But I also tried to pay better attention to Kimi as she motioned to one of the new guards outside sidling our way.

I bent my serpent, stretched pretty far by now but not nearly to any limit I knew of, to touch the guard's mind too. I held up a finger as I felt a slight resistance then heard in Eddie's mind that he really enjoyed the view. He liked looking out at the valley drenched in sun. He missed sitting in the sun, but his eyesight couldn't handle it anymore. He didn't know we were back here at all.

It was kind of like having the TV and radio going while reading a book all at the same time. I couldn't really focus on all of them at the same time, but I was vaguely aware of what each mind had in it. I shook my head at Kimi who looked ready to pounce on the guy if he came any closer. She nodded understanding, so we both squeezed in a little tighter into the bushes to attempt to stay hidden. Finally, Eddie walked back over to his post, a shady, secluded spot, after catching a glimpse of the valley in the sunlight.

I gave my head a little shake as I came out of Eddie's mind. Kimi noticed and gave me a questioning look.

"I don't know," I whispered. "These guards. Their minds are…weird. I don't know…gummy…if that makes sense."

"No," she whispered back, "it doesn't. What are the boys up to?"

I let Kimi take watch while I paid attention to Liam and Wiki. They moved slowly in order to avoid making any noise. The hallway ran much longer than it would have seemed. Long, steep stairs led down to a dead end. When they got to the end, the guards were nowhere to be found. They stood staring at blank walls wondering what to do until Liam made the decision to come back for us.

"They're coming back," I told Kimi moments before they materialized in front of us. I looked up at them and felt disoriented again to be looking at myself. "I can stay in your minds when you transport." It could prove to be useful information.

"Interesting," Liam put in as he and Wiki crouched in the shrubbery with us.

"Hitchin' a ride, huh?" Wiki sounded a little upset by it.

I sent my mind out to search the guards now on duty as Liam and Kimi started talking.

"There has to be some kind of hidden transport device at the end of the hall," Liam said.

"Ella," Kimi asked me, "can you find out how to use it?"

"Sure." I quickly dug through Eddie's mind. He was the more pleasant of the two. I was definitely getting much better at this. "There's a secret piece of rock. You just have to push it so it will transport you down to the main level."

"That should be easy enough," Kimi said.

"Wait," I stopped her, "There are guards at the other end. We'll have to go through invisibly. They'll know it's been tripped, but hopefully they'll think it was just a fluke." I pulled out of Eddie's mind announcing, "These guards are just muscle. They don't know much more."

"All right," Liam said, "Wiki, take us all into the hallway."

"Hang on folks," Wiki reached out to touch Liam's and Kimi's shoulders. I reached over to grab Kimi's arm as the woods around us disappeared.

We reappeared in the long stone hallway in front of the dead end of rock. Everyone else watched as I walked over to the wall in front of us. I pointed to the wall saying, "These three projections have to be pushed in the right sequence then whoever is standing in the circle here on the floor will be transported to the main level." I indicated the circle of flat stone we stood on.

"Ok," Liam said and held up his hands. In the dim light it was hard to see if anything had happened, but he stated, "Now no one will see us."

"Be ready for anything down there," Kimi added. "If anything goes wrong, Wiki will have to get us all out." She looked at Wiki, but he just shrugged.

The four of us positioned ourselves on the circle of stone. I reached up to press the three rocks. One on the right, two on the left. Everything around us smeared together as if Wiki was transporting us again, but I don't think any of us were ready for what we saw.

We materialized on the edge of an enormous cavern with our backs to the wall. Directly to our left sat two guards whose job it was to check everyone coming in. We were very exposed with dozens of people moving around the large cavern. I immediately backed up toward the wall, but Kimi stopped me and motioned for us to all step off the platform away from the guards. They had seen that the transporter had been tripped, but no one appeared on the platform.

"What is it?" A small, wiry guard asked the other as he stepped forward to investigate.

"I don't know," the second one with platinum blonde hair said as he looked over the platform. "It doesn't just go off by itself." He narrowed his eyes to scan the area. I reached out to his mind just as Wiki tripped and scuffed his shoe on the platform. With so much other noise in the echoing cavern, no one could have heard him, but the guard still inspecting the area looked straight at him.

Before anyone could do anything, the guard pointed at us. "There," he shouted, "intruders!"

Chapter EIGHT

We reappeared back at the Storm base lobby. Wiki had grabbed us and disappeared before anyone could get to us in the Shadow base. But now they knew that we had their location. That could cause big problems for everyone. As we all straightened up from our crouch I informed the group, "Calls himself a 'seer.' He can see through images and illusions. He could see the distortion in the light from Liam."

"I'll go back and get our packs," Wiki offered.

"We'll update Jancarlo," Kimi said as the three of us marched down the hall to his office.

After we reported everything, Jancarlo asked, "So, how do we get past the seer? If he can see through Liam's reflections, is there somewhere you can transport to, where he won't see?"

"It was just a giant room," Kimi answered, shaking her head. "I don't know if there's anywhere to hide in there."

"But maybe if we can transport to the other side of the room," Wiki came in the room, "they won't see us."

"Are you ready to try again, then?" Jancarlo asked him.

"Sure," he said, "I can pop in real quick."

"Not without Liam," Jancarlo insisted.

Wiki shrugged, "Fine, but it'll just be a quick jump in and out."

"Yeah, but just imagine if someone saw you just 'jump in'," Liam offered. He stepped over to Wiki, putting his hand on his shoulder. Something resembling anger flashed in Wiki's eye moments before the two men, once again, disappeared, but I'm sure I imagined it.

We only had to wait for a minute or so, but it seemed excruciating. Finally, both men reappeared in the same spot. Liam removed his hand from Wiki's shoulder, "We found a spot we can transport into, behind some large crates. They look like they haven't been moved in a while, so I think we'll have time to get some more stuff together if we want to make it a longer trip this time."

"It doesn't need to be a long trip. We just want to get Ella in there to get as much information as she can." Jancarlo turned to me. "Try to get to Ross. Find out what he's up to. If you can't get to him, try anyone as highly ranked as possible." He turned back to Wiki and Liam. "Make it as short a trip as you can."

"Wait a second," Kimi spoke up, "you're sending them alone?" She didn't sound offended. More like she thought she hadn't heard him right.

"They'll be fine, Kimi," Jancarlo sounded confident, but he looked back to Liam. "In and out." Liam just nodded, putting his hand back on Wiki's shoulder.

I walked over to Wiki and placed my hand on his other shoulder. I met Kimi's eyes, "Don't worry. We'll be right back."

"You have one hour," she said sternly.

The air around us distorted the room. Liam told Wiki we were ready.

With a nod, everything around us shimmered. We appeared back in the large cavern we had been spotted in less than fifteen minutes ago. Large boxes strapped to wooden pallets rose in front of us. I saw some of the boxes said "explosives" on the side. Others said "fragile" and "flammable". No delicious fruits and vegetables here. Some of the boxes on the top drooped open, but they looked like they wouldn't be going anywhere anytime soon. No one saw us, but we knew the guard who had seen us still hovered at the transportation pad. I immediately wrapped my serpent out around us so I would know if anyone approached as we crouched behind the dusty crates.

"Let's go," Liam whispered.

Even though we were invisible, I felt exposed as we inched out from around the crates. Everyone around us went about their business and their business looked like war. It wasn't like walking into the Storm People headquarters. Our base gave the feeling of an office building, even a hospital, maybe. This felt like boot camp. Underground boot camp. People barked orders and ran drills. Actually, since we had made an appearance, they might not be drills. Some were on one side of the cavern fixing military-type vehicles. Hallways led off the main cavern in different directions. We edged our way around the cavern trying to avoid everyone when Liam tapped me on the shoulder. *Which way?* He mouthed.

I held up a finger for him to wait then reached out to the mind of one man walking into a hallway. He was headed to the barracks. That wouldn't get us anywhere. I abandoned his mind to find a woman that had come out of another hallway. She had come back from the infirmary. I would keep that one in mind if I couldn't find anything else. But it was unnecessary. I found another woman in the next hallway on her way to contact Ross. I curled my finger at Liam and Wiki for them to follow me.

The third hallway would take us inside the line of sight of Neil, the guard that had busted us earlier. But he needed cause to activate his eyesight, so I just pointed him out for Liam and Wiki to watch. I listened to the thoughts of the men and women around us as we tried to slip past all of them. We had to skirt dozens of people and obstacles. Once, Wiki almost got hit by a flying wrench. Apparently, the mechanic had the power to move objects, because the jeep he worked on hovered in the air unsupported.

We finally got to the third hallway and started to edge our way down it. At this point Wiki started to fall behind. I figured he was just covering our backs, at least I assumed if we needed to get out fast he would be right behind us. Liam motioned to him impatiently to keep up with us. I wondered to myself if maybe Liam wouldn't be able to bend the light around him if he fell too far behind.

The hallway we entered couldn't have been used very much. It had a few crowded offices, but it seemed the administrative duties played a lesser role to the military-type preparations. We walked further down the hall and didn't run into anyone as we came to a big open area. On one side loomed a fire throwing practice area as big as a three-story house. The stone walls were completely covered in black soot. Opposite the practice area, up a flight of metal stairs, stood a large office surrounded by glass with an observation deck wrapping around the front of it. The windows around the office were spotless.

I motioned to Liam that the woman I had seen coming down here had gone in the office. I checked to make sure we were clear first then whispered, "I'm going to check her out. Give me a few minutes."

"We'll keep an eye out," he assured me. I slipped my serpent through the office window into the mind of the woman.

Her name was Sarah. She did a lot of the administrative work. Just like any good administrative assistant, she knew almost everything about the entire operation. She moved things with her mind which made it seriously confusing to be in her mind too, but I tried to sift through all the information as best I could. Her mind was a little thicker like Eddie's had been, like swimming through syrup, but manageable, so I ignored it.

Sarah kept things running at the base when Ross traveled. She usually knew his itinerary and objectives. Ross never needed her in South America. She had talked to him briefly on his phone, but he had quickly dismissed the problem of intruders. Strange.

I found a map in her head of Ross's many business locations. I tried to remember the locations he visited most recently. The most complicated one had to be Brazil, deep in the Amazon. It must be important because he had been there for a few weeks, but she didn't dwell on the details so I followed her train of thought.

Sarah knew Ross would be with Eva soon. Multiple emotions attached themselves to those thoughts. She wasn't interested in Ross, but she hated the fact that he relied so much on Eva. Sarah didn't trust her. She didn't like Ross and Eva spending so much time together nor making big plans together. Even more, she didn't like them keeping those plans secret.

That's when she thought of them, the big plans Devin Ross had for the People of the Storm, at least the ones Sarah knew about. I got weak in the knees, but I tried to keep it hidden. Ross had so much animosity in him it had made him very powerful. He indoctrinated the idea of wiping out the Storm People in every person he met. Unfortunately for us, many people bought into Ross's plans for one reason or another but they also believed every lie he told as well. Sarah had her doubts, but this is what she had signed up for. She was prepared to see it through. Eva Winford and Perry Anderson had major roles. She knew Aaron would take Perry's place in the Amazon to follow through with one plan. Then Eva and Ross would head to the Rockies. For what, she had no idea. I didn't know who these people were, but I didn't want to waste time going down any of those rabbit holes.

Sarah had informed Ross of the intrusion and had been told not to take any action until he told her. She thought they should immediately evacuate. There had to be something he wasn't telling her. She also assumed it had something to do with Vincent.

A vision of Ross and Sarah swam in her memories so I listened in. They stood alone in the office. Uncertainty adhered to this memory. *I'm just not sure you should be taking what Vincent says so seriously,* Sarah said to Ross. She knew his temper, but she also knew he needed her. He couldn't afford to brush her off the way he did so many others. She also knew he regarded her opinion higher than others. *He speaks nonsense most of the time. How can you trust anything he says?* she asked him.

Ross's face remained even. *I appreciate your concern, Sarah.* He didn't sound like he cared at all for her concern. *But Vincent puts forth a lot of effort to get any message through. He wouldn't say anything unless it's of the utmost importance.*

Sarah nodded. It made sense. If Vincent could say anything coherently, there must be a reason.

So, we'll find this young woman with brown hair, Ross continued. *We'll see what her powers are and if she'll help us. If not, we'll kill her. It shouldn't inconvenience any of our plans to check her out.*

He said it with so little feeling that a chill ran up my spine. He had been talking about me, and here I stood not fifty feet from the same place where he had said it. Maybe Liam had it right. I shouldn't have come.

When Sarah turned back to menial tasks, I figured I had gotten as much information as possible, but had somehow forgotten how to breathe. I tried to take slow, deep breaths as I turned to Liam to leave.

I must not have hidden my distress very well because as I looked at him, he said, "That bad, huh?" I could only nod. He pursed his lips, "Let's get back to Jancarlo. Now."

We both turned to find Wiki, but he was gone. Maybe he had never even come with us. We quietly peeked around the corner. Nothing. "Wiki," Liam whispered as loud as he dared. We stood for a moment in silence. Then Wiki appeared out of the darkness with his hands stuffed in his pockets. His usual jovial grin had vanished. I thought maybe he had picked up on the severity of the situation from me until someone else materialized next to him. I don't know much about guns, but the one this guy held looked like it weighed as much as me! I figured it would make quite a mark.

Liam immediately moved in front of me. With his face only half-turned toward me, he put a finger to his lips. I remembered we were still invisible, but I had no idea about Wiki.

It didn't matter. Wiki stared at the ground, but remained well outside of arms reach. "Sorry," he stated dully. I touched his mind for only a moment before he disappeared.

The guy with the gun pointed it almost exactly at us, "Don't move," he barked. "I know you're there."

I immediately reached out to his mind to see his bluff. He knew we were somewhere nearby, but he didn't know exactly where. He had to stall until Neil came.

Liam glanced at me and I shook my head. He reached back to grab my hand pulling me silently around the guard, away from the point of the gun. "If you don't show yourself," he said, "I'll just spray the entire place until I find your bodies."

Just as we got behind him we heard a voice down the hallway say, "They're behind you, you idiot!"

The guy with the gun swung around, bringing his elbow into Liam's head. Liam got thrown into me, which threw me into the wall. With a deafening CRACK everything went black.

Chapter NINE

I woke up with a horrible headache. I wondered if what had been happening had been a dream. Scratch that. I mean, a nightmare. As I eased my eyes open, I saw dark stone all around me. At least I wouldn't be blinded by light. I lay on what seemed to be a tiny, lumpy cot. I was close enough to see stains and smell something fetid. I could imagine the germs creeping all over me. I groaned a little from the throbbing in my head.

"Ella," Liam sounded on the verge of tears. "Are ye okay?" I could hear an Irish accent to his voice. He dragged himself over to my bedside kneeling next to me. I could feel his warm breath on my cheek.

"If getting hit by a freight train is 'okay', then sure, I'm somewhere in that category." I sat up, but Liam stayed on his knees in front of me. We were in a small holding cell, complete with thick, iron bars on the dense door. No windows, no light, and only darkness beyond the bars.

When I focused on Liam, I saw a long deep cut on his cheek with at least four swollen bruises elsewhere. "What happened to you?" I asked in a panic.

I leaned over him to inspect his face, but he just waved me off, "Oh, you should see t'e other guy. Well, other guys. T'was hardly a fair fight." I gave him a stern look as if to say, *Tell me everything.* He sighed then answered seriously. "After I accidentally knocked you out, they came after you. I put up a fight, but they eventually got us down here." After a pause he said, "We've been down here for an hour or so. I was startin' to worry about you."

I remembered my guilt when he had used Gretchen's healing stone on me first the last time and resolved he should use it on himself first this time. "Do you have one of Gretchen's stones?"

He nodded, pulling it out of his pant pocket. "It doesn't work in here though. We're in a dampening field. It negates all powers."

"How does that work?" I asked. "The dampening field?"

"Just how it sounds," he said. "We've been messing around with isolating and suppressing powers for as long as we've had 'em. It takes a certain type of power to do it, but it's useful."

With this news I immediately tried to reach out with my mind to his. Sure enough, I couldn't find my little serpent anywhere. My heart ached and I thought I could feel eyes on me. I knew Liam must be much more uncomfortable.

"I guess we're stuck here for a while."

Liam nodded, "Yep."

I moved over on the cot, patting the spot next to me. Liam cracked half a grin heaving himself next to me. We both leaned back against the cold wall behind us.

We sat in silence for a moment until Liam spoke up. "Maybe Wiki will send help."

My face fell. I didn't know how to tell him this. He had known Wiki a long time. They must be at least somewhat friends. "I don't think Wiki will be coming for us. Or telling anyone where we are."

"What do you mean?" he asked with an edge in his voice.

"He betrayed us," I said. Better to get it over with, right? "I looked into his mind a second before he disappeared."

"Can't say I'm surprised," he said, unemotional to this revelation.

Now it was my turn to be shocked. "What do you mean?"

"He hasn't been himself lately. I know you can't tell, but he's been edgy and even reclusive lately," he said.

"That's reclusive?" I asked.

Liam nodded. "It is for Wiki."

I let these thoughts sink in, then asked, "Why would he do it, though?"

"I have some theories," Liam sighed, "But I'm not sure."

"How long have you known him," I asked. "What's his history?"

Liam grinned again, half-heartedly. "What? You don't already know?"

"No," I admitted, angry at myself. "I never looked into anyone's minds in the Storm People except yours and Gretchen's. Well…" I figured now was as good a time as any for a confession. "I used Jancarlo's thoughts to get him to let me come along."

"I knew it," Liam said with a chuckle.

"But I've tried not to pry into anyone's mind. Even the first time I met Wiki, I didn't look too deep. I stayed on the surface."

"Maybe, when we get back," Liam consoled me, "we should talk to Jancarlo about re-evaluating whether that's a good thing or not. Sometimes we need to know who we can trust."

I nodded and Liam continued. "Wiki and I got struck about the same time, but on opposite sides of the world. We were brought up very differently. He was young and an orphan and had to make his own way in the world. He had no one for support. No one to trust with his secret. He's always had a problem trusting anyone because of it. So, it surprised all of us when he set his sights on Kimi. She has had no tolerance with him. I think he's a little offended."

"But is that really a reason to turn on your own people?" I asked exasperated. I couldn't understand such a reaction.

"Sometimes being offended is all it takes to turn someone who loves you into your enemy. Wiki is very good at holding a grudge." His face fell as he said it, but it quickly shifted before he added, "I'm sure money has something to do with it too."

Then I remembered the plans I had seen in Sarah's mind. I sat bolt upright turning to Liam with wide eyes. "He has no idea what he's doing." I could hear the fear in my voice and tried to calm myself. "He couldn't possibly know what they're planning. He couldn't betray us to that."

Liam's eyebrows pulled together sharply. "What are they planning? You never said."

"He's building an army," I said boldly. "Ross is using people in other lands, especially the Amazon. The uncontacted groups there are strong, mentally and physically. But he's careful with his manipulations. He's convinced them the Storm People are trying to kill them all. But he's basically bullying anyone who doesn't agree into helping him."

Liam's jaw dropped. "No."

Getting into a stride I continued. "That's not all. He has someone named Perry who funnels electricity through a person's body when they're shocked so they don't die. Then they can also gain the powers they want. Not only can he choose what powers he wants the person to have, but he can give anyone multiple powers. Sarah knows what powers everyone has. She keeps track of it all, but Ross has several powers and he doesn't answer to her."

"Ross has multiple powers," Liam nodded as he said it, almost like a confirmation. "He's been extremely confident the past little while, but we had no idea."

"He's planning something else," I said grimly. "Sarah didn't know what, but she has an idea it's big. Even bigger than the army he's building. Like the army is just the first step."

Liam put his face in his hands, "Do you know how big the army is yet?"

"They're gathering anyone they can coerce worldwide, but the majority of it will be brought from South America and transformed here. They figure with all the powers they'll have, they won't need as many people. The goal is to have five hundred, all capable of fire throwing, limited transportation as well as moving objects." I stopped, thinking maybe I had given him too much.

Liam met my eyes, his face unreadable. "When?"

"Sarah was trying to contact Ross after we showed up the first time," I said. "She assumed he would want to move up the timeline because of it. They'll start gathering tomorrow. They could be fully charged and at the Storm base in as little as three days."

Chapter TEN

We talked about a lot of stuff that day, or night, or whatever it was. We both rested occasionally, but we had no sense of time. We estimated that transporting hundreds of people would only take part of a day, but giving them powers then healing them would take a little longer. At least a couple days with everyone working around the clock. While sitting in a dank cell we had no way to know if they had at least started transporting everyone.

"Kimi gave us one hour," I said, voicing our last hope. "They'll come for us soon, I'm sure."

"By the time the Storm People can set up a rescue, the Shadow will be bringing in the South Americans. We have another transporter, but she can only take two at a time and she can only go short distances. At least she can go somewhere she's never been before, that's her big advantage."

"You know Charlotte will never get in here. The dampening field will stop her." The voice came from outside the door so we knew who it was immediately. "Besides," Wiki added, "only one of the Shadow can get you out of that door. I couldn't open it if I wanted to," he said with a little bitterness.

We both jumped to the small window. Liam moved slower from the many bumps and bruises he had, but I think the anger compensated for everything else. "What are you doing here?" he growled through the small window when Wiki's face appeared.

"Easy, Liam," Wiki sounded very smug, "I just came to talk. I'm going to be busy for the next little while, so I thought I'd take a minute to say good-bye."

"You mean gloat," Liam grumbled.

"Whatever."

"Always looking out for number one, aren't you?" It wasn't really a question, but I think Liam needed to hear the truth from Wiki.

"The guards said you'd figured things out. You won't be alive much longer to tell anyone so I might still be of some use as a spy." Wiki didn't sound excited about the prospect. From what Liam told me, as self-centered as he was, he didn't go out of his way to serve anyone else.

"Why did you do it, Wiki?" I asked. I just didn't understand how anyone could allow something like this to happen.

"You'll understand after you've been used for as long as I have," he said with some heat in his voice. "I'm a glorified airline without all the benefits."

"You could have left whenever you wanted. No one forced you to stay," Liam said.

Wiki's face crumpled in pain for a moment, but then the anger came back. "Someone did keep me there.

You know how she is, Liam. But I'll never be good enough for her. I'm nothing like you." I got confused at this retort. There was more history here than I knew. I guess I should've scrutinized Wiki's past when I had the chance. I looked to Liam for an explanation. I would have questioned him about it, but the look on his face stopped me. Liam glared at Wiki with so much anger I was surprised his face didn't burst into flames. It would've if it had been Kimi. Instead, I turned back to Wiki.

"What are you talking about?" I thought maybe if I kept him talking, we could work this out.

"Liam knows. Ask him," he answered.

"I asked you. What made you turn?"

Wiki turned his glare on me and simply said, "Hate." He turned away, calling back to us quietly, "Good-bye and good riddance."

I moved slowly over to the cot by the wall with Liam close behind. He kept his face turned toward the floor. I tried to catch his eyes, but he seemed to be purposefully avoiding mine. I looked away with a small sigh. He would talk when he was ready.

"Kimi," he finally said. I glanced over at him, but his eyes still studied his shoes. I didn't know if he would go on.

After a few more minutes silence I finally had to ask, "So he's just upset Kimi doesn't like him? That's ridiculous! I mean, people say 'a woman scorned' is bad news, but geez, don't piss off Wiki!"

Liam cracked a grin and shook his head. "Wiki has always been jealous that Kimi…well…" he paused for a moment, scrunching his face up like he had a bad taste in his mouth then finished, "Kimi preferred me."

A love triangle?! That's what this was about?! What had I walked into?! If we ever got out of here, I'd be putting my little serpent to work!

I started out tentatively. "Well," I hemmed, "I guess she is more your age." More than what?! Me?! What a stupid thing to say!

He just snorted in response. He glanced up at me, then I think the implications of what I said hit him. His grin toppled off his face. With a second look at me, his hand lifted as if to reach out to me, but he stayed his hand. "No, wait," he stammered out, "I mean, Storm People don't really look at age…that way."

"You don't?" I asked.

"No," he seemed to breathe again. "Otherwise, I'd be stuck dating centenarians!" He blanched slightly. "That'd be awful. Even Gretchen is technically younger than me. No," he continued shaking his head, "Storm People learn to ignore years and judge by maturity, but Kimi and Wiki are kind of…complex."

I took a deep breath, nodding, "Well, we have plenty of time for a good long story." I sat there looking around the cell. I'm a patient person, besides if we ever got out of here, I would get the story myself.

"It's not a long story," he finally muttered without much emotion. "Wiki has always liked Kimi. Kimi's never liked him. At all. Not even a little bit. She's as civil to him as she can be, but she can't stand to be around him. She thinks he's a huge coward, and she can't stand cowardice.

She had a thing for me a couple of decades ago, but I told her I prefer her as a friend. We've been friends ever since. Unfortunately, it's not good enough for Wiki." He met my eyes again. "He's always thought we're keeping something from him."

I shook my head at the stupidity of it. I couldn't even think of anything to say. Liam's head bobbed in agreement. "Like I said, Wiki really knows how to hold a grudge."

"He's going to aid killing hundreds of people, just for some stupid broken heart?" I continued shaking my head with my lips pursed. "That is cowardice. I don't blame Kimi." For more than one thing.

We sat lost in our own thoughts for who knows how long. My stomach growled at the darkness. My fingers and toes eventually drained of feeling. I rubbed my hands, blowing into them to spread some warmth. Liam reached over to cover them with his. He blew warm air into our hands, effectively warming both pairs. I immediately forgot the wedge from the cot shoving into my butt cheek. After a few more minutes of warming ourselves, I wondered out loud if Charlotte could make it here.

He scanned the window in the door nervously. Then he whispered, "She can make it to the base, but I don't know if she could make it in here to us. She would have to get us out the old-fashioned way, with keys."

"Or a big hammer."

We agreed on that, but Charlotte could only make a location jump of about a hundred miles at a time. We were thirteen hundred miles away from our base.

"Even if, after a few hours, Jancarlo allows her to come get us, it will still take her at least thirteen jumps to get here." We kept our voices low because of what Wiki said about the guards hearing us.

"Do you think Kimi would come?" I whispered.

"She wouldn't stand for it if Jancarlo didn't want her to come. She might allow Kin to go instead, but no one else."

It was silent for a moment until suddenly a shuffling sound came from outside the cell door. We hadn't heard any noise come from the other side of the door other than Wiki for hours. Or it seemed like hours, anyway. Liam and I looked at each other to make sure we had both heard it. With unspoken consent we crept quietly to the door. As we got closer, Liam firmly grabbed me by the arms, guiding me to the side of the door with my back against the wall.

With his eyes still on the window, he put his fingers to his lips for silence. Then he stood next to the door, peering out into the darkness.

"Who's there?" He whispered it, with a firm demand for a response.

"A friend," came a man's voice. The voice sounded familiar, but I couldn't quite place it. "Stand away from the door," the voice said softly.

Liam grabbed my hand, pulling both of us away from the door into the cramped space we shared. He brought my hand behind his back even farther so I had no choice but to stand behind him peeking out from around his shoulder.

The door suddenly burst into white-hot flame. If I had been next to it, I would've been fried. The fire stopped as quickly as it had started, exposing a clear path into a cold, stone hallway.

We crept to the doorway waiting for a trap to be sprung. As we passed the threshold, we saw a tall, pale man with red hair standing so close to the wall he looked like he wanted to melt into it. A man behind him was slumped on the floor. I figured I didn't want to know what happened to him. I recognized our rescuer and instinctively reached out to his mind as soon as I saw him, mentally embracing my little serpent.

Liam looked at him warily then motioned to the charred edges where the door had been. "Fire starter?"

"No," the man said, "It's a trigger. I'm a rock mover. My name is…"

"Eddie," I finished for him.

His eyebrows creased in confusion. He glanced over at Liam as if expecting that he knew him as well. Liam just glanced at me then addressed Eddie, "You were the guard at the entrance when we came in earlier."

Comprehension dawned on his face as he nodded answering, "I knew I heard someone, but I'm well past caring whether or not someone gets in. But I do care if you get out."

"Why?" Liam asked suspiciously.

"Fair question," Eddie allowed. "I made a mistake joining these people. I want out. I thought you might trust me if I help you." His speech was refined. He sounded like he didn't belong in this part of the world or this decade.

He braced himself as if expecting the why-should-we-trust-you?-because-you-have-to argument. Instead, Liam turned to me.

I nodded to him. As I waded through Eddie's mind, the first thing I noticed was that it was clearer. The stickiness had dissipated as though someone had washed his brain out with soap. I could sense some residue on the edges, but for the most part his mind moved and shifted easily.

Eddie's thoughts lingered on the sunshine he had seen earlier while on guard duty. He wanted to live a quiet life looking at the sunlight whenever he wanted. He thought of the woman he had lost. They had fought, so he had been angry and drunk when he met Devin Ross. He now knew Ross held nothing but empty promises.

I also saw it was now late evening. We had spent more time in the cell than I realized. Eddie's disappearance would soon be noticed, if something else didn't give him away first. He risked everything in helping us, but the reward would be far greater. I pulled out of his mind when I knew he would do whatever we needed. We could trust him. If I ever thought otherwise, I wouldn't hesitate to check again.

After I gave Liam a second nod, he looked back at Eddie. He gave a wave of his hand as if to say, "Lead the way."

Eddie's eyebrows pinched together in unbelief. "Just like that?" he asked.

"We'll talk on the way," Liam said, but I figured he would try to keep our powers a secret until he knew more about this man.

We started off down the hallway like shadows, following our new guide. After a few minutes, Eddie threw his arm across our path to stop us. He put his finger to his lips to keep us quiet while he inspected the walls. He motioned for us to follow him to the other side of the hallway a few paces down. We faced a blank stone wall. In confusion, I dipped into his mind. He could hear the guards from here and knew they were coming for him. However, he knew of a hallway hidden in the rock. He wondered how he could get us to go in without us thinking he was trying to trick us. At that moment I heard the guards, through Eddie's mind, down the hall saying, "Check the prisoners." Trying not to think about it too much, I closed my eyes and dove into the stone wall.

The stone was just an illusion, so I reached back through, yanking Liam into the hidden space. Eddie followed us through then took the lead again. Liam seemed calm but dragged behind hunched over. I reached out to his mind as he motioned with his eyes to his forehead.

I've already made us invisible. I need to use the stone to heal myself before I can go much further.

I tapped Eddie on the arm. *Stop!* I mouthed to him then pointed at Liam.

I helped Liam sit down on the floor next to the wall while Eddie looked around us anxiously. Liam pulled out Gretchen's healing stone. He gently lifted his shirt to expose a big, dark multi-colored bruise. He pressed the stone to his ribs with a cringe.

I think they broke my ribs, he said in my mind, *but this should take care of it.*

He moved the stone, taking a deep breath. His breathing evened out and color returned to his cheeks. When he gave us a nod, Eddie beckoned us on. I helped Liam stand, but he was already stronger. Eddie pulled us close to him to whisper, "The guards are trying to find us now. We have to get out of here. We'll try to use some of the tunnels to go deeper into the base. I'll find somewhere for us to hide for a while."

Liam eyed me, I figured to see if we could trust Eddie. I probed Eddie's mind again to see him plotting a course through the maze of tunnels in the Shadow base. He tried to think of somewhere to go that wasn't used very often. I nodded back to Liam, and Liam gestured for Eddie to lead the way.

We ran through hallway after hallway, keeping clear of everyone. Hundreds of tunnel-like hallways snaked through the base. Many more than I had originally thought. Hidden tunnels added to the maze-like effect. Eddie knew how to navigate them pretty well. He stopped at one point, bringing us in closer. "We should be safe for a little while in a room just around the corner, but there's someone in our way. A woman named Mia. She's small, but her power is speed, so she's dangerous. If we can get past her without her seeing us we should be able to stay hidden until we can figure a way out of this."

"What's she doing?" Liam said to Eddie, but I reached my mind around the corner to check. She was shadow-boxing, just practicing to keep busy while on guard duty.

"She's guarding the transporter to Vermont," Eddie answered.

"What's in Vermont?" Liam asked suspiciously.

"We're not going to Vermont, just past the transporter," Eddie clarified.

"Well, if that's all, we should be able to walk right by her," Liam said.

"How?" Eddie said in confusion.

"No one can see us," Liam whispered. "I can manipulate light. We've been invisible since you let us out of that cell."

"Well, that would have been good to know." Eddie whispered back a little harshly.

I shushed him as Liam fought back a chuckle. I tried my best to give Liam a stern look, knowing full well I hadn't exactly disclosed my own powers.

"All right," Eddie whispered again, "let's just walk by her slowly. Hopefully she'll never know we're there."

We followed his lead, but having done this before, we were probably more comfortable with it than he was. The three of us tiptoed into a larger, circular area with hallways leading off in opposite directions. We passed dangerously close to the woman who was, like Eddie said, "small, but dangerous." Her fists were a fuzzy distortion of movement in front of her as she beat the air. I knew I would never want to get in her way.

We slipped past the circular area into the far hallway then into a hidden hallway off to the left. Large stones, much like the one at the entrance to the base, mirrored each other all the way down the hallway. Eddie used his powers to move one of the rocks so we could slip into the room beyond. It impressed me how silently he could lay the rock down again.

The empty room we entered had the same cold darkness like everywhere else, but an added eerie sensation prickled my skin. I thought we had hit a dead end until I noticed some plaques on the walls around us. I stepped closer to read one.

Here lies a brave man who fell in the attempt to obtain
His just privilege, but remained denied.
His memory will live on in the powers of others.

Chapter ELEVEN

I tried to take a deep breath but couldn't find it. I stepped away from the plaque in fear only to find another with the same words at my back. Graveyards had always given me the creeps. "What is this place?" I asked Eddie after he had replaced the stone. My hands shook.

"This is where they entomb the men and women who tried to join the Shadow but died in the attempt," Eddie said, confirming my fears. "They don't use it much anymore because they've been able to keep so many people from dying. But every single person in the Shadow is a hardened killer. They watched each of these people die without blinking. Don't ever forget that."

"Why?"

"Because someday you might have to do it to them."

Eddie slumped down on the stone. I wondered if it was from guilt for all the deaths, even though he had nothing to do with them. I would have reached out to touch his mind, but he looked up at me, "So what's your power anyway. Are you a transporter and conveniently forgetting to tell me?" His eyes flashed over to Liam as he said it but then returned to me.

I looked at Liam touching his mind instead to make sure he wanted me to say anything. With a sigh he asked me, *Are you sure we can trust him? Is he being honest?*

I checked Eddie's mind again quickly, but found nothing different. The thought of helping us was attached to a strong emotion. When I sampled it, it was definitely guilt with a little hope in the mix. He hoped that helping us would make up for what he had been a part of. I nodded back at Liam who shrugged his shoulders at me.

I guess we should tell him then. Go ahead.

I turned back to Eddie, who waited patiently for us to finish the nods and shrugs. "I read minds," I said simply.

"Oh," Eddie said in surprise. Then he smiled. "That's why you trusted me so easily." Contrasting the first impression we had of him, his smile showed what a personable man he could be under different circumstances.

"Eddie," Liam asked, "how did you hear the guards back in the prison? You must have really good hearing."

"I offered to be one of the early guinea pigs for adding to our powers," he said. I think he expected us to be surprised with this discovery, but he didn't know I already knew about the multiple powers. He continued after a short pause. "I hoped a second shock would kill me then I wouldn't have to worry about Devin Ross's war anymore. Instead, it worked just like they had hoped. They gave me super sensitive hearing. I didn't sign up for any more volunteer work after that. I think when Ross started dictating what powers we would receive without deference to our opinions, is when I decided I had had enough.”

“Can you tell us about the other people here? Are there any that might feel the same way as you? Do you have any friends that might help us?” Liam asked.

“I have a few friends, but there really is ‘no honor among thieves’. Everyone here is power hungry. And I mean that literally. They’re hoping that after Ross wins this war, they’ll get the powers they want. Ross sells his war like he’s the guy trying to protect everyone, but to the people he works closest with, he promises power over the mortals. He’s the one really trying to take over the world.”

“How do you know all this?”

“Just by talking to people. Most soldiers here are blood-thirsty or power hungry or both. There are people here who were promised they can take over companies that laid them off. Some have been promised whole cities or states for their help. He guaranteed your buddy Wiki could see to the imprisonment of the entire People of the Storm.”

“But Ross doesn’t want imprisonment,” I interjected, remembering Sarah’s thoughts.

“He’ll promise anyone anything. I think the only people who know what he’s really doing are Ross himself and Vincent,” Eddie said.

“What kind of a role does Vincent play in all of this?” Liam asked.

“Vincent isn’t coherent all of the time. His is a difficult condition,” Eddie replied. “It ruined him when he got shocked. Before Ross talked him into taking his first shock, he could accurately guess the result of situations. Now," he shook his head, "he sees everything. It's too much for his mind. Half of the time he says things that sound ludicrous, so most of us have a hard time believing anything." Eddie looked up at me and said, "He knew about you coming, though."

"So I've heard," I answered.

Eddie shrugged, "I guess it would be hard to tell you something you don't know, huh?"

I realized he probably thought I continued prying into his mind. "Don't worry," I said, "I won't look into your head again unless you want me to." After a pause I added, "or I stop trusting you." I wanted him to know if I ever wondered where his loyalties lay I would just look into his mind. It wasn't much of a threat, but I'm not much of a fighter, so it's all I had.

"Well, first things first," Liam spoke up, "We need to get some supplies then figure out how to get out of here. We have to get this information back to Jancarlo."

Liam did some scouting by himself, which I protested, but he got some food in a small pack. Then we stopped to think about where we could go.

"We could easily take the transport to Vermont," Eddie offered.

"No," Liam shook his head, "We would still have to get to the Storm People on our own while they're busy looking somewhere else for us. Our best bet is to try to get out the main way."

"How are we supposed to do that? There's always a seer at the transporter," Eddie said.

"Is there some way to contact the Storm People?" I asked.

Both men stared at me. Liam said, "You tell us."

I thought for a moment. "It would take a while for me to get there and I'm not even sure I can go that far."

"Phones and computers are out. We have what Gretchen calls 'residual lightning' in our makeup. Anything with a computer likes to go nuts around us," Liam said.

"Ah," I muttered. "That explains the phone when I tried to text my aunt."

Liam turned to Eddie. "How does it work for the Shadow?"

Eddie shrugged. "Electronics work fine for us, but a cell phone won't work down here, and I think the only computer is in Sarah's office. It's one of The Boss's ways of controlling us. No contact with the upper world."

"Maybe we can…" Liam didn't get a chance to finish his thought. Eddie shushed him, holding one hand up to us and the other to his ear. He heard someone coming. He slowly put his finger to his lips, pointed to me then to his forehead. I sprang into his mind as fast as I could.

Someone's coming. He said, *They're in the hallway. They're being very quiet so I think they might be listening for us. Can you communicate with Liam in his mind?*

My brow furrowed. I had never tried to put my own voice or thoughts in someone else's mind. I didn't know if I could do it, but now seemed like the time to try.

I bent my mind to be in both men's minds at once then tried to push my voice into their minds.

Can you hear me? I said into their minds.

I concentrated on pushing my words through to both men. To my surprise I heard, *Yes!* in duplicate.

Liam's eyebrows lifted in surprise. *Well, this is convenient.* He said in our minds.

Indeed. Came Eddie's response. Not only had Eddie heard my voice in his head, but he could hear Liam as well. I realized it was not just me pushing my words through to them, but they had to also concentrate on pushing their words to the others. Liam must have been concentrating on it every time he had talked to me.

Do you know who's out there? Liam asked Eddie.

He shook his head. *It won't matter. They'll hear our heartbeats and know we don't belong in here.*

We'll have to fight our way out then. Liam thought.

As he said it, I pushed my serpent through the large stone door to see who we had to deal with. In silence we listened to the thoughts of a woman named Cindee. She was young but passionate. She hated traitors even more than she hated the Storm People. Everyone in the Shadow was hunting for the traitor and two escaped prisoners. Her extremely sensitive hearing was her first power ever, but recently she had gained the power to create fire, not just throw it. She planned to heat the rock to turn our room into an oven. She would know we were dead when our heartbeats stopped.

We heard the plan in her head as the rock blocking our path turned bright orange. The room flooded with heat. I immediately beaded with sweat.

Suddenly Eddie stepped in front of the burning rock. I didn't think anything was happening for a few seconds until the stone walls shook with a loud explosion. The rock in front of him flew across the hallway on the other side. A boot stuck out from the wall as if it had grown from the rock itself to mark the remains of Cindee.

Eddie turned to us. "We need to get out of here, now."

"Agreed," Liam said as I bobbed my head. "We need to head straight for the main transport. We'll have to make a run for it." He grabbed my hand shouldering the pack at the same time. As we all ran out of the room together, he said, "Ella, stay in our minds so we don't have to talk out loud."

Eddie took the lead again. I noticed we took a much straighter path than before.

I entered both men's minds to immediately hear Eddie say, *Everyone must have heard the explosion. They'll be headed this way.*

Try to move around them, they shouldn't be able to see us. Liam said.

As he said it, we hit an intersection of tunnels. Sure enough, two groups of two people each headed toward us from the sides. We ran straight down the hall past the pairs. As we ran, I made sure the groups had not seen us. They continued to run toward the explosion.

I breathed with relief until we saw a much larger search group running straight at us. At first I thought we would be fine because no one raised the alarm. Eddie stood off to one side. Liam and I pressed our backs against the other side. Unfortunately, the group consisted of six people, five large men and one similarly muscular woman. They stretched themselves to cover all of the space in the wide hallway.

We were almost in the clear when one man with blonde dreadlocks bumped up against Eddie. "Wait," he yelled. The whole group stopped to look at the man, pointing guns and hands in Eddie's direction. Eddie tried to edge away, but he scuffed his foot. The whole group of people exploded in his direction. They threw fire and rocks at him. Some blindly grabbed in the vicinity to try to get at him. Being a rock thrower himself Eddie kept the rocks off of himself, but he had to dive out of the way of the fire. It wasn't bright or strong, but it was enough. Finally, one of the men's fists connected with Eddie's chest.

"Here!" he yelled to the group. There were so many in the group that they couldn't use their powers very much, which might have saved his life. Liam and I couldn't just stand there watching. We started in on the group from behind.

I didn't know if I would help or hinder, but I attacked a woman from behind anyway. I wrapped my left arm around her neck to punch at her head with my right. I connected with her ear. I'd been hit there before with a fly swatter, and I knew it really hurt. She screamed, cringing away, but she recovered quickly. As she turned to try to grab me, I dropped to kick at her legs. It wasn't pretty or perfect, but it did the job. A few crunches and she plunged to the floor like a bag of rocks reaching for her mangled leg.

Again, she recovered too quickly for my liking, but I liked my odds with the invisibility advantage. Then I realized how outnumbered we were. Liam had been doing pretty well helping Eddie, but the powers of the others were proving difficult. Eddie used small pebbles like bullets to pummel the others, but they had a rock thrower to counter his attack.

Liam had gotten his hands on a small knife from someone in the group and sliced at the backs of everyone's legs. Even though the Shadow would stab us through the face with a smile, Liam tried to keep from seriously harming them. I tried to head toward him but got tangled up with one of the other men. In half a second his arms squeezed around me. I tried to resist the urge, but a scream tore from my lips as he compressed me. Liam ran for me but was grabbed by someone else while Eddie got snared by the blonde guy who thrashed him without mercy.

"Is that all of them?" one of the men asked the group in general. The woman stood now but leaned on another man with a murderous look on her face.

A smooth, familiar voice ghosted down the hall, "Not quite."

Chapter TWELVE

I couldn't see anyone, so I immediately reached out with my mind. Sure enough, Kimi had come to the rescue. She had a whirl of martial arts moves spinning through her head. I could tell she needed to go for my captor first, but she was afraid of hitting whoever he held as well.

Without thinking about it, I yelled into her head, *Go!* then thrust the back of my head into my captor's nose as hard as I could. I didn't hit him as hard as I wanted to, but his grip slacked enough for me to drop to the floor as Kimi threw a ball of fire into his chest.

Kimi and Liam flowed around the Shadow. With the addition of Eddie, they turned into a blur of fists and feet taking down man after man. As I watched from the floor, I noticed someone else enter the fray. She moved from spot to spot, never staying in one place long enough for anyone to get a good jab at her. She bounced around making sure no one could get at their guns and generally confusing the enemy. It had to be Charlotte.

Kimi didn't take prisoners. She put a ring of fire around the group that no one, even our own group could get in or out of, except Charlotte. Meanwhile she and Liam finished off the ones hampering us. When all of them were either dead or unconscious (I didn't want to know which were which), she put out the containing fire. Only then did she take off the black cap she had on.

As soon as she did, she appeared in front of us. I had no idea she had something like that. Obviously, it had Liam's powers in it. I could see how Wiki might confuse their relationship.

"Good to see you," I said when I saw her.

"You're late," she said sternly, but she winked at me, adding, "Then again I didn't wait the whole hour before I insisted we put together a rescue."

"Good thing," I said.

"Now is not the time to talk," Liam chastised us. "We need to get out of here." He said this as he turned to Charlotte who stood next to him. "Take Eddie and Ella to the surface first," he said.

"Wait," Kimi said, "don't you think we should have someone to watch him?"

"We can trust him, Kimi," he said motioning in my direction. She nodded that she had received the message.

Before anyone could move, a man tumbled out from the wall next to me. His hair reminded me of Einstein or Mozart with bright white tufts sticking out in all directions. His face was prickled with white stubble, but I could see the edges of frail cheekbones underneath. The scariest part of him were his eyes. A solid white lens twitched under his lids with no pupils, irises or even little red veins. He tumbled toward me as if blind. I caught him in my arms out of reflex. His voice came out in a strained whisper as if every word tortured him, "Don't... Gretchen... Must... go... Gretchen."

"Who is that?" Kimi asked sharply.

"Vincent," Eddie offered with narrowed eyes.

"He wants to go to Gretchen," I said quietly.

Liam and Kimi looked at each other then back to the old man in my arms.

"Someone else is coming," Eddie said.

Again, Liam and Kimi looked at each other. Kimi pinched her thin lips together. "We'll take him with us. Let's go."

We quickly transported out of the Shadow base to the surface. Charlotte first took me and Vincent to a prepared campsite. Then she came back with Liam and Eddie and Kimi last.

Vincent mumbled a continuous stream of nonsense, waving his arms around as if lazily swatting at flies. He sat on the ground next to the fire with Eddie nearby. Eddie understood Vincent's plight personally and took it upon himself to help the old man. He tried to get Vincent to eat, but the old man just continued to mumble, ignoring Eddie's efforts.

Since the first word out of his mouth was "Don't," I hesitated to look into his mind. I figured I would wait until we were all back safely before I dove in. Although clearly not cognizant, the frail old man unnerved me for some reason.

"The Shadow will be combing the hills looking for us," Kimi said. "Wiki knows Charlotte is only capable of up to a hundred miles at a time."

"He'll try to intercept us first," Liam responded. "He knows that when we get back to the Storm Base, he won't ever be able to return there without backup."

"I'll sense anyone who shows up. That's how my powers work," Charlotte said. She was a tall, slender blonde who looked like she belonged on the cover of a magazine, but she came across very business-like.

"Good." Kimi began gathering gear. "We've got to get everyone back to the base as soon as possible. Jancarlo can protect us better from there."

"It will take about fifteen or twenty minutes for me to get two people at a time back to the base," Charlotte said. "Or we can have a half-way rendezvous point."

"No," Liam shook his head, "it's more important to get someone back. Kimi and I will stay behind unseen. Start with Ella and Vincent. Those are the two most important people to get back right now. Then Eddie." He nodded to her, "Go now, but come back as fast as you can."

I did the math in my head. Fifteen minutes both ways meant if Liam was the last one back, as I suspected he would be, he wouldn't be back to the base for an hour and fifteen minutes. He would be a sitting duck for an hour. I met his eyes as Charlotte stood up to start transporting everyone. "Be careful," I mumbled as everyone waited for me. Then, feeling a little self-conscious, I glanced at Kimi. "You too."

"Don't worry, Ella," she said, "just get your information back to Jancarlo."

I hurried over to Charlotte who was helping Vincent stand. We supported him on both sides while the air around us began to shimmer. After the now-familiar breathless feeling, we stood near the road just south of Cheyenne. I thought something might be wrong when we didn't transport immediately again so I turned to Charlotte. "We have to take a breath between each jump," she said, reading the question in my eyes. "Otherwise, we're not breathing for nearly fourteen minutes."

She gave me a knowing look, so I nodded my agreement. We did this over and over until I lost count. Eventually, we landed in the lobby of the People of the Storm base in Georgia. I breathed a sigh of relief, but Vincent continued to mumble in my arms.

Charlotte looked at me sternly. "Take him to Gretchen," she said, shifting Vincent's weight to me "I'll go back for the others." She shimmered out of sight.

Good thing Vincent weighed next to nothing. He didn't seem to be conscious of our surroundings at all. He kept trying to sit down, but as I started moving toward Gretchen's office, he moved his feet too. A few steps before the office door, I saw Jancarlo and Kin running down the hall toward us.

"Ella," Jancarlo's relief oozed out of his voice. "We were so worried about you guys." Even though he hadn't known me long, I could read the truth of the words in the lines of his face. Then his eyes landed on the man with me. "Who's this?"

I ignored the question and simply said, "I need to get him to Gretchen."

Jancarlo nodded to Kin who quickly ushered us down the hall and into Gretchen's office. I steered Vincent to the small vinyl couch by the wall. Jancarlo drew a chair for me next to the couch. I thought for a moment I might be able to fall asleep in it.

"Kin," Jancarlo said seeing my fatigue, "get them some water and blankets."

Kin hurried off to the back of the room and wrenched open the supply closet. Jancarlo stared at me. "It seems you have quite a bit to report." He paused, then asked hesitantly, "Where's Wiki?"

I tried to look at him, but shame of not having seen the coming betrayal pushed my eyes down at the floor. I shook my head. "He's working with Devin Ross," I forced out of my clenched teeth.

I didn't dare look up at Jancarlo for a few minutes. I watched as Vincent absently mumbled and waved his hands. I could make out a few words, usually "danger" and "death" but the occasional "joy" could be heard too. He also continued to say Gretchen's name. I glanced at Kin's back while he stood at the sink. The water in his hands steamed to boiling until he finally noticed and dumped it into the sink. It landed with a hiss and he ran fresh cold water for our drinks.

As Kin brought the water to me, Gretchen came in the room. "What's going on?" she said. She had known about the mission but hadn't expected to be brought in for an emergency. Her eyes rested on Vincent on the bed and me in the chair. "Who did you bring back with you, Ella?"

"This is Vincent," I answered to the whole room. "He asked for you."

"The man who tells the future for the Shadow?" Jancarlo asked.

"Yes. He specifically asked for Gretchen."

Jancarlo gaped at the seemingly delusional man in front of him. Vincent didn't seem aware of anything and certainly not able to speak coherently. Jancarlo gave me a look of skepticism asking, "Have you checked him?"

I knew he was going to ask that. "No," I said with a shrug, "the first word out of his mouth was 'Don't.' Somehow, I think it was directed at me."

"But it could have been part of this rambling, right?" he asked waving in Vincent's direction.

"Yes," I admitted, "but…" I couldn't explain it.

"Ella," Jancarlo put his hand gently on my arm, "I know this can be frightening, but we need all the information we can get." He seemed so confident I couldn't refuse.

I knew I had a responsibility to do my part. And I wanted to help, but it hadn't turned out well. No one else could get the insight I could. No one else could unriddle this man. I remembered something my mother told me once. *"Courage is not the lack of fear; it's the taking of action in spite of fear."* I knew I had to try.

As I reached my mind out to Vincent's, I watched the old man. He seemed so harmless. The split second

before I touched his mind, his body went rigid. His white
eyes locked with mine.

Chapter Thirteen

An overwhelming sense of sounds, sights, emotions, even smells crushed my senses as soon as I breached his mind. I couldn't sort through anything. Confused beyond my sanity, I knew there would be no chance to inspect anything. I couldn't watch the pictures of people I didn't know, doing who knows what, with millions of emotions churning about my mind. I felt other people's pains. I heard millions of people's thoughts. I saw millions of people's futures. I knew what forced Vincent into his incoherent state. A shrill sound grew louder in my own head. In horror, I recognized it as a prolonged scream. I wondered for a moment where it could be coming from, then I understood. I could hear myself screaming, but I couldn't make myself stop. I couldn't remember what I was doing. I couldn't remember my name. I wanted to cover my head with my arms in confusion, but I didn't have any arms.

Suddenly, in front of me, someone vaguely familiar appeared out of the chaos. He had white tufts of hair and stubble on his chin. I tried to remember where I had seen him before, but I couldn't think straight. His brown eyes expressed warmth and concern. If only that screaming would stop, maybe I could think. He eyed me tenderly, saying, "You need to go back."

Go back? Back where? What was he talking about? He reached a gnarled finger out to my forehead and touched it just below my hairline on the left side. It started to burn. I screamed from the pain. Instantly, I remembered what I was supposed to do. Go back. I pulled my mind away as hard as I could. This time, I welcomed the darkness.

When I first started waking up, I had no idea what had happened. I lay in my little hotel-like room at the base. Oh, yeah, the Storm People. Yep, totally normal. Of course I belonged here, but I felt weird. Did I get run over by a bus? My entire body hurt, my head most of all. Even with the room only lit by the usual single light bulb, I could sense someone else there with me. I rolled over in the bed to see who sat in the chair at my desk.

Liam lifted his face to me. Gently, he said, "Are ye really awake dis time?"

"This time?" I asked. "How many times can one person wake up?"

"Ah, you're making sense," he grinned at me. "I t'ink you might actually be awake." He came over to the bed slowly. Sitting on the edge, he placed his hand on my shoulder. "You look like crap."

"Gee, thanks," I grumbled, rolling my face into the pillow. "Why do I feel so sore?" I asked as I tried to sit up.

Liam produced some pills and a glass of water from a table. As I took the medicine, he told me what happened with Vincent. "They told me once you entered Vincent's head, you went completely rigid like you were having a seizure. You collapsed to the ground, screaming your lungs out. You t'rashed around on the ground screaming for a good five minutes, they said. By the time I got back, you were unconscious, and they had brought you in here. Gretchen couldn't do much to help you. She healed you from your fall, but whatever else you experienced was in your mind."

I scrunched up my face trying to recall what had happened. When it started creeping back to me, I had to take a deep breath to keep from getting overwhelmed just by the memory.

"How long was I out?" I asked. I expected I had been unconscious a few hours or so, but I didn't expect what I heard.

"A day and a half," Liam answered solemnly. I stared at him dumbstruck for a moment, then the timing clicked.

"The Shadow. The people! They're going to hurt them! Maybe even kill them! Then they're going to come after us!" I almost launched myself out of the bed, getting louder with every word.

Liam laid a gentle hand on my shoulder to keep me from tumbling from bed. "Easy," he said, "we're making preparations, but there's nothing we can do right now. We need to gather our people. That's the transporters' jobs. And get everyone trained. That's security's job. And shore up our defenses. That's Jancarlo's job and anyone who can help him. Your job right now is to get stronger." He got up and opened the door, sending someone outside to get Jancarlo and Gretchen.

"You must be starving," Liam said, turning to face me. I noticed he was cleaned up and in much better shape than the last time I'd seen him. At least he hadn't been at my bedside the whole time. "I'll go make you something to eat."

"You don't have to do that," I said, not wanting to make him go to the trouble. I tried to stand up, but the room immediately started spinning. So fast I didn't know how he did it, Liam scooped me up, returning me to the bed. As he laid me back down, I noticed how warm his arms and hands were. He considered me for a moment, mirroring the look in my eye.

"It doesn't look like you'll be going anywhere," he said to me gently. He stood up straight. "I'll be right back." He scuttled out the door so fast I wondered if I had done something wrong.

I didn't have much time to worry about it. Before the door had a chance to close, Jancarlo and Gretchen came in. They were happy to see me awake, but their smiles didn't quite reach their eyes. I remembered the impending threat of Ross's army.

"I'm so happy to see you awake," Jancarlo said as Gretchen placed herself on the end of my bed, cradling my hand in hers. "Now maybe Liam will get something done around here." My eyebrows scrunched together as I skeptically asked him what he meant. He just huffed, "He hasn't left your bedside for more than a few minutes at a time. It was all I could do to get him to take a shower. I told him he'd wake you with the smell alone."

"Why would he do that?" I asked.

"Don't you know?" he said.

I suddenly found an interest in my quilt.

We sat in silence for a minute. At that moment, I was extremely tempted to reach out my mind to Liam in the kitchen. But I held myself to my own standards, trying instead to focus on the immediately impending dangers.

"Did Liam report everything?" I asked Jancarlo, finally finding the courage to look back up at him.

"Yes," Jancarlo said with an air of returning to business, "he reported what you learned from the assistant. We're all on high alert right now. The Shadow are probably working around the clock to transform everyone they can right now. Especially since they know we found them. We estimate the attack could happen in the next 48 to 72 hours. We're assembling a team to head to South America to speak with the leaders of the indigenous there. We hoped you would be up for it when you woke."

"Sure," I said, but I began wondering if I could stretch my powers that far and stay safely in bed at the same time. Probably not.

Gretchen looked at me. "Your energy pathways were toasted, but I restored them. I'm going to have to study how your mind works while you look into other people's minds. I need that knowledge in order to help you more in the future." As she said it, I realized I had forgotten all about Vincent.

I leaned forward to Jancarlo. "What happened to him? Where is he?" I was afraid they had locked away the harmless old man, or even worse, maybe he had been left somewhere unattended.

"You mean Vincent?" Jancarlo clarified.

"He's fine," Gretchen reassured me, waving her hands at me. "It took some work, but I've been able to heal him a bit. He can talk some and make more sense, but he says it's still very hard to handle all the information he's receiving. I'm still working with him. We're hopeful we can help him control the visions. In fact," she said, standing up, "I should probably be getting back to him. You should be okay now. Take it easy for the rest of the day. I know you've been unconscious, but you'll still need sleep tonight to start fresh in the morning. Then you should be able to train and help with preparations where necessary."

Before she left, Jancarlo asked her, "Have you been able to work with Kathryn any more today?"

"Yes," Gretchen answered. "We have a stockpile built up. Let's hope we don't need it." She slipped out the door and Jancarlo turned back to me.

"Kimi requested you have a training session with her as soon as you're up for it. I'll tell her you can join her in the morning. Sound okay?" He looked at me for approval, and I nodded. "After that, I have a special request for you."

"Sure," I said, although I just wanted to curl up in bed and forget anything was happening around me.

"Liam and I discussed the detriment of not having reliable communications." I nodded, thinking of Wiki, but waited for him to go on. "The woman I just mentioned to Gretchen, Kathryn Noahson, channel's other people's powers. She can funnel them into herself for her own use or copy them to store in objects for later use."

"Like the stones Liam uses for healing," I said.

"Yes," Jancarlo nodded, "or Kimi's hat."

I had forgotten about that. Her hat must have had Liam's powers embedded in it. I briefly wondered if the hat was a common tool for the security staff or a special gift. I brushed the thought aside as Jancarlo went on with his request. "I wondered if you would be willing to have your powers put into objects for us to use. Liam and Eddie told me how they could hear each other's thoughts while you were in contact with both of them. I hoped you and Kathryn might be able to create some kind of communication device for the Storm People to use."

"That sounds like a great idea," I said, curious what it would entail.

"Wonderful," Jancarlo smiled. "I'll have Kathryn contact you to start the process."

As he said it, a knock came at the door. He leaned over to admit Liam, laden with two trays covered with an exquisite meal.

My eyes popped open when I saw bowls of stew alongside large salads with breads, wedges of cheese and fruits. Liam reddened when he saw Jancarlo standing there. Obviously, he had hoped not to have an audience for his thoughtfulness.

Jancarlo allowed him to slide into the room past him then turned to leave saying, "Looks like a meal for two. I'll leave you two to… uh…eat." For the first time since I had known him, Jancarlo floundered for words. He hastily swept out the door, closing it behind him.

Liam set the trays on the table. As I got up to join him, he watched me carefully. "Don't worry," I assured him, "Gretchen said I'm okay."

"All right," he said. He seemed to relax some, but he still insisted on pulling a chair out for me. I humored his old-fashioned nature.

I waited until he sat down to help myself. The food was delicious. I'd never really learned how to cook especially well, but the leftovers at the Hot Cookie Café had always made me want to learn.

"This is amazing," I said as we ate the stew. "How did you make it so quickly?"

"Stew has to…well, stew," he said. "I threw it together earlier today." He shrugged, humble as always.

"I guess you've had the time to pick up all kinds of things," I said.

We ate and discussed the situation, but seeing as no new solutions to our dangers had presented themselves, the conversation drifted.

"Do you do this for all the new recruits?" I asked, sweeping my hand to indicate the meal.

"'Course not," he said puffing out his chest. "But we could be invaded any minute. I plan on cooking every meal like it might be my last."

"I guess it's a dangerous life," I said.

"Not usually," he said. "I don't think the reality of the danger has hit any of us yet. We've never had this kind of trouble before." He looked at me from the corners of his eyes. "Trouble seems to follow you."

"No kidding," I said. "First my mom, then the lightning strike and now this. Daisy and Missy are better off without me." I knew he was joking, but I couldn't help thinking the same thing. "Maybe I should leave. I wouldn't want to bring any more problems with me."

"Nonsense," he said seriously, locking his eyes with mine this time. "Trouble can be good for the soul."

Moving to safer territory, I asked where he was from. Liam hailed from County Galway in Ireland. I didn't have much history of my own, so I asked him about his, but after a few minutes he evaded the questions by turning the tables on me. "Where are you from anyway?" he asked.

"I was in Pennsylvania until my mom died. Then moved to Florida to live with Aunt Daisy," I said. As he waited for me to expound, I sighed. "Really, there's nothing to tell. I was raised by a single mom in the same small town for most of my life."

"What was your mother's name again?" He asked earnestly.

"Evelyn," I said. "Evelyn Hemlock, why?"

"I swear I've heard that name before." After a moment of thought, he shook it off. "Oh, well," he sighed. "I guess I've been around too long."

As we cleaned up the table, I started thinking about a shower. Before Liam had the chance to leave, I asked him, "Where are you headed now?"

He got a very solemn look on his face. "We have a lot of preparations to make. We're working on getting the word out to all our people that we're in danger. We need all the manpower we can get down here. Then I'll help out wherever Jancarlo thinks I'm of most use. For now," he sighed, "I'm going to meet with Jancarlo to discuss our next moves. T'ere might be someone I need to go see." I hadn't thought he might be going somewhere. I guess I made it evident on my face. He winked at me. "Don't worry," he said, "I'll be seein' ye before I leave," he said with the flicker of Irish brogue in his voice again.

"You should go take a nap," I suggested, "you sound tired."

He cocked his head to the side. "Why do you say that?"

"Your accent," I pointed out. "You start talking with an accent when you're tired."

He gave me half a grin then looked away hiding his face from me. He twisted to open the door but turned back to me. "Don't let Kimi push you around too much." He winked and slipped away.

Chapter FOURTEEN

Gretchen was right. Even though I thought I had been sleeping for a day and a half, I slipped into a dead sleep easily that night.

The next morning, I felt okay but wanted to stay under the covers. I figured she would hunt me down anyway so I forced myself down the hall to face Kimi.

I found the big set of double glass doors into the gym. It looked like any gym with workout equipment, a large weightlifting area and mirrors covering one wall, but it also had mats stretched out on the floor for sparring rings. Against the far wall, two glass doors and a row of windows looked into a huge arena on the other side. The windows had scorch marks on them.

The arena was as big as four football fields and as tall as a five-story building. Enormous boulders lay scattered like small mountains randomly over the arena with old-fashioned torches burning on the walls. It must have been used for practicing with powers because scorch marks marred everything and all the boulders looked like they had been moved recently.

When I found Kimi pounding a punching bag, I almost returned to bed. But she spotted me and strapped a couple gloves on my hands. She showed me a few punches, but mostly blocks. She kept saying, "You need to use your strengths," which I assumed meant I wasn't a strong enough puncher. Finally, she put her hands down to glare at me through narrowed eyes.

"What's wrong?" I asked, remembering the abuse to the punching bag.

"You're holding back," she said with a scary gleam in her eye. "There has to be some way…" Her voice trailed off as her eyes wandered in the mirror to the other people in the gym. Her eyes landed on one man sitting at the weight bench. "Tony!" she yelled.

Tony looked at her in confusion. A chill went up my spine when he wandered over to our sparring ring.

Tony had to be seven feet tall with no less than four hundred pounds of solid muscle. I couldn't find a neck anywhere, and his shaved head topped off the foreboding features nicely. Kimi grinned as she watched the blood drain from my face.

She put a hand on Tony's arm because she couldn't reach his shoulder. "Tony here is one of our top fighters. His power is super-human strength. He may be big, but he definitely doesn't fall hard. Don't let his size fool you, he's quick." Then she turned to Tony. "But he could use a humbling. Tony, don't hold back with Ella."

When she mentioned "a humbling," his smile melted away. Tony didn't look very pleased with me as he lifted his fists to fight me. Kimi stepped up to put her hand between us. At this point most of the others in the gym gathered around, curious to see this tiny little girl humble Tony.

I tried to get my knees to stop shaking as I lifted my hands in defense. Kimi shouted, "Go!" as she scooted out from between us. With a tremor, I realized there was nothing stopping this miniature giant from squashing me.

I have to admit, I really doubted Kimi's lucidity for a few minutes. Tony's fist came flying toward me, and I silently cursed her stupidity. Tony wasn't going to take it easy on me, either. I knew he really wouldn't hurt me, just embarrass me, which could possibly be worse.

From sheer terror, I dodged his gloves every time he tried to hit me. The air from his fist whistled past me, and I knew if I didn't stay out of the way, he would surely knock me cold. Finally, I got caught off guard by his foot in my stomach. He was nimble for such a massive man! I had to have flown at least twenty feet. A warm body stopped me. I sucked in the air that had been forced from my lungs as Kimi made her way over to me.

She stood over me with her arms crossed. "Stop holding back, Ella."

I stared in shock at her back as she walked away! What did she want from me? I had told her I didn't have that much fighting experience. Did she want this guy to kill me? What was she thinking putting me in a ring with him? As I dusted myself off, it hit me like another punch from Tony. Of course... "thinking"... I hadn't been using my powers.

I had decided I wouldn't use my powers on friends or people who knew I had the ability, but Kimi was showing me that there are times I'm expected to use my powers, even on friends. I would have to figure out a way to use Tony's own mind against him. I just wondered if he knew what my powers were.

I slowly made my way back to the large mats where Tony waited for me. I took a deep breath as I dove into Tony's mind before I even got to the mat. A thought formed in his mind of where he would kick me next. Thankfully, he actually *was* taking it easy on me. He planned on kicking me into the balance balls. So nice of him.

Although difficult, I found the most miniscule messages being sent out of his mind into his muscles. The muscles responded instantaneously, but this time I stayed out of the way much better. Every swing of the fist began as a thought before being sent to the muscles necessary to make the move possible. Being able to slow down in his mind, I could interpret the messages before they were sent out. Every time he lifted his foot, he thought of it first. Hence, I avoided the balance balls. The people around us started to relax. Kimi mumbled, "Finally," with a small eye roll.

Tony's face contorted in frustration. His internal monologue got harsher with himself, making me feel bad. The only problem was that he waited for me to fight back. I tested him out a little bit. A bruised rib later I figured out he had a lot of moves programmed into his muscles directly as reflex actions. If I punched at his head his arms knew the exact way to react without him thinking about it first. I stuck strictly to defense.

We danced around while we both wore down. Then it hit me. I had to go around his defenses. After testing his reflexes a little more while listening to his internal monologue of his own faults, I found a move that might be able to compromise him.

I jabbed with my left, watching as he pivoted with his left, but, as he always did, he leaned a little too much. I took full advantage by sweeping under to trip him. I knew he would try to roll as he went down, but I launched myself onto his back before he could get his shoulder underneath him. We ended up almost side to side with my arm wrapped around his neck, or chin, or shoulder, or whatever it was.

"Time!" Kimi yelled, raising her hand. I released my opponent with my arms and my mind, seeing as he probably could have just rolled to squash me, but Kimi had made her point. I needed to be paying attention to my opponents' thoughts, no matter the etiquette. Tony stood up first, quick to escape the embarrassing situation. Surprisingly, he offered me his hand. If nothing else, he was a good sport. He vaulted me to my feet then shook my hand briefly before he lumbered off in the direction of the weights.

"Thank you, Tony," Kimi said to his retreating figure. "You're just what Ella needed."

The crowd dispersed while Kimi strode over to me. "You're wrong," I said as I wiped sweat off my forehead.

Her eyebrows shot up to her forehead. "Oh?" she asked.

"Tony doesn't need a humbling," I informed her.

"Really?" she said scrunching her brows back together. "He always seemed kind of cocky to me."

"He's actually really hard on himself. That's what made it so easy to find a weakness," I explained to her.

"Yes," she said smoothly, "after you finally caught on."

She took me into an adjacent room that was completely empty except for a line of punching bag dummies against the far wall. Opening a closet door, she tried me out on different weapons to see if I liked any. I really took to the staff. It was easy to use and graceful, but not so easy to carry around.

"Well," Kimi said at one point, "if you ever get into trouble, find yourself a broom closet."

"To hide in?"

That got a smirk out of her.

With every punch and swing, grief and pain threatened to overwhelm me as thoughts of the things Jack, Ross and whoever else might be planning for Daisy and Missy. I had written myself off as unable to help anyone. Until Kimi.

"Kin and I will be doing regular training classes three times a day. We need everyone to be in peak performance if there's an invasion," Kimi said as we unwrapped our hands.

"What do you mean, 'if?'" I said not bothering to mask my shock. "They've already started transporting. Probably transforming too!"

"We know," she assured me, "but Jancarlo is hoping we can get a peaceful mission out to the leaders of the people in the amazon to prevent any bloodshed."

"Even with the newest recruits out of the picture, there's still the Shadow intent on killing us. With Wiki able to transport them all into our lobby at any moment," I said.

Kimi's face darkened. The same look of rage she had had with the punching bag came back. With a firm but low voice she said, "Which is why this training is so important." She stood up and I shuddered to think she might order me to start everything all over again. Instead, she said, "Be here in the morning at seven for a class with Kin."

I nodded as she stormed out of the gym.

Chapter FIFTEEN

I grabbed something to eat in the kitchen on my way back to my room. After a shower, I put on some normal clothes then headed down the hall again. Kathryn had left me a message on my door to see her as soon as possible.

Although I hadn't known what it meant at the time, I remembered seeing a sign on a door that said "Kathryn Noahson" on my arrival. I found the door just down the hall from the laundry room and let myself in.

Kathryn was a tall, strong-looking woman with a gentle face and skin the color of deep, rich coffee beans. She greeted me with a wide grin, holding out her hand. "You must be Ella," she said. "It's nice to meet you."

"You must be Kathryn," I said, shaking her hand. Yep, she was strong. "Nice to meet you too."

"So, you're our mind reader, huh?" She surveyed me up and down, appraising. Then her eyes zeroed in on my forehead. "Has anyone talked to you about what we're doing here?" she asked.

"A little bit," I said. She motioned me toward a chair next to a table laden with a variety of different objects. As I sat down, I said, "Jancarlo told me you put powers in objects. He hoped we could make some kind of communication device."

She nodded her head and gave me a few more details. "When I touch someone, I can use their powers for a small time. While I have your powers, I'll move them from me to the object that we choose. It doesn't hurt at all, although at times it can take a lot of energy out of me. I'll start with just duplicating your powers to a lesser degree. I'm not sure how powerful you are, so it could be dangerous for me if you're more powerful than I am." She swept her hand over the table to the variety of objects on it. String, cloth, rocks, wood, metals, liquids, glass shards, and gems covered every inch. "First and foremost, we must figure out what material is best to store your powers in."

Kathryn pointed to my scar. "Most people's powers originate from their scars or in the vicinity. Is that how yours works?"

"Yes, it's almost like I have another appendage I use to reach out to touch other people's minds."

She pursed her lips in thought then asked, "Do you ever get flooded with information?" After I confirmed, she asked, "Is there any way you filter it?"

"It's kind of like a snake smells the air with his tongue," I said. "I can get a taste of a thought or a memory without diving completely into it. I can also just be in the front of someone's mind to hear the immediate things they're thinking. That's how I communicated with Eddie and Liam. Although," I added, "they also had to concentrate on sending me what they wanted to say."

She listened pensively while I described all of this. "All right," she said, rubbing her hands together. "All I want you to do for now is try to penetrate these objects, but remain in them. See which one is the easiest."

I started with the wooden objects. They must have been made out of different trees. I breached them easily enough, but I couldn't keep my mind in them. As soon as my mind stopped inside, the wood seemed to turn to grease and my powers would slip right back out again. I had gone through a number of objects before this, but I had never tried to stay in an object. It proved to be rather difficult. I tried the metals to no avail. They were difficult to enter, and once again, I couldn't remain in them. The moment I tried to stop inside the object, I would ricochet out the way I came.

Then I came to the rock. I almost cried out in pain as my serpent began getting pulled in many different directions the moment it stopped forward progress. I had to jerk out of the rock or pull together again on the other side. "I don't get it," I told Kathryn, "I could stay in Liam's mind while they went into the Shadow base and that was through rock."

Kathryn nodded, "Yes, but you didn't try to remain in it. Your powers stayed in motion." I narrowed my eyes in confusion and she sighed. "You didn't try to read the rock's mind, did you?"

I shook my head. "Of course not."

"Well," she said, "that's essentially what you're trying to do here. Going through something is one thing. Trying to use your powers on it is another." She brought my attention to the next items I would attempt. "I have a feeling it won't be so difficult with these rocks."

I took a deep breath while reaching my mind to the small ruby the size of a dime. To my surprise, the gem was comparable to the substance of mist, easily allowing my powers to remain in place. The brilliant red inside emanated a calm, soothing atmosphere. "Oh," I said out loud. I looked up at Kathryn, who had a satisfied look on her face. "How did you know?" I asked.

She grinned at me. "Just going off the responses you had with the other materials. I think you'll find you can remain in most valuable gems, if you so desire. So," she exclaimed picking up the ruby, "your powers have expensive taste."

I blushed a little at the statement. I had never been "high maintenance" so to speak. I didn't even own any priceless gems myself. Now I would make the Storm People spend a fortune to try to communicate with each other. "Sorry," I muttered.

"Don't apologize," Kathryn told me as she held the ruby up to her eye to inspect it closer. "Usually if I can use a gem, it's easier on me."

She put the ruby back on the table in front of her. "Make sure your powers are well away from it," she said. "We'll need a matching stone." She looked around the room casually as if looking for a pen. I thought she might have to make a notation to ask Jancarlo to acquire another one for her. Instead, she moved over to a small safe behind her desk. It couldn't have been locked because she popped it open to produce a black velvet bag.

My eyes bulged when she scattered the contents of the bag on the table in front of me. There were green, blue, yellow, red, pure white stones and many other colors, all different cuts and sizes. They had to be worth hundreds of thousands of dollars, but she battered through the priceless pile as a child would rummage through a pile of Legos looking for what they need. "We'll stick with a ruby for now." She selected another ruby about the same size, a little more squared cut, and set it next to the other one. Then she swept all the other gems back into the bag to return to the safe.

"One word of caution," she said as she returned to the table staring at the two rubies. "After I let go of you, don't touch me again until after I have transferred power to the stones." She reached her hand out to me while focusing on the gems.

"How will I know when you're done?"

With a hint of a smile on her lips, she simply said, "You'll know."

With that, Kathryn put one of her hands on mine much the way Gretchen had done. I watched as she sat very still with her eyes closed for just a half a second. Suddenly, she jerked her hand away. At the same instant, I saw her forehead, at the same spot I had my scar, start to glow. I did a mental check to realize my own little serpent had noticeably diminished. Smaller and weaker, but thankfully, still there.

The glow on Kathryn's head became a brilliant golden light that elongated into a snake-like appendage. I knew I was seeing, for the first time, what I would look like if my little serpent were visible. It was like finding an old friend.

I sat still, watching as the serpent snaked its way over to the squared ruby on the table in front of Kathryn. It touched the small gem. Slowly Kathryn reached up to her forehead where the appendage was attached and wrapped her long fingers around the shining serpent. At this point her whole face squeezed together as if in great pain. I started to panic as she tilted her head to the side, as if trying to hear something, then opened her mouth in a silent scream.

"Kathryn?" I began to reach out to her but stopped myself. I watched in horror as she pulled at the serpent. It had many tendrils attached to her forehead, but a few of them began detaching.

With her eyes clamped shut, she closed her mouth. "Just a little more," she whispered through clenched teeth. With a painful sound between a scream and a groan, I watched as her serpent finally detached itself from her forehead. She slowly moved the end that had been attached to her to the other ruby on the table. Both rubies glowed a brilliant golden for a moment, connected by the serpent between them before resuming their normal crimson color once the connection disappeared. After all that, I wondered if it had even worked. The two rubies sat staring at me with no hint of the bizarre event. I did a mental recheck to find that my own powers had resumed their strength.

I turned back to look at Kathryn as she feebly pushed herself away from the table. Her eyes rolled back into her head as she collapsed to the floor.

Chapter SIXTEEN

Gretchen sprang into action when I burst through her door looking for help. She brought Jancarlo along too. Together, we helped Kathryn onto a couch in the back of her workshop. She worked with Kathryn for just a few minutes then announced to us, "She's fine. She just needs rest." Looking at me she smiled warmly. "I knew your powers were strong," she said, "but I had no idea just how strong. Kathryn will have to rest for quite a few hours to recover from this." The smile disappeared as she turned aggressively on Jancarlo. "And I will most certainly be on hand if she wants to do it again."

However, his attention wasn't on Gretchen. He picked up the small rubies on the table. "I'll have Charlotte help me test them," he told us, then moved to the door. "Thank you for your help, Ella. I'll send Tony to come help move Kathryn to her room." He excused himself by politely nodding to Gretchen.

"Don't worry, Kathryn will be fine," Gretchen said after he'd gone. "Sometimes this happens. I'll wait here with her until Tony takes her to her room. Why don't you go back to your room and relax. It must have been a busy day for you."

I agreed then thanked her for her help. As I left the room, I caught Tony coming toward me. I forced half a smile, hoping it didn't look more like a grimace then concentrated on the carpet like my life depended on it.

I grabbed a quick sandwich from the kitchen more out of habit than hunger. Back in my room, I had only just finished when I heard a knock at the door. Liam had promised he would see me before he left.

I threw open the door but caught my breath when I saw who stood outside. His white frizzy hair had been tamed down, but he hadn't bothered to shave the white stubble on his face. He stood with his eyes downcast and his hands behind his back. But as he looked up at me, I could see his eyes had changed back to the warm brown I had seen in his mind.

"Sorry to bother you, Miss Hemlock," Vincent muttered between glances up at me. "I wanted to come by to thank you personally."

"Oh," was all I could answer at first, but I managed to invite him in.

Vincent folded his hands in his lap as we sat together awkwardly at the table. I couldn't get over how different he acted. Instead of mumbling and waving, he seemed introspective yet observant. He also didn't seem as fragile. Probably because he had so much more control now.

"Like I said, Miss Hemlock…"

"Please," I interrupted him, "Call me Ella."

He gave me a timid little smile. He acted almost like a little child. "Ella," he said with what sounded like relief. "I'm grateful you got me to Gretchen to be healed. I have to apologize for any harm that might have come to you. The only reason Devin Ross is looking for you is because I told him you would be key to this conflict." He sighed, staring down at his hands. "For my own benefit, I selfishly told him you were important. For that, I apologize.

"I knew once you and your friends got to the Shadow base, I would escape with you." He finally looked up to face me. "I'm so sorry I had to send him after you in order for me to get out." He dropped his eyes again. "Everything was so confusing. The amount of information I received every second of the day was…well…you know what it was like." He glanced up at me and I remembered the onslaught of information that had attacked me when I entered his mind.

As I recalled it, the same sensation of losing myself threatened to overtake me again. My hands started to shake, so I shoved the memory away again. Vincent watched the tremors. The corners of his mouth dipped as his eyes dropped again in misery. "I'm sorry for any pain you might have suffered. I truly am." He looked up at me and his eyes sparkled as he said, "I knew you wouldn't listen to my warning, but I had to try."

I shook my head slowly, muttering, "It *was* for me."

"Yes," Vincent continued, "I'm so sorry."

I pushed the rest of the memory away, trying to smile. "I'm glad you're better. Whatever it took to get you here, I'm glad you've been healed."

"I'm not completely healed," Vincent admitted with a shrug. "Gretchen has done as much as she can. I'm still able to see others' futures, but at least I can ignore most of the visions or concentrate on the ones I want to know."

"Well, at least it's more tolerable," I smiled at him. I had a faint inkling this chit-chat had not really been why he came to see me. "So, if I tried to read your mind now, what would happen?"

He gave me half a smile. "You would probably be fine, but at the same time it might be really hard for you to find anything you wanted."

"So, I can't communicate with you in your mind?"

"We might be able to, but it would be very… tumultuous. Similarly, I won't be able to use your communication device."

He said it very matter-of-factly, but my eyebrows jumped up a little. I started to ask how he knew about it, but stopped before the words got out. More to myself I said, "Oh, of course. I guess we'll be successful then."

"In many ways, Ella." He answered me with an air of mystery as his eyes bore into mine. "I dare not say too much for fear I might change things or make you second guess, but I will say this. You have an important role to play in the saving of this people. You're a very powerful person, Ella."

"You know what's going to happen?" I asked, but of course he knew the future. "You have to tell someone," I said adamantly. "Have you talked to Jancarlo?"

He held his hands up slightly. "I talked to Jancarlo," he said calmly. "He knows what I can tell him. I'm helping him in any way possible that I can. Unfortunately, I told Devin Ross a lot of the same things."

I struggled to comprehend what he might have told Ross, what he might or might not be saying to us. It would be easy for him to hide anything from me. I never wanted to enter his head again as long as I lived and that was saying something. I just sat there stunned, knowing this man knew what the future held for all of us, but he couldn't or wouldn't tell us much.

Vincent finally stood up slowly. "I should be going," he said. "You need your rest." He stepped to the door, and I followed him out of habit. Opening the door, he turned again to face me. "I enjoyed seeing you, Ella. I thank you again for saving me from such agony." With a slight nod, he ambled back down the hall.

I gave him a whispered good-bye as the door swung shut.

Chapter SEVENTEEN

That night I dreamed of Vincent's death with me screaming over his lifeless body. We were in the mountains with trees all around us. A howling storm had just started to blow in. I woke in a cold sweat, not knowing what to think of the mysterious old man. He seemed harmless enough and willing to help, but he also seemed to be holding back. I wanted so much to like him. After all, he had helped me maintain my sanity enough to get out of his mind. I felt as if there had been an intimate connection forged between us, but I resisted reaching out to him. If I couldn't look into his mind, I would have to learn to trust him the old-fashioned way.

While I pulled my hair back into a neat braid, I wished I could have breakfast with Liam, but I didn't know how to contact him or where he might be. While feeling a little empty as to plans for the morning, a knock at my door interrupted my musings. I answered a little slower after my surprise visit yesterday, but when I saw Liam leaning on the door frame my spirits couldn't help but lift.

"Would you like to have some breakfast?" He asked with a slight grin. Either he enjoyed teasing me or he could read minds too.

"I'd love to," I said with a wary smile.

Before I could move to cross the threshold, he exclaimed, "Good." A tray laden with a large variety of pastries, fruit, toast and jam and two large glasses of orange juice materialized from around the corner where he'd been holding it.

Although I tried, I couldn't keep the echoing smile from spreading over my face. I moved aside with a wave of my hand as he brought it into the room. As he leaned over to put the tray down, I noticed what looked to be an old cap in his back pocket, but he didn't say anything about it.

We had a quiet little breakfast, chatting casually. Liam was so easy to talk to. The last person I'd been able to talk to like this was my mom, so in the back of my mind I knew this quaint little existence would most likely come to an abrupt end.

Once we finished our breakfast, Liam reached back to pull the flat cap out of his back pocket.

"I brought you a little something," he said, setting it on the table. It looked like the type an old-fashioned golfer would wear, wide in the back and pinched together at the front to a short brim. It was a dark tweed and, although weathered, it appeared very durable.

"What's this?" I asked feeling a little embarrassed at his generosity.

"Just a little something," he said, shrugging his shoulders. "We used to call it a paddy cap. I think Americans call it a flat cap."

I considered the cap, waiting for a punch line but slipped it on my head. Being so focused on Liam's reaction, I didn't see the air around me shimmer in the dim light. "How do I look?" I asked, but he didn't meet my eyes.

He chuckled. "Why don't you go look in the mirror?"

I narrowed my eyes at him, once again debating if I should stick to the standards I had set for myself and not read his mind. But I stood to go look in the bathroom mirror. I gave a little gasp when I realized I couldn't see myself at all then relaxed as I got the joke too. I came out of the bathroom shaking my head. Liam still didn't look at me. I tilted my head to the side. "Can't you see me?" I asked him.

"Not the way it works." He wiped his hands with a napkin. "I bend the light so I and others, can see each other or not. But when I have Kathryn put my powers into an object, I don't have the power to make you visible anymore. That's why I couldn't see Kimi when she showed up at the Shadow base."

While he talked, I tested my cool new gift by creeping around behind him. I debated on flicking his ear but settled for leaning close to him and allowing my breath to tickle his ear. "So you can't see me at all?"

He about jumped out of his skin, so I gave him the benefit of the doubt. After he took a deep breath to steady himself, he turned in my general direction. "Maybe I shouldn't have given it to you," he said while his eyes wandered around me.

I giggled as I took the cap off. "This could be lots of fun." I put the hat on the table and sat across from him again. "Thank you."

"Fun though it might be," he countered, "I hope it keeps you safe when I'm not around."

I sobered up at this. "Are you leaving?"

He nodded. "I have to go see someone." I waited for him to go on. He studied me then took another deep breath. "Remember when we first met, I told you about a man who attracts lightning?" I nodded. "He has some history with Ross. I need to let him know what's going on. I don't know if he'll be able to help, but we have to try."

A thought occurred to me so I hesitantly asked, "Can lightning still hurt us if we've already been struck once?" I thought it sounded like a stupid question. I had never really thought of lightning being a big problem before. Now that I had lived through a strike I guess it seemed like even less of a threat, but I realized I could be dead wrong.

Liam looked very serious. "Lightning can kill any of us. If we survive another strike, it can change or even take away all our powers. Mother Nature is unpredictable that way."

I swallowed, letting the danger he faced sink in. I tried to put on a brave face. "But you'll be careful, right?"

"Don't worry," he said. "Nathaniel and I go way back. We're good friends. The lightning only gets bad when he's excited or angry. He usually stays pretty calm when I'm there. That means less danger."

I just nodded, unsure what to do or say for a farewell. I wished I had the chance to give him something useful.

"I should get going." He picked up the tray.

I followed him to the door and gave him a sheepish, "Thanks again for the cap. And breakfast."

"Don't mention it," he grinned back at me. He looked very serious for a moment, opening his mouth to say something, then seemed to think better and closed it again. He gave me a half a grin. "I'll see you when I get back. It should be a short trip."

"Sure," I nodded.

He threw me one of his winks and whipped out the door.

At the end of a weapons/using your powers effectively class, Jancarlo appeared in the doorway. After a quick word and a nod from Kin, he headed in my direction. "Ella," he said as he approached me, "I need you to come with me to the conference room." He indicated Charlotte who was nearby. "You too."

He approached a few others and our group grew to about a dozen people walking down the hall. We seated ourselves around a large table with Jancarlo at the head. Vincent was already there. On the table in front of Jancarlo lay a thick leather strap embedded with one of the two rubies with my powers. Secured on Jancarlo's wrist was an identical leather strap with the other ruby in it.

Once everyone settled around the table, Jancarlo started the meeting. "Thank you all for coming," he said. "You're all aware of the problem posed by Devin Ross and his followers. We're hoping to put together a peaceful mission to talk to the leaders in the Amazon. If we can make some kind of truce, perhaps it will lessen Ross's numbers. From what we know, they should be coming here any moment." He paused as if considering his next statement, then continued. "Thanks to Vincent and Ella, we know where we need to go and who we need to talk to. I wanted to send a small group, but in order to be effective, it will end up being a little larger than I would like. We'll need Charlotte to transport everyone there, of course." He nodded at Charlotte, and she gave a small nod back.

"Then we'll need Sophia to speak to the people," he nodded at a woman who looked to be in her 40's with strawberry blonde hair hanging in a ponytail down her back. She had sharp features with a long straight nose. The silvery, fern-shaped scar traced along her right jawline did nothing to diminish her beautiful features. I figured from what Jancarlo said, she must be some kind of a translator. After she gave him a quick nod, he looked over at me. "Ella, we could use you there as well, if you're up for it. If we can know what they need before they even voice it, we should be able to take care of this easily."

I didn't know if I could trust my voice, so I settled for a nod.

"We'll have both Kimi and Tony there for security." Jancarlo waited for their acceptance then added someone named Noah who would keep us safe from wild animals. Last, almost hesitantly, he added, "I would like Eddie to accompany the group unless anyone has a problem with it." When he said this, he looked at Tony, but the group as a whole stiffened at the tension.

"You mean the man who came back with Liam and Ella?" Kimi clarified.

"Yes," Jancarlo answered turning to her. "I understand some of you have your doubts about his allegiances. Having been healed by Gretchen, I believe he can help the leaders of whatever peoples we might encounter to understand the true nature of the promises Devin Ross makes. He'll be able to give them hope that the men they already sent to the states can return to their normal lives without interruption." He paused to glance at Tony again. I wondered if the two men had had an altercation.

Tony finally spoke up. "Has Ella checked him?"

Everyone turned to look at me. "I checked him before we even made our escape at the Shadow base. He seemed genuine at the time. We couldn't have gotten away without him, but I can always check him again," I said.

Tony seemed somewhat relieved as his head dipped a couple of times, but he looked at Jancarlo for an answer.

This time Jancarlo just addressed Tony. "We'll check him again, carefully."

Again, his head bobbed up and down. "Then I'll go with him," Tony answered.

"Good," Jancarlo responded. He picked up the leather bracelet off the table. "Also, thanks to Ella and Kathryn, we have an effective communication device. Charlotte has been helping me test its abilities and we've been able to be in contact all the way around the world." I saw some wide eyes in the group. Wow. Could my power really go that far? "We were able to project our thoughts into these rubies and talk to each other. Sophia," he said, as he gave her the leather strap, "I'll give you this one so we should be able to keep in contact the entire time you're in South America. Just make sure the ruby is touching your skin and say my name in your mind to call to me. You'll have to concentrate on pushing your thoughts into the ruby, but once you get the hang of it, it's pretty easy."

Sophia took the bracelet and strapped it on her wrist, nodding. She and Jancarlo exchanged nods a couple of times, so I assumed they were testing it.

"Good," he said.

Jancarlo said "Ella and Kimi, make sure you have your hats." He gave us both a knowing look so I realized Liam must have told him about the hat he had given me. Kimi gave me a side-glance after we both acknowledged, obviously thinking about who would have given me such a gift. I developed a profound interest in the table in front of me. "The only people in the party I want the Amazonians to see is Sophia and Tony at first. Hopefully they'll think she came with only him for security so they won't be considered much of a threat. Once we can get them to talk to us, Eddie can be introduced. Of course," he turned to me again, "Ella you will remain in contact with the entire group and search the minds of the leaders as dictated by Sophia."

I nodded again as I realized what a role I would be playing in hopefully helping these people. Vincent certainly had it right. I looked at him only to see him staring at the table in a daze. I wondered if he was seeing more futures.

Jancarlo heaved a sigh as he stood. "I think that's everything for now. Thank you again, everyone. The group will have to leave first thing in the morning, so please everyone get some rest."

With that, the group stood to go, but Jancarlo beckoned me to stay for a moment. As the last few stragglers headed for the door, I said to Jancarlo, "Glad to see you're not going to try to keep me under lock and key this time." I was only half joking. I wouldn't mind the locking.

"Yes, well," Jancarlo raised an eyebrow at me. "Liam told me how you handled it last time, so we figured we'd save you the trouble."

Once the door had firmly closed behind the last person, Jancarlo looked at me very seriously. "Ella," he said, "I don't want another Wiki. I want you to check everyone in the group, including Eddie, thoroughly." I nodded, but he went on. "When all this is over, we might have to ask you to check everyone that enters the base." He said it more to himself, but I nodded anyway.

I hated the idea of prying into people's minds, but I also hated myself for not having known about Wiki in the first place. Plus, if anyone found out, I wouldn't be their first choice of someone to hang out with.

Chapter EIGHTEEN

As I headed back to my room, I immediately started searching for the members of the team who would be leaving with me in the morning. I tried to focus, but still caught myself standing in the hall going nowhere or staring at the wall. I decided I would go back to my room first, then search the minds of the others.

I sunk into my bed and sent my mind out the door. I figured I would search Eddie first, seeing as his loyalty was the first to be questioned.

Eddie was deep in conversation with Vincent. I slipped into his mind to find his powers all but gone. His mind opened the same boring filing cabinet of memories I had seen in all the minds of regular people on the surface. He could still move small rocks, but no more than his hands could already do. He wondered what kind of life he might have when all this was over. He was trying to enlist Vincent's help to find the woman he had left behind so many years ago. He had agreed to go on this little adventure for Jancarlo, and he would be paid handsomely for it. In the end, he would probably feel indebted to the Storm

People. But then he would be free to start a new life far away from Wyoming, hopefully with the woman he loved. All this man wanted was his freedom. He would never go back to working for the Shadow. After quite a bit of searching, I knew there was nothing new to find, so I moved on to the other members of the group.

I found Noah doing some review work with Kin. Even while sparring, his mind conveyed more peace than any human mind I had entered. Kind of like the deer I had run into while in Wyoming. It was really nice to be in his mind…a little too nice. I actually rattled my mind to force myself to stay focused.

Noah usually didn't stay underground with the Storm People. He worked as a well-respected veterinarian on the surface. No one knew his success issued from his ability to communicate with the animals. He just had to reach out to them mentally, kind of like I did with humans except he could control them, but he didn't do it often.

His wife and friends had no idea of his life here. At times, Liam would show up to ask favors or bring him news, but for the most part he kept his distance from this life. His wife believed him to be on a business trip right now. I guess technically, he was. His only concern was returning home safely. He planned on keeping the animals away from the group so they could do what they needed to do, but not much else. Whether the group succeeded or not had nothing to do with him. Although shallow and self-involved, he did owe a lot to the Storm People. They helped him pay for schooling and helped him out financially when he fell on hard times at the beginning of his career. He could never turn to the Shadow, but he certainly didn't go out of his way for anyone other than himself or his family.

After a little more searching of Noah, I turned my attention to Charlotte.

I squirmed in displeasure when I found her on a date. She'd met a tall, handsome, fire thrower named Ethan. They had been seeing each other for a few months, but she worried if he would still be interested when she came back. They had gone top-side to steal a few moments in a quiet little park. While chatting with Ethan, Charlotte also tried to pay attention in case anyone snuck up on them. She never liked being caught unawares.

Her mind contained a thick fog. The fog stretched for almost a hundred miles helping her sense the locations of people and objects within that distance. For the most part, she could ignore everything moving in the fog until she focused her efforts.

She was also indebted to the People of the Storm for helping her when she first discovered her powers. She had been a misunderstood seventeen-year-old when she was struck. Jancarlo found her when she had run away shortly afterwards. He took her to the base, and she never wanted to go back. She loved the Storm People. She would do anything for them.

She had dated quite a few of the Storm People, including Wiki. I made sure to search through her memories of being with him to see if they ever talked about future betrayals. I found one conversation where Wiki mentioned getting away from the Storm People. When he learned she never wanted to leave, he never brought it up again. They also didn't see each other much after that. I tried to ignore the part about her having a huge crush on Liam for a long time. She had those feelings well suppressed, but they were still there. Even though she looked like she was older than him now, she was actually younger. She wasn't as powerful so her body aged faster than his. Apparently, not many people were as powerful (and therefore, slow aging) as Liam. She still idolized him and Jancarlo quite a bit. Either way, she would never be the one to turn. I moved on to Sophia.

Sophia was meeting with Jancarlo to discuss strategy. I struggled to investigate her mind. Since everyone else's minds I had seen so far spoke English, I hadn't encountered different languages to stifle me like Sophia's. I worried she might easily be able to hide something from me by having it in another language. I continued through anyways because I could still sense the emotions accompanied with the thoughts and memories. Her powers worked like a window shade that she pulled down. Looking through it, she could translate everything she heard. She had separate filters in different colors that changed everything to those languages. Her memories were wrapped in the filters as if she had translated them then left them that way. She only had to hear a few words of a new language in order to make a filter for it. As she talked with Jancarlo, I could see she was worried about what to say to the Amazonian people and what they could do to stop the war, even if they could deter the leaders.

I looked at the shades of different languages, all color coded. I couldn't be sure if it presented itself that way for her. Maybe I could see the different colors because I could see into her mind. I found some memories with the Storm People and took a closer look. Most of her memories displayed a pink hue and sounded like French, so I took it to be her original language. She had been struck more than 50 years ago in France. She had had an affair with Jancarlo's predecessor (I quickly moved past those memories), but seemed loyal to the People of the Storm.

At one point, I found a memory of an argument with Wiki in the ubiquitous pink. I couldn't translate it, but anger and embarrassment attached strongly to this memory of them yelling at each other. I wished I had taken French in school. I dove into the memory deeper, attempting to see it from Wiki's side, but it didn't work. So, I tried to pull one of the shades down to see if I could use it to translate. It worked, but unfortunately, I had pulled down the Russian shade, a hideous orange. I remembered some of her English conversations had been in purple so my serpent pinpointed the English shade. Sure enough, I could hear some of the argument in English.

What goes on between me and Paul has nothing to do with it! Sophia yelled.

'Nothing to do with it?' Wiki scoffed. *I'm getting lessons on morals from a mistress!* He spat back at her.

I didn't hear anything else. At that moment the shade gave a tug. I realized if I held onto it any longer Sophia would know of my presence in her head. I let it snap back into place.

I quickly returned to her fore-mind to see she had halted her conversation with Jancarlo. She told him she felt a tug or pinch on her scar. Oops! He asked her if she needed to talk to Gretchen, but she said the sensation had passed. If it happened again, she would speak to Gretchen. When her thoughts turned to me, I quickly recoiled out of her head and out of the room.

As I searched for Kimi and Tony, I thought about what I had seen. Sophia and Wiki obviously hadn't gotten along. Chances are they weren't in league with each other, but I should probably mention my difficulty reading Sophia's mind to Jancarlo. She could easily hide something from me.

Kimi and Tony lounged in her room discussing Eddie, which I found a little odd, but it didn't seem like an intimate setting so I slipped into Tony's mind. He was a simple man which I could appreciate, especially because it made his mind easy to read. He didn't trust Eddie because he knew nothing about him. He trusted Kimi, Jancarlo and Liam with his life. Therefore, he trusted me. But he had had a brush with Eddie while working out. Even though he knew he shouldn't have said anything, he couldn't help himself. He couldn't stand a traitor any more than a deserter. To Tony, Eddie represented both. The confrontation hadn't come to blows, but Eddie had stood up for himself giving Tony the only reason to back down. If the man respected himself, Tony would give him the same deference.

I moved past an argument that was at the front of his mind to find out more about Tony. He saw himself as a monster, ugly and frightening, which he used as an excuse to be extremely hard on himself. He figured no one could ever love him. Being an abused child meant his parents eventually were taken away, but that just meant he lived on the streets. He had to protect himself, so he started bulking up at a young age. He got into drugs and gangs on the streets, but when he was struck by lightning in the middle of a gang fight in a rainstorm, they abandoned him as well. They left him for dead in the street. That's how Liam found him.

He had a thing for Kimi, but didn't dare say anything. He knew she could take care of herself and couldn't imagine her wanting a guy like him around. The cocky attitude on the outside just disguised the fact that he had resigned himself to a life of solitude, but he would do anything to protect the Storm People. They had been the only ones who had ever been there for him. Gretchen and Sheila (the other healer) had helped him get cleaned up from the drugs. He, also, never even wanted to see the surface world again. He had a fierce desire to safeguard the people who meant the most to him—The People of the Storm.

Once I cleared Tony, I slipped into Kimi's mind. At least only one language stifled me this time. I couldn't even begin to decipher Japanese. I had to slow everything down to the extreme in order to inspect the emotions connected to the memories. I found the memory of her being struck, but it spiraled in disarray as soon as I looked into it. She and Kin had been practicing with metal staffs in a rainstorm as punishment. They had struck each other's staff at the same time the lightning struck them, hence the lightning was divided between them. One would think the energy of the strike would be less for each of them having been split between the two, but it seems the staffs magnified its power. Jancarlo kept telling them theirs' was a once in a millennium occurrence.

They had been with the Japanese society of Storm People for many years but dealing with Jancarlo and Liam on occasion as well. After many years, their family started noticing their aversion to aging. The difficult day came when they decided to fake their own deaths and surrender everything they knew to keep their secret. They chose the American Storm People to join. Everyone agreed it would work out best.

Kimi really didn't have feelings for Liam anymore. She wasn't lying about that. I know I shouldn't have, but I found the memory of when she got the hat. She had specifically asked Liam for it, knowing it would be useful and Kin had one too.

After a few minutes of being in her mind I actually started to sweat. I realized she had her own little fire burning somewhere deep in her mind, hence being able to start her own fire, not just manipulate it. She could use it whenever she wanted and expand it up to a quarter of a mile.

She was an intensely loyal person. Although she had never really liked Wiki before, she really hated him now. As I prepared to leave Kimi's mind, it occurred to me I should let them know about Eddie.

Kimi. I concentrated on pushing it into her mind.

She stopped speaking, holding a hand up to Tony to do the same. "Who's there?" she asked out loud. I wrapped around into both of their minds.

It's Ella. Can you both hear me? I asked them.

"Yes," they answered out loud.

I just wanted to let you know I looked into Eddie's mind. Tony, he really, truly is trustworthy. He's doing this one thing for Jancarlo then he just wants a nice, quiet life away from it all.

If you say so, Ella. Tony said, *I'll trust him.*

Thanks for letting us know. Kimi responded.

I debated for a second about mentioning Tony's feelings to Kimi, seeing as he never would, but decided to keep my nose in my own business. I returned my mind to Jancarlo's office to see that he and Sophia were wrapping up their meeting with light chatting.

Jancarlo, I said in his mind, *it's Ella.*

He faltered for a just a moment then grinned at Sophia. He made his apologies, telling her he had something he needed to attend to. They ended their conversation, and she left the room.

Ok, Ella, he said in his mind. *Find anything interesting.*

Not really, I reported. *I dug through everyone's minds thoroughly. They're all very loyal to the People of the Storm and to you. Even Eddie is determined to help out on this mission. I let Kimi and Tony know Eddie is safe.*

Jancarlo paused for a second then another thought came to his mind. I heard it a second before he asked, *Was that you bothering Sophia?*

Oh, I answered guiltily, *yeah, sorry. Her mind is hard to read. She has everything wrapped in lots of different languages, so I tried to use her powers to translate her memories. I'm pretty sure she's loyal, but it would be easy for her to hide things from me.* As much as I didn't want to throw her under the bus, I forced myself to give a complete report. *As well as Kimi. I don't speak Japanese or the multitude of languages Sophia knows.*

We might have to discuss you getting a translating tool from Sophia, he suggested, *but we'll save that for later. For now, we'll have to trust them. Get some sleep and make sure you're ready to go first thing in the morning.*

Right, I said. *See you in the morning.*

Chapter NINETEEN

The next morning I had one of those what-the-hell-am-I-doing moments. I wanted to stay in bed and pull the sheets over my head. I wanted to pretend I didn't have anything attached to my forehead. I wanted to pretend the dream I was having of my mother was real. I was really back home in Pennsylvania. My mom was making bacon and eggs, and we were going to sit on the couch binge-watching shows on a Saturday. I wasn't assisting a secret society to defend itself from another secret society compelled to destroy them. It actually wasn't a very good possibility that someone would show up to try to kill all of us.

I shook my head and forced myself out of bed. I would be leaving for a mission to the Amazon to talk to people no other outsiders even knew existed.

In my old life, I wandered around like an idiot wondering what to do with myself. I still did. But here, right now, I had people relying on me. I had special powers no one else had. I would live a lot longer in this life, so I had better get used to it. Knowledgeable, understanding people surrounded me to help me every step of the way. I took a deep breath. If I lived through this, would I stay? Should I stay?

The group met at 0600 in the lobby. I got there a few minutes early, but our group already filled the chairs. We had all been outfitted by Kimi, so we had matching uniforms on. The uniforms weren't for looks, they had been specifically chosen for the type of environment and conditions we would be facing. We all had the same basics in our packs. Food, consisting of granola bars that could feed us for half a day each, healing stones from Gretchen's stash, flashlight and batteries, flint, water skins with a power-infused filter, a small but comfortably warm bedroll, a knife, and any other personal items. I had my flat cap tucked in a side pocket.

The trip to the Amazon would take about forty-five minutes one way. Seeing as Charlotte had to transport six people, we would have a halfway point in Southern Mexico. Sophia and Kimi went first, then Tony and Noah, then me and Eddie. Eddie and I had to wait for an hour and a half before our turn to go to Mexico. While we waited, I questioned Jancarlo about any other transporters.

"Yes, there are more transporters all over the world," he told me. "There's Teresa in Europe, Boris in Russia, and a few more transporters in Africa. But they work for the Storm People in other countries. I've been in contact with some of them to ask for assistance, but I have yet to find out if they're able to pitch in. Keep in mind that communication is difficult between our groups, and they all have lives as well."

After a short break in Mexico, we met up with the others deep in the rainforests of the Amazon. I looked around at the jungle we had landed in. I thought I had known what to expect, but this level of intimidation bordered on terror. The canopy hung so thick it seemed like constant rain clouds hovering over our heads. I could tell the sun drifted just out of reach. We stumbled through the brush in the shadows of monstrous trees. A constant drip or trickle from the trees accompanied us. Feeling like I had stepped out of the shower into a sauna, I immediately took off the top layer of my two shirts.

As we set up, I asked Charlotte where on the earth we had landed. "Inside northern Brazil," she said and pointed, "Columbia's that way. There are a few little cities around I can get us to in an emergency, but not for many miles. We're headed that way," she pointed again. "East of here are the people we're looking for. Not even the local Storm People are willing to search them out."

"Why not?" I asked, but Sophia answered.

"They don't like outsiders," she said. "The people we're going to meet are considered 'uncontacted' either because they are extremely hostile toward foreigners or because they have withdrawn so much from modern society as to be unreachable. Either way, they prefer to be left alone. They're aware of the world around them changing, but they choose an inhospitable location to keep everyone away. We can only reach them due to our transporters."

Charlotte took a little bow.

Kimi approached me with a small spray bottle in her hand. "Need to spray you down, Ella," she said aiming the bottle at me.

It didn't have a label on it, but I just assumed. "Bug spray?" I asked as I held out my arms.

"Kind of," she chuckled as she doused me. Back into the shower, I guess. "This has Noah's powers in it. It's much better than regular bug spray. This will keep all kinds of small animals away from you along with all the bugs, but we have to reapply it every day, and it won't keep large animals away from you. That's why Noah came with us."

She stood up after spraying my legs. "We have some other stuff we'll put around the camp to keep animals away from us at night. I will *not* have some critter climbing in bed with me, that's for sure," she said with a grimace.

I followed her to the large camouflage tent that would be home for a couple of days. Tony moved some rocks into a circle for the fire. "Where's a rock mover when you need one?" He muttered as he dumped a huge rock on the ground.

"Where's a super-human strong man when you need one to collect firewood?" Eddie had come out from behind some trees with a big bunch of firewood in his arms. Tony just shook his head and went back to moving rocks.

Eddie put the firewood in a big pile by the fire pit. He tossed a few of the smaller chunks into the now complete fire pit. Then he looked at Kimi. "It's all wet," he shrugged, "I'm not sure if it will light."

Kimi raised one eyebrow while her chin dipped. "It will light."

As she raised her hand to the firewood, I touched her arm. She stopped to squint at me. I looked up at her forehead and asked, "May I?"

She shrugged then turned back to the wet firewood. Full of curiosity, I shot into her mind. From a sauna to an oven. At first, there hung a thick, warm fog, kind of like the fog in Charlotte's mind. But this initial heat would only be warming the wood enough to dry it out. Then the little fire in the back of her mind grew into a flame-thrower with precision, straight out of her mind into her body. The tepid flame shot past me with lightning speed. I screamed, jerking my mind out of the way, but my body followed suit. I opened my eyes to find Kimi hovering over me in concern. I steadied my breath. "Are you okay?" she asked.

I sat up carefully to put my head in my hands, "Remind me not to do that again," I forced out. A few deep breaths later I allowed Tony to pull me to my feet.

While all this had been going on, I hadn't noticed Sophia and Charlotte quietly talking together. With camp set up, Sophia addressed the group. "According to what Vincent told us, we're in the right place to find the people we need. Charlotte is going to take me to look around. We'll be back quickly. I might need to take Kimi and Tony to make sure all angles are covered, so be ready when I get back." With that she nodded to Charlotte, who put a hand on her shoulder and they disappeared.

The rest of us kicked around camp while waiting to see what we needed to do next. Kimi and Tony mulled over strategy for this mission as well as discussing things back home. I settled by the fire next to Eddie with Noah across from us.

"So I heard Gretchen healed you," I mentioned casually to Eddie, although I left out I heard it in his own mind.

He nodded. "Yeah, I guess being shocked by electricity isn't the same as being zapped by lightning. She healed me fast enough."

"What will you do after this?" I asked. I already knew he wanted to find the woman he had lost, but I tried to sound innocent and make conversation at the same time. Maybe he could give me some idea of what I should do too.

He shrugged his shoulders. "Move on," he stated simply. Then he took a deep breath, smiled and said, "And stay as far away from lightning as possible."

"I hope everything works out for you," I said returning his grin. "I still owe you one for getting us away from the Shadow."

After a few more minutes, Charlotte came back by herself telling the group Sophia wanted Kimi and Tony to help her for a few minutes then she would be back for the rest of us. After she disappeared with our security, I decided I should probably take a quick break before being called to action. I told Noah and Eddie I would be right back.

"Be careful," Noah warned, "even a potty break can be treacherous around here. Call if you need anything."

"Sure," I said half-heartedly. I wasn't about to call them with my pants around my ankles. I'd take death.

I disappeared into the jungle but only a few steps away. The brush wasn't very thick so I had to go behind a large tree. If it had been hollow we could've made it into an outhouse. I had just finished when I heard it. A low growl.

Chapter TWENTY

I stood there praying my spray had not worn off yet, when a beautifully spotted cat stepped out of some grass about five feet in front of me. Her golden eyes locked with mine as she slunk toward me. I stared, paralyzed by fear. I had never seen such a beautiful and deadly creature without glass between the two of us. Somehow, that made all the difference. Her top lip inched up to reveal lethal pointed teeth.

My heart raced as she padded softly forward. I decided to reach out to her mind, thinking I might be able to avoid her if she pounced…or watch myself dying through her eyes. Either way it would be enlightening. As with the deer, her mind was calm, but had a distinct edge because of the danger she faced. She acted on instinct. She simply protected her family in the grass. I dove into her mind to search it in what little time I had. If only I could find a way to subdue the feline I might be able to get back to Noah. The fear came from the fact that I stood taller than her. I slowly inched toward the ground. Eye contact showed aggression. I lowered my eyes to the ground.

Unfortunately, this put us on level ground, literally and figuratively. If I had been another large cat, she would still be threatening me for encroaching on her territory. The only way out of this would be to fight off the intruder. Dang.

Even though she was only a few inches taller than my knees I knew the cat had to weigh as much as me. Completely vulnerable, I knelt on all fours looking at the ground. I couldn't back up the way I should because the tree blocked my path. I cowered with the feline just a few feet from me still growling low and soft. I searched in her mind to find out what kinds of sounds I could make that wouldn't be threatening. I couldn't call for help. Opening my mouth at all would just provoke her. I used the calm I heard in her mind to calm myself. I slowed my breathing, begging my heartbeat to slow as well.

Please I thought desperately, *just stop.*

Suddenly the feline stopped her advance. The threat of me in her mind seemed to be edging away. I flinched away squeezing my eyes shut as she gave me a much louder growl. A final warning. After a final inspection of her intruder, she bolted back to her home in the grass. I groaned with relief but gathered my wits to look up at the sound of footsteps coming around the tree.

"How did you do that?" Noah asked abruptly without masking the shock in his voice.

"Do what?" I shot back. "Almost be eaten? I didn't do anything!" He almost sounded angry at me!

"Exactly," he said. He shook his head with pursed lips. "Her instinct to attack vanished. She should've been going berserk!"

"I just tried to look into her mind," I defended myself. "It wasn't easy to ignore my knees knocking together!"

"No," he sounded deadly serious while shaking his head emphatically. "I think you put calm images in her mind. That's not the way she should have reacted. When I told her to go, her mind warred with the instinct to attack and the urging to 'stop.'"

"You told her to go?" I asked.

"At the end," he told me. "We heard her growl and came straight away, but she was already calming. She should have been tearing you to pieces."

I stared at him dumbfounded. I slowly followed the men back to the campsite. I hadn't tried to push anything into the cat's mind. I had been trying to search it. Apparently. it had been shockingly easy for me to put soothing thoughts into her mind, enough to keep from being killed. I couldn't be sure, but I would have to experiment with this newly found talent. Noah agreed he would help me, but just before we could really start talking about our powers, Charlotte came back.

"Ella," she said. "We need you now. Noah, Eddie," she addressed the men, "We probably won't be needing you today. We're just getting a feel for the situation for now. Tonight we'll discuss the plan for tomorrow with everyone. We'll be back in a bit." She turned to me. "Put on your hat."

She waited until I had pulled out my hat to put her right hand on my left shoulder. Once I had slipped the hat on my head, the air around us shimmered. When it stopped, our surroundings still consisted of the same type of towering trees, but the tent and camp had vanished. Removing her hand, Charlotte whispered, "From here on out you do not take off that cap until we are back at the camp." Then she pointed past me to my right to Sophia and Tony who crouched in the bushes about ten feet away. I assumed Kimi remained somewhere close by them unseen. We tiptoed over to join them. I crouched down by Tony, but he continued to stare up at Charlotte.

"I'm here," I whispered to them both. They knew I would be there, but it must have been the proximity of me that made Tony about jump out of his hiking boots. "Sorry," I whispered again. He just took a deep breath and rolled his eyes in my direction.

"Ella," Sophia said, looking in my general vicinity, "I need you to link our thoughts so we don't have to talk out loud."

"Sure," I said as I quickly linked all three minds, but I still had a question. *Where's Kimi?* I asked in their minds.

She's on the other side of the village, scouting, Sophia informed me.

Is that safe? I asked.

I can sense everyone and everything within one hundred miles, Ella. Charlotte said to me, a little offended. *She won't get lost and I'm sure she can handle herself if she's discovered.*

Okay, I tried to back-pedal my naivety. *But would you like me to include her in our conversation?*

Sophia shook her head. *Don't worry about it now. She'll be back soon. What we need from you now, Ella, is to get into the minds of a villager. I need information and a translation for their language so I can talk to them when the time comes.*

Okay, I thought, *Where are they?*

Down there, Sophia jerked her chin at what I had not noticed before. On Tony's other side dropped a sheer rock cliff. The most avid of climbers would be crazy to attempt it. We sat on a ledge cut into the cliff, inaccessible from every angle, unless you're Charlotte. Peering over the precipice, all I could see were treetops. Upon closer inspection I could make out a few wisps of smoke curling out from under the dripping leaves into the sky. The sea of green we overlooked hid the village.

The village is about one square mile, Charlotte told me. *You should be able to find a few minds to dig through.*

Right, I thought back at her. Then to the group I thought, *Give me a minute.*

I pulled my powers out of the minds of the group to drape them down the cliff. It dove into the trees without being aware of them, but I had to swing it around a few times to contact a mind. I found a woman, a mother, cooking something. Her mind was very foreign. Everything looked strange as if I had walked right into the village itself. I didn't understand any of her memories or thoughts. I saw gatherings with large and small groupings, but I had no way to identify anyone or figure out what they were doing.

Frustrated, I kept my serpent in the woman's mind, but bent it to include Sophia's mind on the receiving end. She took a small, sharp breath when she started seeing into the woman's mind with me.

Suddenly Sophia frantically waved in my direction wide-eyed. I couldn't tell what she wanted and she didn't put anything into my mind. She seemed desperate for me to stop. I twitched out of the woman's mind staring at Sophia. She took a choking gasp of air and fell back on her behind. She took some deep breaths, as if she had just run a marathon, carefully placing her head between her knees.

Tony and Charlotte watched her in confusion. Charlotte put a steadying hand on Sophia's back. Sophia's breathing started returning to normal. Between deep breaths she whispered to me, "Too much… information…too quickly."

"Sorry," I whispered back. I must have become somewhat immune to the onslaught of information that had first been overwhelming for me as well. I tried to think back quickly when I had been in other people's heads at multiple times. Mostly I had just been in the front of their minds hearing what they had intended me to hear. I would have to be careful in letting Sophia into the minds of the people. "Sorry," I whispered again as Sophia sat back up into her crouch. "I'll be more careful next time."

Sophia put her hands up, replying to me in my mind. *It's okay. I'll be fine.* After another second, she thought, *Do you know if others will be able to hear us talk to each other while we're in their minds?*

I contemplated for a second. *I don't know*, I said. *Let me try it on Tony.* I bent my serpent to include Tony's mind and tried to send my thoughts just to Sophia. *Can you hear me?*

Yes.

Yes. They both responded. I wrapped my serpent back around to include the entire group again. *Good thing we checked.* I told them.

Checked what? Tony asked.

Ella checked to see if we could communicate while in someone's mind without them hearing us. I guess it won't work. Sophia told them.

Can you maybe transfer thoughts or something, without them noticing? Maybe you can try that? Charlotte suggested.

Not a bad idea. It will also help me get a translation without getting too much information all at once. Sophia agreed. *Ella, let me talk to you privately again for a second.*

After I complied, Sophia told me to try to take a memory out of Tony's mind without him knowing about it. I bent my mind into Tony's again to find a recent memory of the trip here. Trying my best to avoid the other thoughts, I extracted the memory almost as if my little serpent had not only tasted it with its tongue but swallowed it whole. The memory originated, and thus persisted, in Tony's mind, nothing could change that, but I had copied it with my powers and sent it to Sophia's mind. Her eyes widened again and she gave a slight nod. *That will work perfectly!* She told me.

What will? Tony asked.

Sophia gave a smirk. I wrapped back into Charlotte's mind to let Sophia explain it to everyone.

After she finished, Charlotte looked at her watch. *Time for me to get Kimi.* She told us.

Right, Sophia answered. *Bring her back here while Ella and I work on getting a translation of the language.*

Charlotte nodded then disappeared.

I included Sophia's mind while mine dove into the trees again. This time it knew where it was going and it got there in lightning speed. I found the woman still mixing ingredients in a bowl. She hummed softly to herself while thinking of the words to a lullaby. I realized her baby slept on a bunch of blankets nearby. She sung him to sleep with a soft coo. I pulled the words to the lullaby out of her mind hoping they would be enough for Sophia.

Glancing over at Sophia, I saw a glazed look in her eyes. She sat that way for only a minute before she looked at me with a smile. Not just a half-hearted smile, but a triumphant smile. She nodded vigorously so I pulled out of the mind of the woman.

Have you got it? I asked silently. I was just in the front of her mind so I couldn't see the use of her powers, but I knew she would have created a new shade.

Yes. She continued grinning. *That worked perfectly! I have a translation for their language.* Her smile started to falter. *I'm not sure how you're going to be able to use it though.*

Don't worry, I reassured her. *I'm sure we'll think of something.*

Chapter TWENTY-ONE

We regrouped back at camp to eat and try to figure out what our next steps would be. Eddie knew he only played a small part and didn't join too much of the conversation. I'm sure he was also aware not everyone trusted him completely, so he might have been trying to stay out of the loop.

We munched on granola bars as Sophia told us, "I'd like to take Ella back to the cliff to get more information." She turned to look directly at me. "As soon as we can figure out how to get the translating and your mind reading merged in a practical way."

I nodded, swallowing my last bite. "If you give me a minute, I might be able to work something out."

"Sure," she said it casually, but I noticed a little suspicion in her eyes. She moved to sit down next to me on the ground and looked at me through narrowed eyes. "Just don't get too nosy in there." She said quietly while tapping her temple.

I tried to smile, but I think it probably looked more like a smirk. I turned to the fire hoping it would mask my guilty face. I stared at the fire as I reached out again to Sophia's mind. I already knew more about her than I probably should, besides, I needed her translating while I looked into someone else's mind. I figured I'd have to do it without pulling down the shades that made the translation.

After a few minutes of looking around, I knew I needed Sophia translating for me to do anything. I got Sophia's attention in her mind.

I need you translating something. I told her. *Probably into English, so I can understand it.*

Right, she said. *Try looking into Kimi's mind. Find a memory from Japan, and I'll translate it for you.*

As soon as she mentioned it, a blood red shade dropped down in her mind. If I angled one way everything I heard was in Japanese. If I angled to the other side everything changed to English. I would just have to stay on the correct side of the shade. Without having to pull any memories from Kimi's mind, we had an easy solution.

Charlotte took me and Sophia back to the cliff top view of the village. We spent hours looking into the minds of the villagers. Occasionally Kimi or Tony would come back with Charlotte after she checked in at camp. They would check in on us, get updates, then all go back to the camp. Sophia and I silently dug through minds and memories to see how life ran in the small village. It took longer with Sophia in tow than it would have if it had been just me because I had to feed her small amounts of information at a time. A few of them had the same sticky, syrupy feel to their minds and memories, but most were clear enough.

We figured out the leaders, etiquette for visitors to approach, even their dealings with Devin Ross and his people. We tried to get a feel for how the rest of the village saw Ross and his crusade. Many mothers had lost their sons to what they believed to be someone else's fight. The stickiness was thicker in their minds. Their community had been three hundred men strong, but almost two hundred of those had been taken along with many more from other groups. I did the math. Ross had gotten his five hundred easily. They had now been left with old men and young boys to defend their village.

The leaders' minds were the hardest to enter. They weren't just sticky in places, they were rock hard, as if someone had poured cement in their minds and it clung to certain memories and thoughts. Even still, the leaders had begun questioning whether Ross had been helping them or not. These leaders were revered by other groups as well as their own. They often came to ask advice, which is why Ross chose these people to approach as well. If we could get the leaders to somehow talk their own men out of fighting for Ross, we would stand a decent chance, but time ran dangerously low.

The leader was named Namal. He was a practical man who would do anything to protect his people. He reminded both me and Sophia of Jancarlo. The others who led with him as lieutenants: Soobos, Nenglo, and Lem, were also wise and practical. Lem assisted the three main elders, but they held his opinion in high esteem.

As we studied these men and their families, we grew to love their culture as much as they did. Sophia and I both decided we had to do whatever we could to return their loved ones to their homes. We came back to the camp well before the sun had reached its peak knowing what we had to do next.

By the time we got back, Eddie had secluded himself to rest in a tent. He wouldn't have a role to play until the end. The rest of us sat around the camp as Sophia reported.

"They have a tradition," she explained, "when others come to visit in peace, they bring a gift." She tentatively eyed Noah trying to feel out his reaction. "Usually, it involves a large dead animal."

He just nodded as if it made sense, so Sophia continued. "We're going to have to kill something and bring it as a gift. That should immediately raise our status in their eyes, hopefully higher than Ross, because he didn't do it. The more grand the animal, the better audience we get. Noah," she asked him outright, "do you have a problem with bringing an animal here to be killed?"

I think he surprised all of us by his lack of emotion when he shook his head. "Not at all."

"Good." I could see Sophia visibly relax at this answer. She went on to tell Tony he would have to kill the animal. The Shadow could show up any minute, so we had to act immediately.

After the group broke up, I slid over to sit next to Noah. "I thought you would have more of a problem with an animal dying," I said, trying not to sound too judgmental.

He looked at me questioning, "Why would I?"

My eyes widened and I shrugged my shoulders. "I don't know," I stammered out. I felt a little silly. "I thought maybe you connect with them. You know, feel their emotions, understand what they're thinking when they die, that kind of thing."

He just grinned at me, "Ella, did you feel bad for making that jaguar leave you alone?"

"I was terrified," I pointed out, "I wasn't exactly tuning in to her feelings."

"That's just it," he said. "Animals don't feel things the way humans do. They might get excited or scared, but it's usually through association to certain events or sudden changes. They have base emotions and feelings, but nothing as profound or complex as a human. They live on instinct with no free will of their own. Especially the wild ones. They don't have the same choices we do. That's what makes us different. Our choices make us happy or sad, but animals can't choose. They do what they do because they almost have to. Their path is already laid out for them. They react in certain situations the way they do because they've been programmed that way from the dawn of time. When it comes to death, humans all react differently in different situations, but animals all act the same. They try to defend themselves, but if they know the time has come, they stop. I've had animals in my office that are just waiting for death because they're in pain and they know death is the next step. Death is just another bump in the road to animals."

I thought about it for a minute. It made perfect sense. From what I had experienced in just a couple of animals' minds, I knew they saw death as another door to walk through.

Noah interrupted my thoughts by adding, "Maybe if we figure a way out of this mess, we can work together so you can get more of a feel for your powers."

"Yeah, I think that'd be a good idea."

Charlotte used her transporter powers to sense a large animal. Sophia suggested using an animal that the indigenous could eat and use other parts for supplies. "High currency," she called it. Charlotte found a massive thing called a tapir.

Using my powers as practice, I pushed the idea into the beast's mind for him to come our way. Noah stayed in its mind as well to monitor my progress. A little out of my element, but I told it which way to go. He followed my direction readily even with my underlying hesitation. I grew a little more confident, but Noah warned me once he sensed us, he would fight the instructions.

He was right. As soon as the tapir caught our scent, he immediately wanted to run for it. With a little more effort, I got him to walk up to us. As he approached us, he stopped. Sweat beaded on my forehead as I struggled with him. His instinct to run or attack threatened to prevail. Therefore, it caught me completely off guard when he decided not to run. Although he looked like a cow with a really long nose, the fighting instinct shook me.

Noah stepped between us to check the animal before he could pounce. The brute laid his head on the ground as if nothing had happened. He wasn't asleep, but Noah kept him docile. I panted from the rush of adrenaline draining out of me. Trying to gain control over my shaking hands, I collapsed on the ground.

"It's okay, Ella," Noah told me. With the tiniest movement of his finger, the tapir walked past me into the camp. "I'll take it from here." He turned back to me at the last second to add, "Maybe you can try some small animals first."

I regained my breath while gazing at the jungle around me. Small animals, huh? I wanted to be offended. He had a condescending personality, but I knew he was trying to help. I searched up into the trees to discover some monkeys and birds. The birds were fun to watch as they flew around the treetops, but after my latest brush with fangs, even their sharp beaks intimidated me. The monkeys were just plain obnoxious. I figured they would be too big to start with anyway.

My mind wandered closer to the ground to a few insects. Too small. Next to them, scrutinizing them in perfect stillness, sat a very small frog. I took it for a simple tree frog except it sported a brilliant, golden yellow. I watched it eat a few more insects then tried to make it come down the tree to me. It came down steadily as if I had just offered a bag of flies.

I thought maybe it would decide to run away as soon as it saw me, so I prepared to force it, but surprisingly it continued to hop closer to me. It struggled to get through some grass to get to me when Noah came back out of the camp. He watched me as I watched the frog free itself from the grass.

I held out my hand when it was only a few jumps away from me, but Noah yelled, "Ella!" His eyes drilled into the frog, who turned abruptly and hopped away.

"What?" I asked him, "You said start small."

"Anything, but that one." He breathed again as the frog disappeared into the grass. He looked at me with pursed lips. "That's a poison dart frog," he told me. "One of the most poisonous creatures in the world. Those have enough poison being secreted from their skin to kill twenty men. One touch would've killed you."

"Oh," I whispered as I grasped the severity of what I might have done. "But he came to me so easily. He wasn't scared or anything." I stood up to join Noah, moving back to the safety of the camp.

"Yes, well," he said, "they act as if they know of their immunity. They come across a little cocky sometimes."

"Oh," I whispered again. I looked back at the spot where I had almost caused my own death. Maybe I would wait until I got back to play around with controlling animals.

Chapter TWENTY-TWO

Everyone was ready to go when we returned to camp. Tony had the tapir slung around his shoulders. Charlotte transported most of us to a clump of trees just outside the village boundaries. She and I hid there. She could sense if anyone approached, so she would be fine. I would stay with her keeping in contact with Sophia. Noah and Eddie would stay back at camp until Eddie was needed. Sophia and Tony would walk into the village appearing alone, but Kimi would be going with them.

I slipped into Sophia's mind as the three went walking out of the trees. They would be seen almost immediately, but they would walk for a while before the villagers would let them know they had been seen. The threesome walked confidently. Charlotte relaxed, knowing the location of everyone at all times. Kimi and Tony were always confident and Sophia trusted our group completely. I, however, shook in my very sturdy boots.

I watched through either Sophia's or Tony's eyes and after maybe one hundred feet, an arrow came whistling out of the trees overhead, sprouting in the ground at

Tony's feet. We had warned him they would see him as the leader of any group. It would be up to him to correct them. They stopped cold, waiting as two young boys somehow climbed out of the trees while keeping their arrows targeted at the pair.

He told the boys in their own language, as Sophia had trained him, that they came bearing gifts in order to speak to the leaders. Although skeptical of the pair, the boys were more used to this manner of approach than anything else, so they took Sophia and Tony into the village with Kimi following silently.

I helped Tony remember how to say his next lines as they walked. I wouldn't have to be in the minds of the villagers until Sophia and Tony spoke to the leaders. The trio had to approach from the correct side of the village so it would be quite a walk to get to the leaders.

As the small group walked, a few of the villagers peeked from their homes, interrupting their various activities. They didn't like the foreign people who visited, so Sophia and Tony were watched suspiciously. The boys kept their arrows nocked while they walked one in front and one in back. Though it wasn't the most threatening of receptions, we could tell they didn't want us here.

After waiting a moment outside, Sophia and Tony were ushered into the small hut that served as the meeting place for the leaders. Kimi stood very close to Tony who helped her slide inside the hut through the grass that served as a door. Two older men stood guard outside the hut, dismissing the boys to return to their posts.

Tony laid the dead tapir outside the hut but in front of the opening. Inside the hut a few women hovered near the walls and four frail elders sat behind a small fire. In their language, Tony said, "We bring you a gift of friendship and hope you will hear what we have to say." Without taking a breath, he added, "Let me introduce my leader, Sophia." Inwardly, I listened as he hoped he didn't have to say any more, because this was all he had practiced. If he had to explain or answer questions or say anything else, I would have to coach him through Sophia.

The leaders seemed taken aback, they looked between the two people in front of them. Sophia knew they might have a problem with accepting her as the leader, but we hoped having Tony tell them would make it easier to digest.

Namal looked at Tony and asked, "She is your leader?" pointing to Sophia.

Just nod, Sophia told Tony in our minds. *Not speaking will make it clear you're done with the conversation.*

Tony gave a sharp nod.

Soobos pointed to Sophia then carved a matching scar on his own jaw with his thumb. "We have been warned of your people," he said pointing to her again.

Sophia lowered her chin, casting down her eyes. "You have been lied to," she said plainly. Sophia decided candor would be the best way to approach these practical people. We hoped they would see through Devin Ross's silky lies.

The group in front of us shifted uncomfortably as the other people in the hut murmured their disbelief. At that point I shifted into only Sophia's mind.

I'm going into Namal's mind, so I can hear what he's thinking, I told her. *I'll try to share what I can, but don't push anything through to me.* I also made sure to be only in the front of his mind, so she didn't get too much information at once.

Once in his mind, I tried to gain access to Namal's memories of Devin Ross or anyone he worked with, but something blocked my way. Something strong. Solid. I couldn't tell what it was, so I pressed up against it trying to find a path around or through it. Nothing.

I explained to Sophia about the blockage in Namal's mind.

Figure out what's going on, she told me. *But hurry. I'm not sure how long they'll allow me to speak with them before throwing us out.* Then she turned her attention back to their encounter as I sent her what I could.

I could see that Namal thought the others wouldn't agree, but he didn't see Sophia and Tony as a threat. He had originally been against even allowing Ross into their village. The conversations with Ross were blocked. How had Ross gotten this man to agree with him?

Namal's son had left with Ross, although there were no emotions attached to the memory, which struck me as extremely odd. Wouldn't a father worry about his son? Be sad to see him go?

He hadn't originally wanted to speak with Ross. I could see through the barrier that Namal had originally tried to throw him out, but somehow, through the cement wall on the memory, he seemed to now be willing to speak with anyone from outside their village. It was as if, since meeting Ross, he had changed his mind suddenly to accept outsiders. He waved to a young boy in the group to take the tapir, indicating he accepted the gift and would hear us.

I knew Sophia and Tony relaxed when he accepted the gift, but they didn't move or shift their stances in the slightest. "I thank you for allowing us into your village safely," she said when Namal waved to her to speak. They were moved as Sophia spoke their language fluently. "We're very sorry your lives have been interrupted so harshly. We understand you only desire prosperity for your people. Please believe me when I say we have this in common." She allowed them to respond to this statement.

I searched all of the leaders' minds again and again. They were all the same. Solid walls blocking any access to memories of conversations with Ross and his people. I could see them from a distance, but not read them or feel them. Those same blockages served to veer any communication or connections away and no emotion connected to them. I pressed against them again and again. As I attempted to slip around the wall in Namal's mind, I found a few spots where the hard blockage was slightly softer. A thicker, sticky consistency than I had yet to come across. Then it hit me.

Mind control! I practically yelled in Sophia's mind. *That's how Ross got these people to agree! It's the only thing that makes sense. They don't want to be part of the rest of the modern world, why would they agree to get involved in our war in the first place? Mind control! Or at least some form of it!*

All three of them? Sophia asked.

After a quick check, I answered, *yes. And I think, to some extent, some of the others in the village too. Even some of Ross's men in the states are being controlled.*

Can you do anything about it? She asked. *Reverse it somehow?*

The men stared at her across the fire. Namal waited for her to go on. He expected her to ask something of them. Outside his mind, he motioned for her to continue. Inside…I got to work.

When he thought about his conversation with Sophia the block became sticky toward her. Then it shifted away from her. I chased it around the blockage until I found a spot where it was still. I pressed against the sticky memory. It pressed back.

"We mean you no harm," Sophia was saying. "We pray for your way of life here to continue as it always has, without interference. We simply ask that you call your young men back home. Leave our people in peace as we wish for your peace." She said it as plainly as she could.

I pressed against the blockage and the softer spot pressed back. We fell into a rhythm of back and forth.

Namal held his left hand out to Soobos on his left, but his hand shook slightly for a moment. I was making progress.

"You say you mean us no harm," Soobos said, "but we have been warned you will lie to us. How do we know when we call our young men back, you will not slaughter us all in our sleep?"

I pressed against the blockage again. It pressed back. I pushed as hard as I could. It pushed back even stronger.

Sophia had prepared for these questions. When Namal motioned for her to be allowed to answer she tried to speak gently. "Devin Ross took your families away, we want them to return to you. We want your people to be strong. If we were going to attack you, why would we strengthen you first?"

She held her head high, waiting for the questions to continue.

Namal hesitated. He looked at Nenglo, who waited his turn to speak. After a moment, Namal indicated the other man's turn. "Even if we wanted to call back our young men," Nenglo said, "we have no means of communication with them. How will we ever get them back?"

Namal again motioned to Sophia for her to answer the question. "If you will give us a message or token, we will take it to your young men to see them safely returned to you. All we need is your decree that they come back, and we will gladly relay it to them."

At this point, Namal put both hands on his legs. He hunched over as if in thought, but I knew he was struggling internally alongside my mind. Then he sat up straighter. "We..." he faltered, as the thoughts pressed against mine, harder than ever. But as it eased, he spoke again. "We have been told our young men will be returned to us at a later date with no harm done to them. Why should we listen to you and go against the agreement we have already made?" he spoke like a robot, performing the words Devin Ross must have cemented in his mind. Sophia and I could tell he was fighting Ross's ideas. Literally and figuratively.

His mind is stronger when he's not reciting what Ross put into his head, I told Sophia. *Keep talking.*

When motioned to, Sophia chomped at the bit to start talking, but had to calm herself down enough to organize her thoughts. She did all this without moving a muscle. I tried to keep out of it as much as I could. "Did they tell you of the unnatural changes your men would undergo during their absence?"

The entire group murmured. This had the best effect on Namal's mind that I could've asked for. The stickiness thinned further. I pressed and he pressed back. Over and over.

Before she lost her chance to speak, Sophia continued, "You were led into this agreement under false pretenses. You are not honor bound to an agreement when the other party has not been truthful. This is what your own laws state." She said it loudly enough for the entire group to hear but directed her comments to Namal.

Namal held up his hand to silence the small group. Then he held out his left hand to give Soobos a chance to speak again.

Soobos, flustered over her revelation, composed himself quickly. Finally, he asked, "What kind of changes are you talking about?"

Sophia knew we shouldn't reveal our powers to them, it might frighten them out of any help they might be willing to offer. She also knew she needed to be as honest as possible about all the problems they faced. "These powers will permanently impact their lives and yours, if they ever return." She enunciated every word deliberately. "But we have the ability to heal them so they can return to their natural state before they come home. That's what the other people don't know." She looked at the three men pleadingly. "We want to help."

At these words, my mind and Namal's pushed as hard as we could. He was reaching for help. I was reaching to save him. I pressed as hard as I could. As he pressed back, I didn't stop. I pressed into his thoughts until the stickiness thinned to the point that I could almost feel the other side. Like slicing through a thick membrane, the blockage stretched to its limit and finally broke. My mind touched Namal's. The real Namal.

Anger.

Careful! I yelled to Sophia. *He's free, but he's mad!*

I felt Charlotte's hand on my back as I panted. I felt like I had just won a race, tired and exhilarated all at the same time.

In front of Sophia, Namal's head dropped. He panted in time with me then lifted his eyes back to hers. He blinked a few times and shook his head slightly.

He ground his teeth. "Devin Ross," he growled.

Sophia pulled away ever so slightly. "Namal?"

"He's a treacherous liar," he spat.

Namal's companions turned to him. Nenglo shook his head in confusion. Soobos muttered, "We agreed to help…" but there was no emotion behind the idea.

Namal glanced at his companions, then turned an angry eye on Sophia. "We do not allow outsiders into our village. Leave now."

"Yes, I know," she said quickly as he began to stand and usher them out. "I know and I respect that, but—"

Namal took hold of her arm. Tony stood to intercept the smaller man, but Sophia held a hand up to stop him. Sophia allowed Namal to push her out the door as I jumped back into her mind.

Sophia, I said. *I helped free him. I think I can help his friends too.*

Before Namal could push her too far, Sophia shouted, "We can free your friends. All of them."

Namal used the arm he was holding to turn her to face him. "You freed me?" he asked her.

She nodded. "My friend did. She helped anyway," she said. "She can help your friends as well."

They both turned to see the other two men stepping from the hut with placid faces.

Namal's eyes bounced between Sophia, the two men, then Tony. "Will you force us?" he growled at her.

"Never," she bit back. I explained in her mind and she relayed it back to Namal. "Your mind was already working on freeing you. Your friends will probably eventually free themselves as well. But we have the power to make that happen sooner."

He allowed his hand to slip from her arm and jerked his head toward the other two leaders.

On it, I told her before diving into Nenglo's mind.

As I worked in Nenglo's mind, Sophia nodded to Namal and explained quietly to Tony (and Kimi) what I was doing.

Nenglo must have had a stronger will because his mind was easier to free. As he shook his head in confusion, I jumped from his mind to Soobos. Soobos pushed against my powers, and we swayed back and forth to weaken the blockage. Eventually, all three men looked at Sophia with simmering anger on their faces. But she knew the feeling wasn't directed fully at her.

"You saved us?" Namal asked her.

She shook her head. "My friend," she answered. "She's very powerful."

"Powerful enough to save the men from our village?" Nenglo asked.

Sophia nodded. "I think so."

I sagged against the tree in front of me. Charlotte rubbed my back gently. She must have been watching me struggle with the mens' strong minds.

The three men looked between themselves and Sophia. I slipped into their minds. As they nodded to each other, I understood. Their minds were clear and their own again. They were angry at Ross, but had no way to get their men back or even find Ross. They knew they would have to trust us.

"Please," Namal said. "Come back inside."

Again, they entered the little hut, but no one bothered to sit. One of the women in the hut motioned to Namal with a hand, but he waved it away. She stepped back, but her shoulders seemed to loosen from relief.

"We don't have the means to go wage war against a powerful man like Devin Ross," Nenglo said.

"Or you, for that matter," Soobos added.

Sophia shook her head. "We don't want a war with you. We want to return your men to you unharmed."

"Yes," Namal said. He ground his teeth. "By now, Devin Ross has already mutilated them."

"No," Sophia answered. "We can heal them."

When she was met with confusion, Sophia sent me the message. *Bring Eddie.*

"I brought someone with me to prove it," Sophia told the men. "If you allow him to come in, he can tell you everything."

After another brief glance to each other, the men nodded. Sophia turned to Tony, telling him to go get Eddie. Tony nodded his head to the leaders before he left the stuffy hut. Once he left, he retraced his steps back to Charlotte's hiding place in the trees. I leaned against the tree, invisible nearby. It would take him a few minutes to reach our location, so Charlotte had plenty of time to go get Eddie.

When Tony reached our hiding place, he simply looped around the back of the tree emerging with Eddie on the other side without breaking stride. The two men walked confidently back to the village.

Sophia, Tony and Eddie sat across from the leaders of the village. Sophia acted as translator for Eddie. The leaders asked Eddie about Devin Ross and what he knew of his plans. They also asked why he had decided to leave his service and what he planned to do next. As I realized it, I informed him that he must have had a small amount of mind control placed on him as well, but he was able to free his own mind. Eddie told the leaders that they must have had extreme mind control over them, but their minds were already breaking free, they just needed a little help.

He went into detail about his recruitment and the brutality of Ross and his people, but he was just as vague with them about what he planned to do next as he had been with me. When they asked for proof that Eddie had actually been part of Ross's people, he showed them what remained of his scar. Everyone could still see the twisted scar as it snaked up his forearm then across his elbow. The remnants of the scarred skin were still dark. In spots it seemed to make the light waver. The leaders had seen these marks on Ross and his people.

All around, Eddie did well convincing the men to help us, although that part was already mostly done. Seeing his scar healed helped them feel there would be hope for their men when they returned.

While Eddie spoke with the elders, I tried to concentrate on helping Sophia and Eddie. I stayed mainly in their minds, but occasionally slipped into the minds of everyone.

After Eddie had told them all he could, Namal nodded his head and addressed both Sophia and Tony. "You will please wait outside while we discuss this matter." A boy motioned for them to sit in front of the fire outside where they would wait. A faint light covered the village from the canopy of trees, but now the specks of light from the sun started to dim as the sun went down.

I wrapped my serpent around to find the members of our party. It took me a minute, but I found Kimi sitting by Tony.

I'm going to check in with Jancarlo, Sophia informed the group. *Ella,* she said, *I'll scratch my left ear when I'm done.*

I pulled out of her mind as Charlotte asked, *Is someone going to tell me how it went?*

Good, I guess, I told her. I knew everyone else would be listening to my insight as well. *They're scared but more angry. They know there's really no choice but to trust us since they can't get to Ross themselves. They can't rescue their men themselves either. They're just trying to decide how best to proceed.*

As we discussed in silence, Tony pointed out, *Sophia's done.*

I quickly slipped back into her mind. *I told Jancarlo about our progress. He wants us to try to get back as soon as possible without pushing them into a decision too quickly.* She paused then uncertainly added, *He says Vincent told him we have less than twenty-four hours until the Shadow show up at the base.*

A stunned silence followed. *When was he told about that?* Kimi asked almost accusingly.

Apparently, a long time ago, Sophia confirmed, *but he just informed me about it now. He said it was more important for us to concentrate on our mission here.*

I looked over at Charlotte's face to see the anxiety mirrored in everyone's thoughts.

There's more, Sophia told us. *Jack escaped. They think Wiki helped him.*

Jack is the most powerful metal mover anyone knows of, Kimi pointed out. *We've got to hurry and get back if he's on the loose.*

Ella? Sophia called to me.

Yeah?

This is taking too long. Look into the leaders' minds. See if they'll be reaching a decision soon.

Okay. I quickly slipped inside the hut, but before I slinked into Namal's mind, I told everyone in the group, *Don't say anything else until I give the all clear.* Namal and the others were not so much discussing whether or not to help us, but *how* they would help. I pulled out snippets of ideas and strong feelings about the options presented to them. I chose to send these thoughts to the group then gave them the all-clear as I left the hut again.

Finally, one of the women from the hut came out to get Sophia and Tony moments later. They walked into the hut again with Kimi in tow, but unseen. This time I stayed in the groups' minds to let everyone communicate if necessary. Sophia sat in front of the elders waiting for them to speak first.

Namal squared his shoulders. Addressing Sophia, he said, "We have decided to do as you ask, but the men of our village will not follow with just a message or a token. I have decided I will come with you to fetch them back."

Sophia had thought of this answer as well. "I don't think that will be necessary," she told the aged man. "It will be dangerous and you will experience many disturbing things."

"Nevertheless," Namal crossed his arms, giving Sophia a stern look, "I will be going with you."

Suddenly in my mind I heard Charlotte's urgent thoughts push through to all of us.

Someone just showed up. You're going to have company. Get out of there.

How far? Kimi asked.

They popped up just outside of the village. They'll get to you in a matter of minutes.

Is it Wiki? Tony asked.

No other transporters know where we are or how to get here. Charlotte answered solemnly.

At least if Wiki is here, that means he's not transporting people to Georgia, Sophia pointed out.

Or he's done, Tony added like a ray of sunshine.

Would Wiki really want to stay out of the fight? I asked. *Okay, okay!* I shot back when I got an overwhelming response of *YES!*

Every time I slipped into someone's mind their thoughts were tainted with the urgency that the Shadow could show up at the base at any moment. Now, the urgency made my mind itch.

While Charlotte warned us, Nenglo reached over to Namal and lightly touched his arm, a signal that he wanted to say something. Namal motioned for him to speak. "One last question I have for you," he said to Sophia. "What will happen to Ross?"

Sophia nodded solemnly, answering, "We don't want to harm anyone. If we can, we will detain him for as long as need be."

"Please," Nenglo said, "keep us informed so that we may decide if further punishment is needed."

"Of course," Sophia said, nodding. "Now, it's important we leave as soon as possible. We'll come back for you first thing in the morning."

As they stood to leave Charlotte said, *Too late*.

Chapter TWENTY-THREE

Tony swept the curtain of grass wide for Kimi to leave in front of him, but as he, Eddie and Sophia came out of the hut, four men walked up to them. Everyone knew Jack and Wiki when we saw them. Kimi paced close to Wiki unseen, and he tensed. I knew he sensed someone else being there. I left Sophia's and the groups' minds to dig through the minds of the Shadow.

After only half a blink, I knew Aaron Parker, a horrible person who hated the Storm People and wanted them all to suffer slowly. He was tall and bald, but on the older side.

The other man was Roy Simms, and he had been helping the Shadow for so long, he realized he just liked hurting people. He enjoyed watching the pain when a new person got shocked. He had several tattoos across his muscled arms, because he used to be addicted to seeing the blood. Now he used the Shadow to watch other people bleed. Like the other men, he held no trace of mind control.

Aaron didn't seem too surprised to see Sophia and Tony although something like shock pulsed across his face when he ran straight into them. He never even looked at Eddie although Jack watched him with a look of pure hatred on his face.

Aaron looked down at Sophia's scar running her jawline. His eyes narrowed. He squared his shoulders and looked up at Tony who glowered down at him. He relaxed slightly as he remembered the indigenous people surrounding him. His eyes volleyed between the two of them. "What are you doing here?"

"That's our business," Sophia snapped.

"It's our business if you trouble these people. They're under our protection," he shot back.

"Your protection is a lie," Sophia accused bravely.

The leaders in the hut heard the noise out front and emerged to investigate. Namal saw the three scars on Aaron's wrist. "What's going on here?" he asked.

Aaron gave a brief bow to the elder then picked up a thick stone hanging around his neck in one hand. He held it by his chin as he spoke to Namal. It must have been a translating stone of some sort because his words came out in their language. "We have been sent by Mr. Ross to check on you and your people. He hopes you're still in agreement with him about the need to eradicate the People of the Storm."

Namal returned his cold gaze. "There is much we need to discuss," he said. He indicated the hut he had come from. "Please, come sit with us."

Aaron's face grew even colder as his eyes swept back to Sophia. A thick tension hung in the air. Most of the people nearby had slipped away unnoticed. After getting what information I could, I came out of their minds and back to our group.

He's going to try to get you guys alone so they can subdue you without everyone else seeing. I told Sophia.

Everyone waited to see what Aaron would do. "I see," he finally said. "Apparently things have changed." He glared at Sophia then turned back to Namal. "Jack will stay here, while you wait for my return." He said it dispassionately so there was no mistaking it for anything but a threat. "I'll make sure these people leave and don't bother you anymore." He turned back to Sophia and Tony, put down the stone, speaking in English so the indigenous wouldn't understand. "If you value these peoples' lives, you'll come with me quietly. Jack, if I don't return in twenty minutes, kill Namal."

Jack moved his hostages back into the hut with a jerk of his head to the elders. As he walked through the grass behind the leaders, I noticed from Sophia's point of view the thick, metal chain dangling around his waist.

"Follow me," Aaron said as he moved to leave the village. Roy and Wiki followed the group.

Aaron has three scars. I started to report. *That means he has three powers, fire throwing, limited transport and moving objects. Roy is an illusionist. He's also a really good fighter. He has some metal rings on his belt he's keeping hidden. I haven't been able to see what they're for yet, but I know they're to use on the Storm People. He only has four.*

I'm pretty sure I know what they're for, Kimi said. *We've been making some of the same thing. They have a dampening field in them. If they get one around your neck you won't be able to use your powers.*

Kimi, Tony and Charlotte are the important ones to keep those things away from then. Sophia pointed out. *Ella, I'm going to contact Jancarlo.* I snapped out of her mind to focus through Tony's mind on what was going on around them.

After just a few seconds, Tony saw Sophia scratch over her ear like she had before. I slipped back into her foremind. *Jancarlo knows what's going on and the danger we're in. He doesn't have any help to send us immediately, but said he'll send someone the long way anyways. Ella, make sure you stay out of this, so if all else fails you can at least get information back to Jancarlo.*

As she said it, they broke away from the village into a clearing well away from curious eyes. Stepping into the trees they saw at least ten more men all armed with automatic rifles surrounding them.

Oh crap, Tony moaned internally.

What is it? Charlotte asked.

Did you not pick up on the dozen heavily armed men in our immediate vicinity? Tony asked accusingly.

There's no one else in your vicinity! You should still outnumber them four to three. Charlotte shot back.

The men are an illusion, Sophia verified.

Let's hope the bullets are too, Tony mentioned.

Aaron turned to Sophia, "On your knees." Then he looked at the other two men. "All of you." He shot an icy glare at Eddie.

All three of them glared back, not budging. I hated watching it through their eyes. My heart pounded in my chest and I didn't even have a gun pointed at me.

"If you can't count, just so you know, you're a little outnumbered," Aaron sneered. The bluff wouldn't work.

Sophia gave half a grin. "I think you're the one who can't count. See, we know those men," she jerked her head at the men with guns, "are just illusions." She continued to grin up at him stepping a little too close. "Leave this place while you still have the chance."

"I kind of hoped you wouldn't come quietly," he grinned back at her. "Gives me a reason to do this." He whipped the back of his hand across her face.

That's when all hell broke loose. Sophia crumpled on the ground. Tony attacked Roy, but his hands slipped through the illusion. Without warning, he got a dark metal ring snapped around his neck from behind. He touched the ring around his neck then jumped up with his face twisted in a defiant snarl. He ran at the men with the guns, swinging through them to see if he could find one with substance. Horror even worse than I had already been feeling enveloped me as I realized I could no longer enter Tony's mind. All the fake men with guns around them started firing, but sure enough, the bullets weren't real either. It did, however, make it very loud and confusing.

Eddie went for Aaron but was outmatched. After getting a couple of punches in, Aaron kicked Eddie into a nearby tree.

Kimi went for Wiki, but after a few painful kicks finding their mark, he transported away from her. "There's someone else here," Wiki yelled to the others. "It might be Liam."

Kimi tiptoed around behind Wiki and grabbed a fistful of his bushy blonde hair. Pulling his ear close to her mouth she whispered with all the venom she could muster, "I won't be as nice as Liam." Keeping hold of Wiki, she knew he couldn't transport without taking her with him, so she pummeled him with blows. At one point, she finally smashed his head into her knee and Wiki collapsed on the ground. But he must have been faking. When she went to grab him again, he transported away and didn't reappear immediately.

Aaron focused on Sophia, who wasn't much of a fighter anyway. Holding his hand out in the air, another metal ring flew into his fist. He advanced toward Sophia with the ring but found himself being attacked by an invisible foe. Kimi resisted lighting any flames for fear they would be used by Aaron. He disappeared quickly, but not before Kimi got in a few good kicks, then appeared behind Eddie. He clicked the ring around Eddie's neck, but it fell away immediately, refusing to lock into place. Eddie shrugged at the phenomenon then took a swing at Aaron, but Aaron disappeared again.

Aaron reappeared a few feet away from Eddie and Sophia, who struggled to her feet. Kimi tried her best to keep up with Aaron, but he kept ahead of her. That's when Charlotte jumped in.

I hadn't even noticed she had disappeared from beside me, but I saw her through Sophia's eyes as she and Aaron flickered around the clearing playing cat and mouse.

Tony saw Charlotte appear. "I can't find Roy!" he yelled to her.

She solidified enough to yell back. "I'll get him!" Of course she could locate his body, but she couldn't tell what he was doing. When she materialized next to a tree, a couple branches snapped a ring around her neck. She clawed at the ring, screaming, but to no avail. Charlotte slipped from my reach as well.

Suddenly the tree burst into flames. Roy bellowed, melting back into himself. Aaron intervened, moving the flames to Sophia and Eddie. Roy's raging subsided as Kimi was forced to put the flames out before they could surround Sophia and Eddie.

Aaron scanned the clearing, apparently looking for Kimi.

What's he going to do? Sophia thought to me urgently.

I reached out to his mind too late. He grabbed Sophia by the throat from behind, brandishing a long blade that hovered somewhere between knife and machete with a serrated tip. He pressed the razor edge against her throat. "Show yourself!" he yelled. "Or she dies!"

Everyone stopped to stare at Aaron and Sophia. I dug through his mind desperately to give Sophia as much as I could to work with, but I could only send her small images. He would use her as a hostage to get the others. I would've sent information to Kimi, but I couldn't find her.

Tony walked over to join Eddie in front of the pair. He looked utterly defeated without his strength. I knew he would probably blame himself if anyone got hurt.

Aaron turned to Charlotte, motioning with his chin. "Come over here where I can see you."

Charlotte slowly walked over in front of him, but with a look of defiance in her eyes. Roy gingerly stood up, whimpering at the patches of burnt skin covering half his body.

"Show yourself!" Aaron shouted again. He pressed the blade harder into Sophia's neck.

With a look of seething hatred, Kimi appeared when she pulled the black knit hat off her head. As soon as she appeared, a dark metal ring flew off the ground to wrap around her neck. Kimi dropped from my grid as well. With Kimi under control, Aaron yanked her hat out of her hand and shoved it in his back pocket.

Moments later, Wiki and Jack appeared, each holding a thick metal bar. "Good timing," Aaron told them. "Chain them together. Strap them to a tree." He shoved Sophia into Tony's arms.

The metal started to morph into silver chains that slid around everyone's wrists. Then the end of it wrapped around a thick tree trunk.

Sophia, I thought to her urgently, *I can't communicate with anyone that has one of the rings on them! I won't be able to talk to you!*

She thought quickly. *The rings won't stay on Eddie. You can at least talk to him.* Then she had a dark metal ring snapped around her neck and she was gone.

I punched the tree in front of me, but quickly pulled it together to make sure I could still reach Eddie's mind.

Aaron stood in front of Sophia with narrowed eyes. "You must be a translator. We probably don't even need one of these on you." He tapped the ring around her neck. "But better safe than sorry." Then he turned to Eddie. "And why don't the rings stay on you, I wonder."

"They probably don't like traitors either," Roy spat at him.

"It's because you have to have powers for the rings to stay on." Everyone turned to look at Kimi once she said it.

Aaron smirked at her, "I've seen this man move a small mountain," he informed her while pointing a thumb at Eddie.

"They cured me," Eddie said. His face was hard to read, but I knew he hoped the men in front of him would want the same future.

Unfortunately, it only seemed to make them angrier. Aaron yanked on Eddie's arm and ripped back his sleeve to reveal his arm. When Aaron saw Eddie's scar mostly healed, he shoved it away grunting in disgust.

He turned to Jack. "Stay here," he said. "Roy and Wiki, come with me."

I pulled out of Eddie's mind to see what Aaron and the others were up to. He needed to talk to Ross about what to do with us. He came here to babysit leaders so they didn't try anything stupid because Ross knew we would come talk to them, but I couldn't tell if either Aaron or Ross knew what the outcome would be. Wiki could take Roy to be healed then come back. Roy and Aaron would have to trade off watching the elders and taking over for Jack with Wiki bouncing between everyone.

The most distressing part was Aaron's confidence that Ross would have him kill at least one of the leaders as an example. Aaron was a vicious man with nothing but cruel intentions. I desperately wanted to keep this horrible being away from these innocent people.

As soon as I had gotten as much as I could, I pulled back out of Aaron's mind, telling Eddie we were clear and started sending him the information. Careful not to overload him, I let him know where they would go and what they would do. For his part, he sat quietly chained to the others as if nothing were happening. We both noticed Sophia giving him furtive glances. We knew her hopes of communicating but had no way of letting her know what was going on.

I'm not much of a fighter, I told him, *but I have my cap and the element of surprise.*

You should try to contact Noah first, he told me. *See if he can help.*

I sent my little serpent flying through the trees. I didn't realize how fast I could really push it until I tried. I looked into the minds of animals and people briefly as I passed in order to keep my bearings. I knew vaguely where we were camped, but I had no idea how far away. Our camp sat atop the hill with the cliff we had used to overlook the village. If Noah tried to traverse it alone, it could be dangerous. Not to mention, he would be far too late to help anyone. I went back into Eddie's mind explaining the geographical difficulties.

Maybe he can send some animals or something. Eddie suggested.

Then it struck me, *Of course,* I told him. *I just have to find the right frog.*

I saw the question form in his mind right before he came to a realization. *Wait Ella,* he told me urgently, *are you sure you want to kill him?*

No, I said, *just scare him but I guess I'll do what I have to do too.*

After I swept around for a little while, I found a few of the right frogs, easily urging them in the right direction.

Give me a minute and pray this works, I told Eddie. He wished me luck and I pulled out of his mind.

Chapter TWENTY-FOUR

As the sun sunk deeper behind the towering trees, I made use of the little light left.

Jack, I whispered into his mind.

Jack looked around warily. "Who's there?" he said out loud. He looked over at the group bound in his own chains.

They looked at him with curiosity on their face.

Jack! I yelled it this time in his head. Partially because I was mad. Partially because I wasn't sure if he could hear me. He jerked his head to the side, frantically looking around while standing up.

"Did you hear that?" he asked his prisoners.

Sophia was a great actress. She narrowed her eyes at him. "Did I hear what?"

The others weren't so good at keeping straight faces. While Tony, Charlotte and Eddie just had little grins on their faces, Kimi had to turn away from him to keep Jack from seeing the spreading smile on her face. She bit her lip pretty hard, but couldn't help showing her entertainment when Jack yelled at her, "What are you laughing at?"

I know all about you, Jack! I yelled at him again to get his attention back on me. I pulled out his memory of trying to abduct me as an example, but I found many other little misdeeds he had done. One by one I shoved these memories of his past back into his mind. He gave choking gasps as I drove them to the front of his mind. *You haven't been very good, have you?*

"Who are you?" he yelled into the dark forest around him.

Down here, Jack. I focused a picture of the forest floor in front of him in his mind. At this point, I stood just behind one of the many thick trees to his side, but he didn't know. He crouched down to the ground to inspect where he thought the voice came from. From under some leaves three small frogs hopped out. The one on the left was bright green with black spots on it, the one on the right was a vivid red with similar black spots, but the one in the middle, advancing a little further, allowed his brilliant yellow to shine bright in the moonlight. Jack knew these kinds of frogs. He straightened up slightly from his crouch. "You're a frog?" He looked around as if waiting for someone to jump out at him and tell him to smile for the camera. "What's going on here?" He eyed the group warily who smirked back at him.

Don't judge a book by its cover, Jack. I told him.

"But," he paused, "you're just a frog."

The little yellow frog cocked its head to the side as I said, *Oh, am I?*

I started assaulting his mind with information the way mine had been assaulted when I entered Vincent's mind. Some of the images came from that very encounter. I didn't want to give him any information on the Storm People so I poured thoughts from the indigenous and the Shadow into his mind.

At first, Jack put both his hands on the sides of his head. Then his eyes squeezed shut as he shook his head side to side. After only a few seconds he let out a loud yell, falling to his knees. I stopped the battering and allowed him to gasp for breath while on all fours. He opened his eyes to find himself nose to nose with the poison dart frog.

"What are you?" he asked weakly. He moved to sit back, but I saw in his mind as he started to transform some of the metal around his waist into tiny star-shaped metal bullets to kill the frog.

That would be a mistake, Mr. Jackson Samuel Portman, I said, although I didn't have much to threaten him with.

He stopped, but his face contorted in anger. He didn't like the fact that I knew his real name.

"What do you want?" he asked.

Just for you to get out of my jungle and never come back! Again, I assailed his mind with the same thoughts from my experience with Vincent. In only a few seconds, he writhed on the ground, wailing. I probably should have felt bad for him, but I knew what he was capable of. I crammed more information into his mind. While he screamed, I forced more and more on him, rage fueling me. Suddenly, silence. He collapsed on the ground, unconscious.

I stepped into the clearing to wide eyes and slack jaws.

"Ella?" Sophia sounded afraid. "Did you do that?" She motioned to Jack with her head.

"Yeah," I said. I couldn't figure out why they all gaped at me. "What? He's not dead."

"That's amazing!" Kimi finally said, the smile spreading on her face. "But do you know how to take these things off?" She tried to pull at the ring, but had no luck taking it off. "It's the problem we've been having while making them."

"Hold on," I said. I dug through Jack's mind for the second time with him unconscious. I liked him better that way. I knew his mind pretty well by now. It took a moment for me to find the instructions he had received from Aaron. "Yes," I said. I pressed the scar on my forehead to the almost imperceptible break in the ring. It immediately sprung free of her neck.

"The rings stay in place by capturing your powers. Someone else's power forces them off," I explained. "That's why the rings don't stay on Eddie. He doesn't have enough power for it to stay on."

Kimi held out her chained hand and a small flame appeared. It moved to the chains on her wrists and burned white-hot. She jumped to her feet once the chain fell away from her wrists.

Kimi took the ring off Tony's neck with a nod of her head. I did the same for Charlotte and Sophia. With Tony freed, he set to work breaking chains off everyone. Kimi immediately ran over to place one of the rings around

Jack's neck. Tony joined her with the leftover scraps of the chains, fashioning a rough pair of hand cuffs with them.

"Charlotte," Sophia said, "Take him back to camp. Have Noah watch him. Then come back here for the rest of us." She turned to the rest of the group. "We need to get out of here. Tony, you go with Jack first."

"Wait," I said. "They're going to kill them."

"Who?" Sophia asked.

"Aaron," I tried to clarify. "He's going to kill at least one of the leaders. If we leave, he might kill all of them just to make a point."

"We need to bring Namal with us as well," Kimi pointed out.

"All right," Sophia said. "Clear out of here. Get rid of the chains as best you can. Make them come looking for us."

Keeping the chains around was too dangerous, so Tony threw them as far out into the jungle as he could, which ended up pretty far.

Soon Noah joined the group, reporting that they'd tied up Jack with some rope back at the camp. Tony had the brilliant idea of dragging Eddie so it looked like we had dragged Jack somewhere else. I think Tony enjoyed it. Of course, I think Eddie did too. Then we surrounded the place, waiting for the other Shadow people to return.

Tony boosted Sophia and I into a tree to wait. "I'm going to contact Jancarlo again," she said, right before she tuned me out. I wondered for a moment if I were to reach out to the bracelet if I would hear the report or not, but thought it would be like listening in on a phone conversation. She cut her report short turning quickly back to me. "Sweep the area," she told me. "Find them so we're one step ahead."

I swiftly sent my mind out to search the surrounding area. I knew the direction of the village, but I didn't know if they had moved or not. I found Aaron and Roy in the same hut where the leaders had been. Roy had just gotten back from getting healed. Wiki was supposed to be checking in on Jack, so I knew he'd be back any moment to tell them what happened. I didn't wait too long. Wiki popped back into the hut, announcing our disappearance.

"They know we're gone," I told Sophia.

I watched as Aaron roughly jerked Namal to his feet. With the other hand, he took hold of Wiki and Roy connected as well. They transported to the clearing where they had left us. The fragile old leader didn't let the other men see his terror at suddenly being in a different place. He had been preparing himself for strange and horrible things to happen. It took a minute for him to get his orientation in the new spot, but he passed it off as old age to the Shadow group. He was much braver than anyone knew.

I watched as Aaron and his companions pushed Namal along as they followed the drag marks in the dirt. I listened to their conversation and their minds as they stomped through the trees.

"They're following the marks," I relayed to Sophia. "Wiki will be on defense. He's going to be transporting around the area as far as he can see."

"Ok," Sophia said, "tell Charlotte to be prepared to slap a ring around Wiki as soon as he transports close enough to her. Tell Kimi to take Roy, and Tony gets Aaron."

I gave everyone their orders, informing them the others were coming. My heart raced just from the waiting, even though I knew how far away they were. I didn't bother trying to keep up with Wiki. But I sent images of Aaron and Roy walking through the shaded jungle to Kimi and Tony.

All at once, we saw Wiki transport to a spot on the perimeter of our ambush. Charlotte was ready for him. She transported right next to him, snapping a ring around his neck before he completely solidified. With a yelp of surprise, he grabbed at it briefly then turned his attention to take a swing at Charlotte. Too bad for him he didn't hold a candle to her without his powers.

Aaron and Roy came running into the trees where Kimi and Tony waited for them. Although caught unaware, they adapted quickly. Tony tried to get the ring around Aaron's neck, but he kept transporting away. Noah sent in a couple jaguars to keep Wiki in place so Charlotte could help Tony take care of Aaron.

Meanwhile Kimi made short work of Roy. He didn't have a prayer against her. As soon as he appeared, she grabbed hold of him so he couldn't get away from her. She kept trying to get the ring around his neck, but, only with some luck, he knocked it out of her hand. By keeping her attention focused on Roy, any illusions he conjured up wouldn't fool her.

They tussled a bit longer before a monkey swooped out of the trees and picked up the metal ring. Of course, Kimi understood that Noah was assisting her, but a confused Roy took a second glance at the animal. He ended up with tiny little Kimi wrenching his arm behind his back. While he lay face down in the dirt, the monkey snapped the ring around his neck. It was a little strange to see Kimi give the monkey a fist bump, though.

Unfortunately, Roy's capture turned Aaron into a cornered animal. He paid no attention to Kimi's fire, pelted Tony with rocks and branches all while dodging Charlotte's attempts to snag him. Tony took a basketball sized rock to his head, but he only fell to his knees for a few moments. When Aaron pulled out the long blade he had used to threaten Sophia, they all had to keep their distance. They tried baiting him, but he knew the trick. With our group out of my way I could get my serpent in to Aaron's mind. The moment I entered, I heard his next move.

"Namal!" I yelled. Kimi spared a glance up at me, but the others started to move in on Aaron.

The old man was attempting to blend in with a trees while watching the fight, but Aaron grabbed him before he could. Aaron lifted the knife, but when he plunged it toward the old leader, Charlotte realized what he was doing. Faster than a blink, she transported between the two men. The blade sunk with force deep through her heart. Aaron's top lip curled back in a mad dog snarl. He twisted the blade in her ribs before Tony could tear him off her.

Charlotte slipped to her knees with the handle of the blade sticking out of her chest. Tony and Kimi clamped the ring around Aaron's neck while Sophia, Eddie and I converged on Charlotte. Everything seemed to move in slow motion. Charlotte's breath rattled for only a moment then she fell to the ground. Sophia had a healing stone out before we got to her, but it was already too late. Pressing the stone against her chest, the wound didn't change at all. I reached out to her mind hopefully, but heard nothing. Memories, thoughts, feelings. All gone. We encircled her body in stunned silence.

Chapter TWENTY-FIVE

Having seen everything, including the use of our many powers, Namal still offered to bring us back to the village for food and rest. Like I said, he was a lot braver than I realized. He called for some boys who wrapped Charlotte's body in a cloth and carried it into the village behind us. Charlotte's sacrifice for Namal made it no longer necessary to hide from the villagers. We were welcomed as family. Sophia asked Namal if we could bury her somewhere nearby. After all, we couldn't take her body back with us. Namal promised she would be buried with their honored dead.

The rest of the night passed in quiet mourning. We knew we were on borrowed time at this point. Either the Shadow hadn't attacked the base yet or we were too late to get there to help. Whichever it ended up being, we greedily took the time to sorrow.

Memories of my mother's memorial threatened to drown me as I sat in the hut. I repeatedly pushed them away about as successfully as pushing away the tide. Only Sophia and Eddie openly shed tears, but I think we all shared in them. Only I knew Eddie's tears came from his own guilt for allowing Ross to further his plans. He indirectly blamed himself for Charlotte's death. Tony, I believe guessing Eddie's feelings, gently patted the other man on the shoulder.

Aaron and his companions were bound and gagged so we could mourn in silence. Some of the villagers eagerly stood guard around the former threat to their elders. We slept in the main hut where Sophia had met with the leaders, but I don't think we got much rest. I dozed occasionally, but never had a solid steady sleep.

Kimi tried to gently push Sophia and the group to get back to the camp and find some way out of the Amazon. Sophia and Noah insisted it was too dangerous to try to get through the jungle at night. It would be hard enough in the daytime. Eventually, Kimi settled to simmer.

As quickly before dawn as we could manage, we gathered around a deep pit beside the burial plots for tribal leaders. We watched as the boys reverently lowered Charlotte's body to her final resting place. Not much was said as we sat around the fire in the hut afterward. The women of the village brought us fruit and breads to eat, but none of us had much of an appetite. They took good care of us while we discussed what we needed to do next.

"We need to get back to the camp to collect Jack," Kimi whispered into the silence.

"But we can't be dragging those jerks along," Tony indicated the Shadow group.

"It's also going to be rugged terrain to cross to get there," Sophia said. She thought for a moment then came to a decision. "Kimi, you can go, but you have to take someone else with you. Not Tony, we need him here to guard Aaron."

"I'll take Ella." She said it so fast I flinched. I thought for sure she could move faster with Noah. I didn't want to go anywhere. I had been less than useless during the fight. I only gave Charlotte the information that got her killed.

Sophia looked to me for confirmation, but what was I going to say? No? "Get going," she told us. "The Shadow will be getting to the base any moment. We've got to find a way out of this jungle."

Kimi and I bowed quickly to our hosts before we left the village. We moved as quickly as we could. Kimi urged me to jog as often as possible, but the overgrown vegetation made it difficult. Kimi knew the landscape pretty well for not being a transporter. We went around the mountain from which we had gotten our first views of the village. It was more of a hill really, but a tall, steep one with treacherous loose rocks. The villagers had a precarious path they used to get to the top. Once off the path, we were left to our own devices.

With our hats tucked into pockets, we hiked. We didn't talk much as the exertion kicked in but had a few snippets of conversation. I didn't feel much like talking, much as I had since my mother's funeral, but Kimi tried to chat every once in a while. I think she was trying to distract both of us, not to mention that if everyone at the Storm base died, we would be stuck with each other for a long, long time.

I asked Kimi about her history. It was easier to listen. Plus, she was an interesting person, and I loved hearing about her life. I also hoped, talking to her this way, I could cover for some of the information I had gotten while probing her mind for Jancarlo.

Kimi told me of her young life in Japan with Kin. She also told me of their three older brothers. Kimi and Kin were the last with Kimi being the youngest of five children. She grew up getting picked on and pushed around by her brothers, but in public they stood by her every word and action.

"That's the difference between our cultures," she said. "Where I'm from, families stand by each other no matter what in front of other people. It's when you're behind closed doors you really pay for what you've done."

"I didn't grow up with any extended family to speak of, just my mom, so I wouldn't know," I said.

"I can trace my family bloodline back thousands of years to ancient families of Japan."

"Wow. My mom told me once that my great-great-grandmother was a gypsy," I said. Kimi chuckled, but I continued. "She said our last name is derived from the only way she knew to make money. She grew and sold hemlock."

Kimi stopped walking and turned to stare at me. "You're great-great-grandmother grew hemlock…and sold…."

"Poison," I finished for her, "yeah."

I hadn't thought about it for a long time. With my mother gone, I would never have a chance to find out any more about my family.

"Kimi," I asked hesitantly, "how old are you?"

She narrowed her eyes at me. "How old do I look?"

I shook my head. "You know what I mean." To be honest she looked slightly older than Liam, still maybe early twenties, but I knew she had been around a lot longer.

I didn't expect her to give me a straight answer. After continuing to walk for a minute, she finally answered, "I was born in 1953."

This time I stopped in my tracks. "Holy crap, Kimi!" She only paused for a moment to roll her eyes before resuming her pace and expecting me to keep up. "So, what about your family?" I asked her, "other than Kin."

"We stuck around home for a little while," she said. "We got away with looking really young, but we could only pull it off for so long. Our families started asking questions. Dangerous questions. So, we had to leave." She got a weird look in her eye for a moment, then said, "I still remember the look on my mother's face at our funerals." She shook herself from the memory and continued, "We were in Africa for several years, moved to the States about twenty years ago. A lot of the Storm People shift around once people start realizing they're not aging."

"I guess that should make it easier for me to stay in one place," I said. "I don't have many people to hide from."

"I don't know," she gave me a side-long glance, "you might have to hide from Liam."

"Oh no," I groaned.

She seemed to hesitate before saying, "Can I give you a friendly warning?" I gave her a questioning look. "Only because Liam is a good friend." She paused another moment as we climbed over a fallen tree. Once we both landed on the opposite side, I looked at her to finish. "His first love devastated him. I don't want to see him get hurt, that's all."

I couldn't answer. Neither of us said much after that. It seemed like Kimi tried to keep me distracted after that. She even tried racing to keep our pace going faster, but I couldn't possibly keep up with her. I asked her why she wanted me to come with her and she told me I would make the trip bearable. It took us a couple of hours, but we finally started seeing familiar territory.

"We're getting close to the campsite," she said pointing straight ahead of us. I could faintly see the top of the tent through the thick foliage. "Race you to the campsite?"

I threw my mind through the trees and it got there in the split second after she said it. "I win."

She narrowed her eyes at me. "Cheater," she said. Then she scrunched her eyebrows together. "Is Jack still there?"

I swept around a little bit to find him trussed on the ground, "Uncomfortable and miserable as ever. Yes, he's still there."

"Don't let him know what your power is unless absolutely necessary," she said. "It's a good rule of thumb for anyone. Especially when it comes to the Shadow." I nodded my consent before we ran into the campsite.

It had taken us a few hours, but we got there in plenty of time to turn around and go back to the village. Jack grumbled at us when we arrived, understandably upset at having been left so long. He claimed he would've escaped by the time we got back except he wasn't able to get out of the rope. He had a lot of complaining to do.

I gathered what I thought we could use, cramming it into a couple of packs. Kimi adjusted Jack's rope so his hands rested behind his back with a sort of leash connected to them, but his feet remained unfettered.

"Where are we going anyway?" Jack asked grumpily.

"Back to the village," Kimi said. "We'll have to figure out the rest from there."

"What happened to your transporter?" He asked with a smirk. Kimi glared at him. I could swear flames flew out of her eyes.

"Same thing that will happen to you if you ask again," she shot back at him. "We'll be walking."

Jack knew enough to change the subject, but kept complaining anyway. "What if I don't want to go?" Jack taunted. "Maybe I'll just sit down and let you drag me."

Kimi began to retort, but I put a hand on her arm to stop her. "If that be the case," I said gently, stepping closer to him. "There's a little frog I met in the trees who told me she'd be willing to—um—how did she put it—encourage you?"

He flinched away from me but grudgingly agreed.

Kimi and I shared a grin before I took the lead so she could watch the prisoner. Before I turned my back on her, she looked up at her forehead much the way Liam had done before. Unbeknownst to Jack, while I walked ahead of us, Kimi and I spoke mind to mind.

Can you let Sophia know we've got Jack and we're on our way back? She asked.

Sure. It will take me a minute to find her. I kept Kimi in the loop while I whipped through the trees to the village. I quickly found our group sitting outside, brainstorming our next steps. I linked into Sophia's mind to hear her in the middle of a conversation with Jancarlo.

Kimi and I stopped cold at the same time as we listened to the noise on the other end. We stared blankly at the trees in front of us ignoring Jack's questions. The Shadow had infiltrated the base. Jancarlo described how they had appeared just moments ago.

Help is on the way! He yelled through. *I'm sorry, I have to go!*

Chapter TWENTY-SIX

A deafening silence filled our minds when he broke off communication. For a moment I forgot my purpose in contacting Sophia as my mind filled with Liam's face. Instead, Kimi reached out to her.

Sophia, Kimi pushed through. *We're on our way. We'll be there in a matter of hours.*

I'm afraid no matter what we do now, Sophia said, *it will be too late for us to help our people.*

It's never too late! Kimi pushed through forcefully.

I cut off the communication with Sophia, but stayed in Kimi's mind. *I don't understand,* I said. *We've got Wiki trapped here. How did they get into the base?*

There's more than one way in and out of the base, Ella. She told me. The anger over the betrayal seeped into her thoughts. *And Wiki knows them all!*

She tolerated no slowing down after that. She didn't want to chat, loll around or even stop for breaks. She was determined to get us, not only to the village, but out of the jungle.

We had been at it for another few minutes or so when a familiar shimmer started mixing the air in front of me. I prepared my serpent to strike out, thinking it had to be Wiki, when a short, fat, man with a thick, bushy mustache solidified not five feet in front of me.

"Come now, my lovelies, there's no time for formalities." He had a thick Russian accent and a pleasant joviality to his voice.

"Boris!" Kimi exclaimed. I'd never seen her so excited. She yanked on Jack's rope, twisting him around behind her as she ran at the rotund man. She gave him a quick embrace so I didn't bother to probe his mind.

Boris grabbed the back of Jack's shirt as Kimi and I put a hand on each of Boris's shoulders. The familiar sensation of the air shimmering around us took us to the leaders' hut.

Kimi shoved Jack toward his comrades while looking around the cramped space. Aaron, Jack, Roy and Wiki sat shoved up against a wall together. With the rings around their necks, they were helpless to use their powers. They watched us scathingly.

Around the fire in the middle of the room, stood our group. Tony had to hunch over in order to not punch a hole in the roof of the hut. Next to Sophia and Noah, looking as comfortable as possible, stood Namal, Soobos, and Lem. But the only other familiar face I saw made my heart skip a beat.

Liam spoke with Eddie on the edge of the stuffy hut. As soon as I saw him, he gave me a relieved smile. His shoulders dropped as if a huge weight had come off them as he pushed his way through the crowd.

"I heard you guys could use a ride," he said as he threw his arms as wide as he could in the crowded shelter to wrap them around me and Kimi. I was suddenly hyper-aware I hadn't showered or brushed my teeth for days.

However, Kimi shoved away from him. "We've got to get back there, now." She turned to Boris asking, "You can take as many people as you want, right?"

"Ya," he nodded in assent. He turned to Tony in a casual aside, "I transported most of Woodstock once. Very embarrassing, but they were none the wiser." With a straight face the entire time, he turned back to the group. Tony strained against the smirk on his face as Boris said, "I'm ready to go when everyone else is."

"We're ready now," Sophia said loudly. In a lowered voice, she asked Eddie, "Are you sure?"

He bobbed his head. "It's the least I can do."

Sophia gave a short jerk of her head and addressed the group. "Everyone hold on to someone next to you. Don't forget to grab the prisoners." Tony bent over to grab them by their shirts, two in each fist, compelling them onto their feet. Kimi stepped next to him to place a hand on his arm while holding onto Noah's shoulder. The entire group linked together with arms crisscrossing each other.

Soobos and Lem stepped away from Namal to make sure they weren't touching anyone. They would be staying in the village. Namal put one hand on Sophia's shoulder. The other he raised in salutation to Soobos, who returned the gesture.

Liam left his arm around my shoulder, putting his other hand on Eddie's shoulder. I was already situated next to Boris so I put my hand on his shoulder alongside a couple more hands. Once Sophia gave the all-clear the air distorted around us.

We didn't take the same path as we had with Charlotte. I figured Boris could jump further than Charlotte. She had taken us by way of Mexico because she couldn't make long enough jumps to take us through the Caribbean. Either way, we had to circle around to get back to Georgia, but with Boris we got to see some beautiful beaches. At one jump we landed on a little spit of sand surrounded by crystal clear water. The Shadow group cried out because of the lack of shade. Even I must admit, the sudden sunlight stung my eyes after the shady jungle, but I noticed Eddie staring out at the water with a mixture of awe and pure elation. I hoped to find him here someday.

Every time we stopped to take a breath, Kimi would fidget or shift or sigh. Her impatience glared brighter than the sun. But what she expected or wanted to find, I couldn't be sure. She could be eager to get into the fight. Part of her definitely couldn't keep out of a fight. Or she could just be eager to help her brother. I knew she must be anxious to know if he was okay. Either way, she made her desperation to get back painfully obvious to the whole group.

The trip back only took about fifteen minutes, but it still felt like an eternity. When we finally landed topside in Georgia, Kimi turned to Boris. "Take us to the detention area first," she ordered.

Boris nodded, and I wondered how much he knew of our facility. He took us all straight to the detention area, down the hall from where we had held Jack before. Holding cells lined both sides of the walls. Tony quickly dispensed of the four burdens we brought with us. He didn't bother to relieve them of their wrist bonds but threw them unceremoniously into individual cells.

Once rid of the captives, we all turned to Kimi for orders. She asked Boris, "Where is everyone?"

"They're in the arena," he answered gravely.

"Can you tell what's going on?" She asked, trying to get more to work on.

"No," he shook his head. "All I know is where the warm bodies are." He truly looked sorry he couldn't give her more to work with.

"All right," she told us. She looked at Sophia with Namal by her side. "Once we get there, try to direct all of his people to Namal." She addressed the rest of the group, "Whatever you do, don't hurt them. Bring them to Namal."

She nodded to Boris. "Take us in."

Chapter TWENTY-SEVEN

Again, our group linked together. The air shimmered around us. After the now comforting sensation of breathlessness passed, we stood in the workout room looking into the fighting arena.

Just as I had gotten my breath back from the transport, it was knocked out of me again. I couldn't believe the scene before us. The space that had seemed so enormous to me before, now seemed to have every inch occupied. Bodies stirred like a disturbed anthill. Bursts of fire erupted in the air sweeping around people and rock alike. Massive boulders the size of small houses would lift only to fall crushing anyone in their way. I saw people flying through the air as well. Probably the strangest thing I saw was a ball of water floating from person to person. One man had it encircle his head. He tried to drop down to his knees to free himself, but it followed him. Then he tried moving side to side to escape with no luck. Eventually, he slipped into unconsciousness or drowned. I realized the man moving the water sphere would wait until a person passed out then remove the water to slap a metal ring around their neck.

Many of our people lay on the unforgiving stone, but just as many of the Shadow had fallen as well. Jancarlo must have told our people not to hurt the Amazon people because very few of them lay on the floor dead or unconscious.

Without waiting for anyone in our group to tell him what to do, Namal bounded through the door separating the gym and the arena. He knew his part in this, and he would help if it killed him.

Fortunately for him, we were determined not to let it kill him. Our group shot after him unnecessarily. I noticed as we ran into the arena that no one touched Namal. The Shadow thought he was on their side. The South Americans stopped to listen to him. Since he wasn't threatening anyone, the Storm People left him alone as well. He walked through the violent crowd without a single person hurting him.

Many of the indigenous he approached looked shocked to see him there. He talked to them, trying to explain, but it took too long.

"Protect him!" Kimi yelled to Tony, pointing to Namal. Then she launched herself into the brawl, lighting Shadow members on fire from behind.

Liam stopped me before we entered the fray as well, pulling on my arm. "Put on your cap," he said, looking at me very seriously. I jammed it on my head. "Now stay close to me. Let me know if you need me."

I nodded but remembered he couldn't see me. "Okay."

We followed behind the rest of the group. Invisible to everyone but me, Liam grabbed the metal rings to snap them on any Shadow members closest to us.

Most of the Shadow held rings ready, trying to get them on the Storm People. The Storm People had rings of their own. Although not as rough, the metal was just as dark. I wondered momentarily what they were made of.

As I wandered around invisible, I lost track of Liam. No one attacked me, thank goodness, but I struggled with my own incompetence while watching the onslaught around me. I saw Tony and Kin fighting with their backs to each other and stopped for a moment to stare at them in awe. Their arms and legs waved around them at anyone foolish enough to come within their reach. They also swung around each other, one serving as a springboard for the other. The two brawny men seemed to be performing a carefully choreographed dance while lithely dispatching their opponents.

Suddenly, out of nowhere, Neil appeared in the crowd of bodies around me. This was the same man who had seen through Liam's inflections of light at the Shadow base. I was getting seriously sick of this guy. He threw himself at me with a ring in his fist. He probably figured he could overpower me easily, and he noticed no one else could see me. I dove into his mind and reacted to each planned attack before he could make it. I could hear his mounting frustration as every move he decided upon was dodged or deflected. Although more confident with my abilities, I didn't have time to dance around with him forever. Then I remembered the little trick I had pulled with Jack. I compiled all the thoughts, memories, images, sounds, feelings, smells, everything I could think of that I had received when I probed Vincent's mind. Compressing it into one neat little piece of information, I rammed it into Neil's mind.

For one moment his eyes rolled into his head and his jaw went slack. His body jolted with his back arching briefly before he fell to the floor, unconscious. I looked up at Liam who shouldered his way past a few fighters then stood staring at Neil's body. "Ella?" he asked with concern on his face.

"Liam," I said loud enough for him to hear me over the noise, "watch what I can do!" I reached my mind out to the people closest to us pressing the same bit of overpowering information into their minds. One by one, four people around Liam had the same brief seizure then fell to the floor unconscious.

Liam's eyebrows popped up to the top of his head. "Okay," he said. "I changed my mind. I'll follow you. Oh," He pointed at one of the people who had just passed out, "I hope they're not dead, because she's one of ours."

I took off my cap, shaking my head. He grinned at me. Taking some rings out of the hands of the unconscious Shadow members, he snapped them around their own necks.

Together we started moving through the crowd. I would make a Shadow pass out then Liam would lock a ring around their neck. Invisibly, they never saw us coming.

The Storm People they fought would simply shrug and turn their attention to the next foe.

After we had gone through the crowd a little while in this manner, I realized how many people were stuffed in this huge arena. We worked our way forward without any real aim when I came to one of the large boulders dotting the field. I saw someone with dark skin scrambling up the side of it. When I got closer, I recognized Namal.

I looked into his mind to see his plan. From what I could understand, he was trying to get to a better vantage point to address his people. A group of his men helped him climb onto the small mountain.

"What is it?" Liam asked, standing next to me.

"Namal," I said pointing at the elderly man. "He's going to try to talk to his people, but I'm not sure they'll hear or even be willing to listen."

We watched with concern, but still no one touched the old man as he tried to yell from the top of the rock he had scaled. We heard his words, low at first, but we couldn't understand anything he said. He waved his arms around and shook a long stick he had picked up. Those around him quieted to hear the old man. I marveled at the seemingly frail man before us who commanded such an air of authority. He didn't look especially intimidating, just withered with age. But his men all around us took notice of him, pointing him out to others.

His words began to ring clear through the enormous cavern. The dark-skinned indigenous people gradually stopped their actions, unconsciously advancing toward him. Now, the old leader's words got clearer as more of his people would listen. His words began to echo around the massive arena. Everyone stopped to listen. Somehow, everyone could sense the importance. His people wanted to listen. The Shadow must have assumed Namal was there to demand the People of the Storm surrender or something of that nature. The Storm People had no idea what he was saying but must have delighted in the reprieve from fighting. For the first time, I noticed the same rock that had been around Aaron's neck also hung around every one of the Shadow's necks. They could understand what Namal said perfectly.

Suddenly, something he said set off one of the Shadow. I had been waiting for it to happen. "HE LIES!!" echoed from the now quiet crowd. One man stepped forward to yell at Namal. His people didn't like that very much, but he continued on. "He's bewitched by the Storm People!"

"He's an imposter!" shouted a woman next to him. Suddenly multiple Namal's started working their way into the crowd. When one of these apparitions walked by me, I waved my hand through him.

Namal continued speaking to his audience again, but the Shadow had gotten the gist of what he had to say. They would try to stop him now. All at once a man flew into the air. As he rushed toward Namal, I struck out at him and he fell to the ground with a thud. Then others started toward the old man. One by one, I plucked them off before they could come within ten feet of him. To my surprise, the old man took it completely in stride, like this kind of stuff happened to him every day. His men around him, however, were not pleased their revered leader was being attacked. They turned on the Shadow.

Things looked pretty good for a minute there. I thought these guys just might get us out of this situation. Unfortunately, not all the indigenous people could tell the difference between the Shadow and the Storm People, or maybe they were mad enough that it didn't matter anymore. At one point, someone accidentally turned on one of the Storm People. Someone else saw it and turned on the attacker. I wondered how many conflicts had begun simply from a misunderstanding like this.

We had a three-sided war on our hands. Again, the chaos escalated, except this time the indigenous people attacked any unfamiliar face to cross their path. Fire flooded the area as if Namal's people just wanted to burn everyone alive. I couldn't blame them. I was sure they just wanted to go home and end this nightmare. They directed their anger at everyone who had dragged them into this. I stared at Liam sadly, both of us must have thought the same thing.

Finally, Liam said, "We've got to find Jancarlo and see if we can help Namal." As we started forward again, a familiar face streaked past us, slamming into Namal's small mountain. Namal saw it too and yelled orders to his men, of which we didn't understand a word. Liam and I rushed to Kimi's side as she lay in a heap on the cold, stone floor.

Chapter TWENTY-EIGHT

Warm, wet red gushed onto the ground from the back of her head. Her breath came in short, raspy gasps. Liam lifted her up gently, laying her head in his lap. I could see his teeth grinding as he looked between the two of us. He pulled out a healing stone to press it softly to Kimi's head.

As she lay unmoving, her face seemed to shift in my mind, from Kimi to Charlotte then to my mom. Then I began to imagine who might be next. Daisy? Missy? Tony?...Liam?

No! I thought to myself. *We can't keep losing! I can't keep losing!* I'm not sure what my face looked like, but anger grew inside me making my vision go blurry. "No." I said quietly. I rose to my feet while staring at Kimi's still face. "This has gone on too long." I whispered more to myself than anyone else. "This is going to stop."

I looked up at Liam's face with my eyes wide, but I didn't see him. My mind filled with Kimi's still figure. Liam looked at me with a mixture of fear and shock. "Ella, wait," he started to say something, but I swept past him into the crowd.

I looked around at the people fighting. This was ridiculous! What were these people thinking? Kimi had been trying to help everyone! She was the kindest, strongest, smartest person I had ever met. Who did they think they were to keep fighting over her body like this? How dare they think they have the right? The rage inside me grew from a small hot fire to a torrential bonfire.

"This ends now," I whispered again enunciating each syllable. I drew in a great long breath to scream at the top of my lungs as I whipped my serpent through the air. If I could have seen it, I'm sure it would have looked like a helicopter blade slicing through the air at mach speeds. Every person it hit passed out in an instant. Waves of people around me fell to the rock beneath them. Everyone. I wasn't picky. I continued screaming as long as I had breath, which didn't seem long enough to me. As I screamed, my serpent writhed through the air knocking out everyone in the arena. I not only pushed through certain memories I had received from Vincent, I pushed through everything. Everything.

The blaze seared in my chest as I swept through the arena knocking out every living being with a single thought. Some started to run as they saw the wave coming at them, but even the ones with super-speed couldn't outrun me. I could stay with others as they transported so they passed out when they solidified again. I walked on the bodies around me as I headed to the far end of the arena. There was no escape. They had to stand there and take it. I screamed with rage with a final sweep stretching more than two hundred yards to the far corners of the arena.

Once everyone was down, I collapsed to my knees sobbing.

As I knelt on the hard ground with tears pouring from my eyes, I felt a gentle touch on my shoulder. Oh, good, I didn't knock everyone out. I turned and grabbed the person into a bear hug and bawled into their shoulder. Even in my uncontrollable state, I noticed my comforter reminded me more of Vincent than Liam. Small and frail, they smelled earthy, but clean at the same time. They wrapped their arms around me and let me cry.

I thought about the horrible violence I had witnessed. I thought about Charlotte's lifeless body, wrapped in cloth being lowered into the dirt. I could see clearly the enlarged picture of my mother, ringed with red and white flowers at her memorial. It was all we had to mourn. As my tears spilled, I realized I hadn't cried like this since before my mom died. I remembered Daisy telling me that if I wanted to throw things and make a mess, I could. I remembered Missy offering her shoulder for me to cry on. I probably should've taken her up on it, but I resisted. I refused to allow my pain to spill and I didn't even know why. Now that it finally did, I realized it felt good.

Finally, I stopped my sniveling enough to sit back and look at the person soothing me. It was Namal. I should've known. His kind, brown eyes gazed down on me. He pressed his palm to my cheek saying something I didn't understand. He said it with such a peaceful voice that I cracked a pained grin. He grinned back at me and patted my shoulder.

It felt strange to have this man who had known nothing of our people a few weeks ago calmly help me stand up then support me while walking back to Liam and Kimi. This time I tried to step around the bodies littering the floor.

When we got back to Liam, Namal squeezed my hand then touched my cheek lightly. He said something again, and nodding, he walked away from me. I noticed other members of his people waiting for him. They watched me warily and kept their distance.

Though riddled with guilt, a part of me rejoiced at the end of this terrible conflict. I vaguely noticed there were others I hadn't knocked out now running around putting rings around the Shadow's necks. The focus of my thoughts remained with Liam and Kimi.

I turned my attention reluctantly to them. Humiliation washed over me as I wondered what Liam must have thought of my outburst, but I didn't dare look into his mind. I guess seeing Kimi unconscious had been the last straw for even my lengthy temperament.

He stared up at me then graciously took my hand in his. I breathed a small sigh of relief. At least he wasn't afraid of me. I knelt down next to him. He still had Kimi's head in his lap. I slowly looked down at her face again, afraid of how I might react. She looked so peaceful. I guess without all the fighting raging around us, it didn't upset me as much. Whatever the reason, the fire in my chest had extinguished. "Is she going to be okay?" I finally managed to ask.

"I think so," Liam said. "She drained the stone I had, but she's breathing better and she's got a good strong pulse."

"Good," I sighed again. Kimi would be okay.

"That was amazing what you did." Liam looked at me with awe. I had to look away from him, but I enjoyed the warmth of his hand on mine.

"I don't know what came over me," I said as I studied the ground. "Kimi getting hurt…It kind of pushed me over the edge, I think."

"Remind me not to piss you off." Hearing him say it brought back memories of me saying the same thing to Kimi. I looked at him in surprise. He had a mischievous grin and a twinkle in his eye. So he must not think I was crazy. I grinned back at him just as Jancarlo came over to us.

"Convenient rage fit, Ella. We might have to put you on the security team." Jancarlo crouched down next to me smiling broadly.

I returned his smile tentatively. "You're not mad I knocked everyone out?" I asked. "Even the Storm People?"

"Well," he hemmed, "I do wish we had some more help in the task of cleaning up this mess." He looked out over the mass of bodies scattered on the floor of the cavern. "But we did plan for this eventuality." He turned slightly to look behind him. Vincent hovered behind him sheepishly.

I looked up at the old man, but he hesitated to meet my eyes. "You knew this would happen," I said. It wasn't a question, but I struggled not to make it an accusation either.

He briefly glanced up at me. "It was the best possible scenario to play out." He looked back down at his shoes. "Sorry I didn't tell you, but your friend will be okay. In fact, she should be waking up any second."

As we turned our attention back to Kimi, she did, indeed, start to move. We watched her carefully. Her eyes fluttered open. Once they were fully open, she bolted upright but cringed and grabbed her head. "What happened?" she groaned.

Liam smiled at her. "Someone hurt Ella's friend."

Kimi looked up, confused. Then she registered the sea of unconscious bodies around us. She looked at me warily, "What did you do?"

Before I could answer, Jancarlo put his hand on my arm to stop me and said, "That's not important right now." He looked at each of us in turn. "This isn't over."

He stood up, and the three of us followed. I saw who had been left over from my tirade and guilt replaced the anger. I had left Namal with about a dozen of his men. He must have instructed them to help us because they busied themselves putting rings around the Shadows' necks.

Namal's men transported through the mass of bodies. After putting a ring around someone's neck, they would transport the unconscious person into a large group at the entrance to the arena. From there, Boris waited for a large group then would transport them, I supposed, to the holding cells. Namal's men could only transport one person at a time, but they worked hard so they had cleared out about a quarter of the arena in the short time we had been talking.

Gretchen scurried among the wounded. Jancarlo produced a large bag full of healing stones. After we had each taken a couple of stones, he laid the bag on the floor taking a couple out for himself.

"Let's go." He took off into the crowd. As we pressed the stones to most of the Storm People, they opened their eyes relatively quickly. They were confused but oriented themselves enough after a minute to help clean up.

Many of them had other injuries from the attack itself, mostly burns or broken bones. Those we had to use extra power from the stones to heal, but almost everyone returned to our ranks. We lost a few, but they had not been my doing, thank goodness. The few dead were from the initial attack.

As the indigenous people awoke, Namal or one of the others would explain things to them, then they would start helping as well. Liam had the idea to grab one of the translating stones off the Shadow to use for himself, and we all followed suit. It took hours, but as our numbers swelled from the healings it went much faster. We were able to get to everyone before they woke on their own. I wondered how long they would have been out, a day and half like I had been? That couldn't be possible. Jack had woken after just a couple of hours. Of course, I hadn't unleashed my full power on him.

Once everyone was healed and sorted, the South Americans milled uncertainly in the arena. They spoke quietly with each other, wondering what would happen to them now.

Jancarlo pulled Boris aside to request he return the South Americans home in large groups. Gretchen decided to go to the jungle with them so she could work to heal them immediately, leaving Sheila to follow-up with everyone else here at home. With the brown translating stone around my neck, I went to say good-bye to Namal.

I found him talking to Sophia and Jancarlo. When he saw me, he excused himself to greet me. He pulled me into a hug then holding both of my hands in his, he made a small bow. "I don't know if you understood me before when I told you 'thank you.' Everything will be okay because of you. Thank you for being who you are and using your power the way you do. You are an amazing young woman. We owe you our lives." He touched my cheek again then made another small bow.

I didn't know what to say. He was such a brave man and noble leader, but here he was praising me. I felt so unworthy. I struggled with my thoughts, but finally just spit out what I had intended on saying to him, "Thank you for helping us." I wanted to say so much more, but I couldn't find the words.

I inclined my head solemnly to him hoping it would convey all the emotions I felt. When I straightened to face him again, he said, "I pray someday we will see each other again." With that last word, he turned to join his group and they disappeared on the spot.

As I stood there staring at the vacancy, Liam came to stand next to me. "Seems like an amazing man."

I turned to look at him wistfully, "He's the only one in this entire place without any supernatural powers, yet he was easily the most powerful person here."

"I wouldn't say that," he responded with a wink.

I simply turned back to stare at the spot where Namal had bowed to me. "You didn't know him the way I did."

Chapter TWENTY-NINE

It had taken an hour or two, but the Shadow were finally locked up. One by one, we offered them a chance to be healed and leave in peace. Many took the offer. Sheila would heal them, but first she worked on replenishing the stock of healing stones. Her powers weren't as thorough as Gretchen's, but they would still keep someone from death.

Once the Storm People began returning to their somewhat normal lives, Jancarlo ushered me, Liam and others into another meeting. Vincent was already seated at the table again. This time he looked somber.

Kimi and Kin were there along with Tony and Kathryn. As I came in the room, I tried to nod to Tony, who sat on the other side of Kimi, but he turned away from me coolly. Kimi saw the movement, so when I sat down next to her, she leaned over to me. None too quietly, she said, "Don't mind him. He's just upset because you knocked him out."

"Sorry," I muttered half-heartedly in Tony's direction. I heard Liam chuckling next to me.

As the group quieted, Jancarlo motioned to the arena. "This isn't over," he told the group ominously.

"What do you mean?" Tony asked.

"Did anyone notice that Ross wasn't even among those attacking? He isn't done," he said. "This invasion was just a distraction for his real goal." He looked at each person around the table individually as he explained. "Ross was planning on using Wiki to get to him, so that's at least slowed him down, but it won't fully deter him."

I glanced around the table in confusion. Apparently, everyone else knew the details. "What am I missing here?"

Liam opened his mouth to talk, but Jancarlo stopped him, "Ella," he pointed to his head, "I'll show you."

I reached out to his mind to see a scene of a young boy with curly, sandy colored hair, camping with his father. *The father's name was Stanley Ross.* I heard Jancarlo explain. *The boy is Devin Ross. This is a memory of a story I was told. I guess it's how I imagine it happened as I was told it.* A storm raged around them as they raced to tie down the tent. In a brilliant flash of white the father and boy were both struck with lightning at the same time. Miraculously, they both survived.

Soon after they both came around, the boy started setting fire to everything he touched. He was obviously a fire starter. Luckily, the rain put out most of the fires. The father drifted off the ground. He had the power of flight. The rain slowed, but lightning sizzled around them as another man wandered into the campsite. The lightning apparently followed the man. *Nathaniel Van Maren* Jancarlo indicated.

He had a kind, roundish face that reminded me of Liam. His dark brown hair flecked with white hung around his face in long tangles. He had stubble on his chin as if he hadn't shaved for days. He looked to be in his early fifties because I could see gray in his whiskers as well.

The memory continued as Nathaniel tried to talk to the father and son, but lightning raged around them. The pair became even more frightened yelling at Nathaniel to leave. Nathaniel kept asking if they were okay, or if they had been hit by the lightning. Rather than talk to Nathaniel, they took shelter in their meager tent telling him one last time to "go away."

As Nathaniel turned to leave, lightning disintegrated the tent behind him. Again, both father and son were struck, but this time the father didn't wake up. The son wailed in agony at the sight of his father. Nathaniel came back to try to help him, but the boy turned his rage on him. He held up his hands trying to burn him, but the power of fire had been taken from him. Nathaniel heard sirens blare in the distance and knew he couldn't be seen there. "I'm sorry," he said to the boy over the sounds of the storm around them.

He left the boy sobbing bitterly over his father's body. *He always blamed Nathaniel for his father's death. It's what has driven him to gain his powers through other means. It has also spurred repeated attempts on Nathaniel's life. But Nathaniel is one of us and we protect our people.*

The memory ended, so I took it as an invitation to leave Jancarlo's mind. I was a little disoriented when I came out of his mind.

"As you can see," he told me out loud. "Ross is bitter toward Nathaniel. I believe he's going after him. Again."

"What makes it so different this time?" Kin asked. He wasn't asking Jancarlo as much as Vincent.

Jancarlo answered. "This time he has a woman who can shield him and herself from all powers. Her name is Maria." He paused for a moment then continued, "We need to apprehend Ross. According to Ella's intel, he might have something else brewing. We don't know what it could be, so we need Ross. The safety of all our people may depend on it." He paused again to look at the faces in the room. "You'll have to volunteer for this mission. I won't make anyone go. It will be just as dangerous to be around Nathaniel as it will be to detain Ross."

Liam didn't wait half a second before he raised his hand. Jancarlo waved him off quickly. "Yes, Liam. I know you want to go," he said.

I raised my hand, "I'll go too." Liam wouldn't look at me. I thought he might be happy I wanted to come with him, but maybe he didn't want me in danger.

Jancarlo just nodded as everyone around the table willingly volunteered to go as well. I thought maybe Jancarlo would say we didn't need that many people, but he agreed to every offer. "Thank you all. Get your things together. We will leave almost immediately."

At this Kin perked up. "You're going too?" he asked Jancarlo.

"Yes," he nodded, "We'll need everyone we can get."

"Wait a second," Kimi said. She eyed Vincent, "Don't we know if we'll be successful or not?"

Everyone turned to Vincent who took a deep breath to refocus himself. "My vision does not reach that far."

"I don't understand," Kimi pressed.

"At some point during the encounter, my vision stops. I have no idea what the outcome will be." He said very matter-of-factly.

"Does that mean something will happen to you?" I said in concern. Maybe he shouldn't go.

"Possibly," Vincent said looking at me kindly but with sadness. "But if I don't go, I know you won't be successful, so I'm electing to go."

I swear I heard a mouse cough in the deathly silence that followed. We realized the sacrifice Vincent could possibly be making. "Is there any other way?" Tony asked quietly.

Jancarlo shook his head minutely. "Be ready to go in an hour."

"Uh," Vincent raised his hand, "might want to make it half an hour."

Jancarlo nodded then motioned to the rest of us. "You heard him."

We immediately bolted for our rooms. Liam followed me. "Aren't you going to get some stuff together?" I asked him as we whisked down the hall.

"Ella," he grabbed my arm spinning me around to face him. "I'm not sure you should go."

"What are you talking about? Did you miss what I did in the arena?" I waved my hand in the direction of the battle we had just come from. "I can help. I'm not about to let you go and get yourself hurt if I can do something about it."

"I'll be fine," he insisted. "I told you I'm fine around Nathaniel."

"But not necessarily when he's being attacked," I pointed out.

Liam hesitated, avoiding my eyes. "I'll be fine. I just want to know you'll be okay."

"Don't worry," I said. I pulled my cap out of my back pocket to slap it on my head. "I'll be invisible." I took the cap back off so he could see me smile at him then turned to get back to my room. "I don't want anyone to be able to find me by the horrible smell though," I said as he followed me again. "I've got to try to get a quick shower."

When we got back to my room, I thought Liam would head to his own room to get anything he might need. Instead, he asked, "Can I wait for you?"

I shrugged. "If you want." I grabbed some clean clothes to dash into the bathroom. I took the fastest shower I had ever taken in my life. It had to be some kind of world record. Dragging a brush through my hair, I came out of the bathroom to see Liam still sitting at the table in the corner of the room.

"You're fast," he muttered.

"Can't be late," I teased. I didn't have anything to bring. Very few healing stones had been left to use. Jancarlo had a couple of them and would probably use them judiciously. I wrapped my hair up out of my face, stuck my cap in my pocket then turned to Liam to leave.

"Ella," he hesitated. He found a profound interest in something next to my left foot. Something clearly bothered him, but I still couldn't figure out what. I opened my mouth, thinking I would try to say something comforting, but before I could get anything out Liam said, "He's my grandson."

Chapter THIRTY

I was slack jawed, caught completely off guard. Maybe I should have looked into his mind for this. I just stood there like an idiot with my mouth hanging open. I guess I had never considered the idea maybe Liam had another life like Noah. I didn't quite know what to say, so I muttered something stupid like, "Your grandson?"

He was quiet for a minute then asked, "Do you want me to show you?"

Okay, I told myself, *get a grip. He wouldn't be willing to show you if he wanted to keep it quiet.* Before I could start making smart comebacks to myself about him coming clean and really wanting nothing to do with me, I shook it off. I pounced on his brain like that jaguar in the jungle.

When I entered his mind, I saw the same woman I had seen in my dream ages ago in Wyoming. She sat at a mirror brushing her dark red hair around her heart-shaped face. She hummed softly to herself, or maybe to her bulbous belly as she occasionally reached down to touch it. *Sinead,* Liam told me in his mind, *my wife.*

You have to understand, he added quickly. *We got married very young. It was common back then. We were only seventeen.*

The scene quickly shifted to show Liam out in a large field working in the soil. Clouds roiled over his head. Without warning, a bolt of lightning streaked at him from the sky. It connected with the tool in his hand, then his head, throwing him to the ground.

The scene shifted again to show Liam out in the field on a clear day, but he wasn't working the land. He was practicing making things disappear. His hands shook, and he squeezed his eyes shut between each attempt. He seemed disturbed by the ability, but still he worked at it. He must have been working to control it.

The memory shifted again revealing Liam and Sinead deep in an argument. I could make out that he had told her what happened, but I couldn't understand what they said or why they fought. Sinead pointed to her head, yelling. I think she claimed he'd lost his mind. Liam shook his head motioning to the table next to them. Pointing his palm in their direction, the flowers on the table disappeared. Sinead shrieked in fear and ran into the next room. Then the scene shifted again.

Liam pleaded with Sinead while she climbed, with surprising ease despite her pregnant belly, into a wagon pulled by two horses. A man who seemed to be Sinead's father or older brother sat in the wagon with creased brows. He watched sadly as the scene played out. Sinead, pregnant with their first child, was leaving her husband forever. Liam fell to his knees weeping as the wagon filled with those he loved rolled out of sight. I thought the memories would end there, but then Nathaniel Van Maren's face swam in my mind. Clean shaven with his hair shorter and not as wild, he told Liam, *Ciara McCurdy was my mother.*

The memories ended, so I slowly withdrew from Liam's mind. "Ciara McCurdy was the unborn baby I never met," he said. "I found Nathaniel after he had been struck. That was a good half century ago." He shuffled his feet. "I wanted you to know before you see him."

"So," I hemmed, "you're okay with me going now?"

"I'd rather have you where I can keep an eye on you, but I'm torn because I want you to stay safe as well." He narrowed his eyes at me then added, "If you'd rather stay, that's fine too."

"No," I answered quickly, "I want to go now more than ever. If I could've had an extra moment with my mother before she died, I wouldn't hesitate. Family needs to be protected."

We awkwardly left my room together walking back out to the lobby as my head swam in confusion. He wanted me to be safe, but he didn't want me to meet his grandson? I couldn't help but notice the guilty emotions connecting the memories I'd seen to his thoughts of me. I gave my head a small shake to rid myself of the thoughts. I figured I'd worry about it later. For now, we had someone to protect.

We met the others in the lobby. We waited a few minutes, but not the entire half hour. Boris had already begun transporting those who were ready. He agreed to take everyone willing to go to Nathaniel's home in the Northern Rocky Mountains, but he already warned us he didn't know how long he would hang around. He worried about lightning strikes, but he also wasn't sure any of this would affect the Storm People in Russia, his home. I found out he could transport up to five hundred miles at a time by sensing everything around him the way Charlotte had. His senses got stronger with proximity, so Boris agreed to stay nearby to keep track of the group, but he would keep well outside of lightning strike range. He also told Jancarlo that he would bring along any stragglers. As for the rest of us, we would do whatever it took to capture Devin Ross.

Although not as well organized as our group to the Amazon, I took comfort in our numbers. While I had showered, Jancarlo used the time to recruit others to assist, so there was about forty of us. Jancarlo briefed the group before we left. Kimi, Kin and I would keep our invisibility caps ready at all times.

In just a few jumps, we all stood on the side of a mountain with the tips of the Rockies over our heads and the tops of trees spread out around us.

I took in the nobility of the behemoths of earth surrounding us. Our location in Wyoming had been gentle, rolling hills compared to these beasts. I'm not sure what I expected, but just looking around us made me feel small and insignificant. I could make a small giant of a man pass out with a sting from my little serpent, yet it was hard not to feel like a bug that might, at any moment, be squished by a gigantic shoe. The clouds hanging overhead made it feel like a fluffy blanket had been pulled over my head to muffle all outside sound. Even though it was still the warm side of fall, a chill wind bit at my nose and cheeks at this elevation.

Occasionally thunder rumbled in the distance with a small flash of light overhead. It seemed quiet, but we knew it to be the calm before the storm. You've never seen a more jittery group of grown people because of a few dark clouds.

Liam made the group invisible before we left, mostly so we didn't shock anyone if we appeared briefly on a busy roadside somewhere. Once we stood in the mountains, a slight shimmer revealed some of our group. I knew Liam would keep tabs on everyone.

With a nod, Boris disappeared immediately after he dropped us off. He seemed like a nice enough man, but I think his loyalties remained in Russia. I wondered if we would ever find someone as loyal as Charlotte.

Looking around, I didn't see anything at first. I knew we were well away from civilization, but I wasn't sure where. I asked Liam quietly, receiving a quiet response.

"We're in the Rockies on the border of Canada and the States. It's really hard to get here without a transporter." He looked at me knowingly. "Believe me," he said, "I've tried."

He started across the clearing we landed in so we all fell in line behind him. As we got closer, I finally noticed a small building, a little log cabin nestled in the trees. A chimney let out puffs of smoke to let us know someone was home. Not that we had anywhere else to go. Piles of chopped wood lay stacked neatly on one side of the cabin with an ax and wedge for splitting nearby. The cabin sported two hinged cutouts, makeshift windows without the advantage of glass, one on either side of a front door. Apparently, these opened if you needed light or air, but the rest was solid wall, no glass. I guessed Nathaniel didn't want the inconvenience of occasional shattering glass.

Liam rapped his knuckles twice on the unadorned door. We heard no movement inside, but the air around us began to stir. The wind picked up while the clouds swirled ominously. I felt the air crackle above us.

"Nathaniel," Liam called out, "it's me." He didn't elaborate. "We need to talk."

The air around us calmed only slightly. I think the "We need to talk" put Nathaniel on edge. We finally heard the door scrape open a crack to reveal his face. His beard looked like a dead animal on his face. His hair hung almost to his shoulders in dirty clumps. He looked only a few years older than he had been in the two memories I had seen of him. He didn't say anything as he drank in the group surrounding Liam.

Finally, he looked at Liam. "Back so soon?" he said. "You and your friends must have a death wish." His voice was surprisingly smooth for such an unrefined demeanor.

Liam must be used to this kind of attitude because he simply said, "You need to talk to Jancarlo."

Without hesitating, Nathaniel swung the door open to step through. He wore simple jeans and a flannel shirt with a t-shirt underneath. He looked at us all curiously, but his eyes doubled back to me then my scar. After an uncomfortable amount of time staring at me, he glanced over at Liam, who met his eyes for a moment, then he turned back to Jancarlo.

"What can I do for you and the People, Jancarlo?" Nathaniel asked.

"We came to warn you. Ross is headed here again," Jancarlo said flatly.

"Why should I care if Ross is coming here?" Nathaniel retorted. Then in a whisper he added, "He's more than welcome here."

Liam dropped his gaze to the ground. I started to reach out to his mind, but painstakingly pulled back. I would not intrude on his private thoughts.

"I know how you feel about him," Jancarlo said, "but this is bigger than his dispute with you. We need to try to apprehend him."

"Do what you need," Nathaniel waved his hand at Jancarlo then swung his gaze back to me. What was he looking at? "I'll not try to stop him. Now or ever." Then he addressed Liam, "Your friends are under the mistaken impression I want to be saved."

"It doesn't do any good to have you hurt," Liam pleaded gently.

Nathaniel just shook his head at him. "Care to step inside?" The invitation was meant only for Liam. I could tell without touching Nathaniel's mind that he did care for his family.

"Maybe later," Liam said.

Nathaniel just shrugged and shuffled back into his small cabin. Liam watched him with a sad look on his face then turned back to Jancarlo. He glanced at me for only a split second.

Jancarlo turned to Vincent. "How long do we have?" he asked.

"Five minutes. It'll take them longer to get here with their own transportation."

"All right." Jancarlo addressed the group, "Kin and Kimi, get everyone into a position with a view. Liam, we don't need anyone invisible until I tell you. But once they show up, no one can make a sound. Is that clear?"

We split up into two groups. Jancarlo, Vincent, Liam, me, and about half of the group spread out in the trees to the left of the cabin. As we sat down in the trees to wait, Jancarlo whispered to us, "All Ross knows about the attack at the base is what Vincent told him before he left the Shadow. He wasn't always cognizant, so a lot of what he told Ross was up for interpretation. He didn't tell Ross Ella's powers, just that she would be important. He said he only did that so Ella would somehow find her way to the base. He knew he would be rescued along with Ella."

"What did he tell him about the outcome?" Liam whispered urgently.

Jancarlo checked through the trees again then turned back to face Liam. "He only said, 'They will all fall.' Obviously, that's exactly what happened. Everyone fell, literally. Ross didn't care whether the South Americans and Shadow were victorious or not. He just wanted all of the Storm People busy or incapacitated, so he's coming here expecting not an ounce of resistance." He turned to look back down the mountain again as he said, "But he's still coming well-armed."

Kin, Kimi, Tony and the rest of the group were hidden to the right side of the cabin. I figured they already knew all of this. Even spread throughout the trees, I could still see everyone. It wasn't a large group, but hopefully it would be enough.

After a few minutes, Vincent tapped Jancarlo on the shoulder. "It's time."

Chapter THIRTY-ONE

"We need to disappear," Jancarlo said turning to Liam. The air shimmered around us as we all stood up to peer through the trees. I stared at the far side of the cabin, but I could no longer see our people on the other side. The air around us electrified as the flashes overhead became more frequent. Even Nathaniel knew something was going on.

We watched the sun lower. As the last lingering rays disappeared behind the trees, the reason for Jancarlo's anxiety came into view. At first, I thought someone, probably Ross, was carrying a big rock up the hill. Bigger than a beach ball, I watched as it bobbed into sight. Then I noticed that rock sat on top of an even bigger one. As it came into view, to my horror, the larger rock split into three sections—a torso and two arms.

I tried to remember to breathe as I watched the giant humanoid-shaped rock stride up the mountain under its own power. What I took to be simply depressions in the rock were eyes. It had no mouth or nose, but its hands sported well defined fingers. I guessed that he stood at least twelve feet tall, well over the height of the small cabin. For a giant, possibly four or five tons of walking rock, I was surprised by how lightly he strode, but he still left deep depressions with each step.

Behind him, almost unnoticed by everyone, walked Maria Gomez, Eva's sister. She walked cautiously in front of Devin Ross himself, with Eva at his side. Jancarlo wasn't kidding when he said Ross would be well armed.

Jancarlo nudged me so I tore my eyes away from the mountain walking our way. He pointed to his head and I snapped into his mind.

Start trying to find weaknesses. He told me. *See if you can get any information.*

I could only nod. I started to turn back to the small group that approached the little clearing in front of the log cabin, but stopped when I caught a brief glimpse of Liam's frantic eyes. With an ache in the pit of my stomach, I realized Liam would be the first person to throw himself between Nathaniel and the walking landmass coming toward us. I recalled all the things he had done for me then considered the idea that I'd never be able to repay him. I thought of all the questions I had for him. Thinking he might never answer them, I felt a vice close around my heart. I wanted to get to know him much better, but in that moment, I realized we might be out of time.

His eyes bore into mine the moment they met. He reached his hand out to take mine. He squeezed my fingers gently. I cast a side-long glare at Jancarlo when he insisted in my mind, *This is not exactly the time!*

This might be the only time, I retorted. I looked fleetingly at Liam who, like me, had seemed to relax a little.

With renewed determination, I swung my serpent around, launching it into the approaching enemy.

I tried the real people first. I worried about trying to do anything with the rock monstrosity, so I saved him for last. I dove at Maria first, only to find my powers disappeared every time I tried to attack her. I silently huffed in frustration, shaking my head a little bit. All Maria's walls were up, so I moved on to Ross.

He moved cautiously, looking into the trees as he marched behind his two protectors. As soon as I drove forward into his mind, my mind got cut off as well. I pursed my lips, shaking my head again. Liam and Jancarlo watched me silently.

I moved on to Eva. A minor player, but at least I might be able to get information. Sure enough, the way was clear. I nodded my head to the others and penetrated into Eva's mind with savagery. I dug through, trying to find out about Ross's plans. Her powers made the rock bodyguard possible. I pulled out a memory of her animating the giant and prepared to send it to Jancarlo. She had gained a few other powers, but hadn't had much time to explore them yet.

There was also something else. Something very obscure. She had a couple memories of going somewhere far away with Ross. I didn't have time to explore where they went, but I could tell it was a cave deep underground. Ross took her just outside the cave to wait for him while he talked to someone, but he never let her come in. She didn't know who he spoke to, but she knew he got instructions and advice. He claimed to be protecting her by not letting her come into the cave with him, but she wondered if he just didn't completely trust her.

Eva loved Devin Ross deeply. She would do anything to help him take his revenge on Nathaniel. She knew she was exposed to the powers of any of the Storm People that might show up, but she trusted BamBam to watch out for her.

Wait. I stifled a snort as I realized she had named the giant rock walking with them BamBam. Wasn't that some cartoon character? I guess it fit, but it seemed silly enough to make me shake my head. I restrained a giggle as I swallowed that little gem. I couldn't wait to show it to Liam. My joviality vanished when I saw in Eva's mind that BamBam had something up his sleeve. He could throw fire.

Despite the danger posed by BamBam, Eva's thoughts made it clear that Devin Ross was clearly the most powerful enemy. We couldn't use our powers on Ross at all. With his multiple powers, of which Eva knew many, we were sitting ducks if we tried to approach him. Our invisibility hats would stop working around Maria, our fire wouldn't reach him, our rocks would fall to the ground. To top it off, it worked only one way. Ross could use whatever powers he wanted, but we couldn't.

Last, but certainly not least, I focused on BamBam. I remembered what had happened when I tried to enter rock with my powers in Kathryn's office. It didn't feel great, so I wasn't looking forward to it again, but I forged ahead anyway.

At first, it was the same as pressing through anything, but once I tried to stay to see if I could read his mind, my own mind was pulled in a myriad of different directions. The crystalline formations of the rock split my serpent millions of ways. My face compressed as I suppressed a cry. I couldn't stay in his mind, if he had one.

I yanked out to dip into Eva's mind again. I got what I could then turned to Jancarlo to divulge it.

I noticed Kin and Kimi behind us at that moment. I don't know if they had always been there or if they showed up while I looked into Eva's mind, but I included them in the briefing. I sent them the memories slowly so I didn't overwhelm anyone. When I finished, Jancarlo consulted everyone. *Should we have Ella take out Eva so they're at least one person short?*

I could tell he looked to Kin and Kimi as strategists. Kin answered him, *Ross has extra hearing and some sight. He knows someone else is here already, I'm sure. Have Ella take out whoever she can, as soon as she can. We'll pick up the rest of the pieces later.*

I can still use Eva's mind while she's unconscious anyways. I supported Kin's suggestion.

Okay, Jancarlo said as the others nodded. *Do it Ella. Let's tip our hat.*

Chapter THIRTY-TWO

We all watched as Eva's eyes rolled back into her head. She melted to the mountain floor with a graceful thump. Ross stopped as if suddenly frozen in time. Unfortunately, BamBam kept moving under his own power. The rock monster looked at Eva then swept his eyes into the trees. I had vainly hoped he might not be able to move without Eva conscious.

"Eva?" Ross called to her. When she didn't respond, he looked into the trees as well. "Who's there?" He asked maliciously. "Jancarlo? That you?" He looked around some more. "Liam, you must be here!"

Jancarlo squared his shoulders as he stepped from the trees. I reluctantly watched Liam follow him. When the air shimmered around them, Ross's attention snapped to their faces.

"We know what you're doing here," Jancarlo said to him.

"I should've known you two would survive," Ross sneered at them.

Jancarlo gave him a humorless grin, "You have no idea what happened in Georgia, do you?"

"'They will all fall,'" Ross quoted Vincent's words. Although he said them bitterly, he was confident in the meaning.

"And so they did," Jancarlo reported to them, "Everyone."

"At least we killed most of the Storm People then," Ross raised his voice in excitement.

"No," Jancarlo shook his head, "Actually, I think only three or four died."

"Three," Liam corrected him.

Ross couldn't hide his arched eyebrows. "What do you mean? You just said they all fell."

"They did," Jancarlo waved at Eva on the ground, "just like that. But it doesn't mean anyone died, and she's not dead either."

"What did you do to her then?" Ross yelled.

"That's not important." Jancarlo's face looked grave. "What's important is that we want to talk to you." He pointed up at the rock giant. "Call off this attack."

It was Ross's turn to grin at him tauntingly. He knew he had the upper hand. He shook his head barely enough for us to see. "I don't think so," he said. Then he directed his words to the mute giant. "BamBam," he called up to him, "Bring me the man in the cabin!"

At this, the giant stomped forward, no longer treading softly. Suddenly our group attacked from all angles. Ross watched in shock as fire soared at his bodyguard, rocks pummeled him, even plants grew out of the ground around his ankles trying to trip him up. I saw birds swooping down out of the air and a couple of bears staggered out of the forest to try their luck on the rock giant. I guess Noah decided to help after all.

Unfortunately, it only slowed the giant a small amount. He pressed on through the attack, swatting his hands as if moving through a cloud of mosquitos, which the birds somewhat resembled. A few more of our group with speed and strength powers actually attacked BamBam head on. Tony was one of them. I noticed Kimi's face harden when he bounded past her.

As our group tried to attack the rock behemoth, no one noticed the door to the cabin open. Over the tumult, we did notice the sky darken and clouds thicken. I couldn't guess what made Nathaniel upset, Ross attacking him again or the fact that we would all risk our lives to protect him. As lightning struck the tops of trees in the forest nearby, we heard Nathaniel roar, "STOP!"

Everyone stopped to look at him, even BamBam. Lightning struck around everyone. No one dared move. Hair stood on end. Electricity filled the air itself. "Leave them alone!" shouted Nathaniel directing his order at Ross. "I'll go with you."

"Nathaniel," Liam shouted to him over the charge in the air, "that won't help us!"

Nathaniel looked at him sadly. He looked like a man defeated. "But it won't hurt you." Nathaniel looked back at Ross. Without moving a muscle, lightning streaked out of the sky toward him. Maria flinched away, raising her hand to protect her face, but there was no need. The bolt flashed from the sky, but at the last second swerved away to strike the ground next to them. Ross stared at Nathaniel, unmoving. Again and again lightning screamed out of the sky to glance off, as if they had an invisible barrier set to protect only them.

After a minute of this, one of the bolts shot out from the pair into the trees straight at me. I hadn't really been paying attention to anyone around me until someone slammed into me from the side, knocking me to the ground. I closed my eyes and covered my head in protection from the brilliant light. When the lightning ceased, I looked up at my hero as he sunk to the ground. I snapped into Jancarlo's mind. *Vincent took a bolt for me.*

Is he okay? Jancarlo asked.

I don't know. I crawled over to him as silently as I could to feel his neck. *There's a pulse.* I said.

Good. Make sure he's out of harm's way.

I pulled the frail old man into some shrubbery, hoping it wasn't poison ivy or something. He would be covered from view for the time being. It would have to do until this ended.

Finally, Nathaniel gave up. Ross stared at him. "Are you finished?" Ross asked. Without waiting for an answer, he blinked his eyes slowly and a metal staff appeared in front of him. Floating between Maria and himself the staff was split into sections at the top directing the lightning away from them. It looked like a naked umbrella with very short spokes. "You can't touch us," he told Nathaniel. Then looking at Jancarlo he said, "None of you can."

Behind me, I heard both Kin and Kimi say in unison, "We'll see about that." Without another word to each other or anyone else, they both leapt through the trees. I wanted to scream out to them, but my voice clogged my throat as everyone else bolted from the trees as well.

Ross's eyes widened when he saw the numbers. He screamed to BamBam for protection. The giant swept his arm at the group of people. With every swipe of his basketball-sized fist he knocked aside our people, but he still couldn't get to them all. The group as a whole tried to get between the giant and Ross. They forced the giant back to the side of the cabin, but he kept swinging. Tony climbed his back to get at his head, making deep grooves in the rock, but BamBam didn't relent.

Some of our people went for Ross and Maria. Either our people weren't great fighters, which I doubted, or they weren't used to fighting with their fists and without their powers because Ross took on most of them easily.

Jancarlo, Liam and even Nathaniel all entered the fray. Jancarlo had brought a dampening ring, but he only had one. He was bent on getting Ross, no matter what. He fought well, but Ross could do any number of things from throwing fire, anticipating his moves, or dousing him with water then zapping him with small currents of electricity.

Maria was no novice either. She took on Kin and Kimi both. I guess they figured strategically they would have a better chance at Ross if they took down Maria first. Kin had a ring as well, but he wasn't being very successful at putting it on her.

Meanwhile, Liam, Nathaniel and most of the others weren't having any luck with the giant. It was all they could do to keep from getting squashed by the enormous feet. Throwing their powers into the mix only hurt our people. Once a fire flared, BamBam would manipulate it away from himself back at the Storm People. I imagined pounding my fist against a rock. That's how this fight was shaping up.

By this point, I had at least come out of the trees. I wondered if I should help with Ross and Maria. But I would only be helpful there if someone knocked Maria out or got a ring on her. So, I decided I had better help with the giant.

He smashed trees and rocks trying to get people at the same time. Fire snaked its way through the attacking crowd to burn several of our people. I didn't know how I could help or what to do. I couldn't even get through the crowd of people surrounding the giant to even try taking a swing at him. Which would just hurt me anyways.

So, I stepped out of the way and tried to think for a moment. Noah and I had talked about my ability to control animals. I debated bringing more animals to our aid, but abandoned the idea. I didn't want them getting hurt just to protect us. Then I remembered Noah's theory on why I could control animals. Because they didn't have a free will of their own. They did things because it was programmed into their being. I wondered if this rock monster had a free will. I knew it could be a long shot and it would probably hurt, but I dove into the rock again, trying to find a foothold. Or a mind-hold. Or whatever.

Distracted, I had to do a double-take and rip my mind from the rock giant again when I saw her. Tearing through the trees with her brown hair, the same color and texture as mine, streaming behind her. She wore tan cargo pants and a tank top that looked like it used to be white. When she burst into the clearing, she threw her hands toward BamBam and a nearby stream flew through the trees into the monster's face.

"Mom?" I struggled to breathe. Here she was. In front of me. Alive. "What…? How…?" My head began to spin.

"Ella!" My mom began to lower her hands, but the water dropped from BamBam's face, allowing him to see his attackers again. He took a swing at Tony before my mom could turn her attention back to him. "We'll have to catch up later, honey," she said as she swirled the water around BamBam's head.

"Liam," I screamed, pointing at my mom, "cover her."

Liam gave a quick jerk of his head, and my mom disappeared again, as well as several other members of the group. I guess Liam decided that they would have the advantage if BamBam couldn't see any of them.

I attacked the rock again. This time, I tolerated the pain a little longer as I watched BamBam fight with the invisible group around him. Most of them were knocked out, having probably taken a stone fist to their head or body. Jancarlo had a ring around his own neck but continued to fight like a wild animal with Ross. Kin's ring now lay on the ground broken in two, smoldering, but he and Kimi kept up with Maria. Only a few Storm People were left fighting the giant. The animals had disappeared, making me realize Noah must have been knocked out or worse.

Tony sat atop BamBam's shoulders bashing away at his head. His hands dripped red, but he continued to beat at the rock. He made a good-sized dent in the giant's head, but BamBam kept swinging. Liam fought to keep the giant's hands busy so Tony could hack away at the head. Water pooled around BamBam's feet forcing him deep into the earth. It slowed him, but only made him look like he was wading through shallows on a seashore.

I tore my mind away from the devastation around me to focus on staying in the rock's head. I could feel my mind being torn in a million different directions again. I always tried to enter a person's mind through their head. The mind was in the brain, right? But as I tried to stay in the giant's mind, I didn't get pushed out of the rock, but down…into the rock. Instead of resisting the pull, I let it go, just a little. It wasn't like the time I tried to enter inanimate rock. This time the individual pieces of crystalline formations were connected with energy. They worked together. As soon as I let it pull me in, the pain subsided. With relief, I allowed my powers to move through the millions of small spaces making up the walking stone. Once I had filled most of the animated rock, my scar began to burn. I knew in an instant as my mind spread through the rock giant my power needed to detach from me, but I had no idea if I would get it back where it belonged or if I would even stay conscious. I didn't know if anything I was trying would be effective or if I dared attempt it.

As I fought with my indecision, I looked up to see Tony being ripped off the giant's head. BamBam was wading through a small, summoned ocean, so my mom was still out there. Liam must have been out there too because I couldn't see either of them. I figured I should probably do the same thing, so I donned my cap.

While I struggled deciding if what I was trying would even help, BamBam got a lucky swing. My mother popped into view as BamBam caught Liam in the chest. Liam flew into my mom and both of them bounced off the cabin wall to land directly in front of BamBam. My mom recovered slightly to stare up at the monster as he lifted his giant foot to squash them.

I knew I couldn't wait any longer. I wanted more time with my mother. She was here and she was going to stay here. With a thought and a gut-exploding pain, I squeezed my eyes shut and mentally ripped my serpent from my head, launching it fully into BamBam.

I didn't see anything for a moment, but then blinked my eyes open again. I stared down at my mom and Liam with a giant rock foot hovering over them. With a little effort at controlling a new body, I pulled my stone foot back to set it down away from the two.

Liam slowly opened his eyes as I did this. I'm sure he thought that he should be a bloody boot stain by now, but he didn't know I had gained control of the giant. My mom searched the rock giant and everywhere around her in utter bewilderment. I looked around as Nathaniel wobbled to his feet. When he saw me standing over Liam, he ran for me, but my mom yelled at him to stop. I watched patiently, not knowing how to tell them it was me. The giant had no mouth, but I had a feeling I wouldn't be able to talk anyway. I looked around as others of our group came around as well. Nathaniel, Liam and my mom held everyone at bay. I turned to the sound of his voice when Ross stumbled toward me.

"What are you waiting for, BamBam?" he yelled up at me. "I said to kill them all."

I narrowed my eyes at him. If I could've growled, I would've. Then, yes, I pulled a King Kong. I grabbed him around the torso, lifting him up to stare him in the eye. He barked at me to put him down between crying out in pain, but I shook my head. I brought my free hand to wrap around my throat then pointed at Ross.

Liam's smile spread across his face. He ran over to an unconscious Jancarlo to retrieve the ring from his neck. While Ross cursed me, or my host, actually, I set him on the ground locking his arms to his side to keep him still. Liam ran over with the ring in his fist. He was almost to Ross's neck when my grip began to loosen on him. He must have been using his powers to move the actual rock, but he had to put up quite an effort. I fought back, trying again to squeeze my gigantic hands around his body. I had no nerve endings in this body, so I didn't know how tight I held him. Liam, seeing us struggle, darted forward to snap the ring around Ross's neck. As soon as the ring locked in place, my grip overcorrected before I could stop myself. If I had been in my body, my stomach would've churned when I heard the bones crunch. Blood dripped from his mouth. In shock, I yanked both hands away from him. With vacant eyes Devin Ross's mangled body crumpled to the ground.

Chapter THIRTY-THREE

Devin Ross and all his secrets and plans were dead. Liam took the ring off Ross's neck and closed his eyes. Although he had no love for Ross, Liam had a sanctity of life in general. I was just glad I hadn't felt Ross's body in my own hands.

Liam passed the ring to Kin who had Maria pinned on the ground. She sobbed uncontrollably as he put the ring around her neck. She succumbed to her defeat as he zip-tied her hands. She had watched Ross's death in despair, so she knew it would do no good to fight. Kimi administered a healing stone to Jancarlo nearby. I turned back to Liam and my mom, figuring I had better try to explain. I pointed into the trees I had come from. I knew my body lay somewhere nearby, but no one could see it. Everyone watched in confusion.

Suddenly it dawned on my mom. "Ella?" she whispered up at me in astonishment. I nodded vigorously then waved an enormous paw at her. I met with many wide eyes as realization swept through, but our victory stopped short when Kimi cried out to Tony.

Liam and I followed her as she ran past me twenty feet behind the back of the cabin. Tony lay at the base of an enormous boulder jutting out from the mountain. He lay unconscious, looking like he had been rolled in red paint. She screamed for a healing stone with more passion than I had ever heard her muster. Someone used their powers to throw one through the air into her waiting hand. She pressed the stone to the back of his head assuming it would probably be where the most damage had occurred. She only held it there for a moment before Tony's eyes trembled open. He looked up at her with a half-smile, "You look like you've seen a ghost," he slurred.

She shook her head. "Don't scare me like that," she said. She moved to press the stone against his hands, but Liam reached down to stop her.

"Kimi," he said softly, "There are others unconscious as well. We need to heal them."

She stared back at him with flames flashing in her eyes. "Then send Boris for Gretchen. I'm going to heal him."

She turned back to Tony, but he reached up and clutched her wrist himself. "I'll be fine." He moved her hand, still holding the stone, away from himself so Liam could take it from her. "See," he said straining his face into a full grin, "I'm still stronger than you." Although it had seemed like he had moved her hand without any resistance, she had been putting up a fight.

"Stubborn," she sneered at him, but her face melted a little, almost into a smile.

I rolled what I could of my eyes. I left them alone in order to help Liam and Jancarlo any way I could.

I used BamBam's massive hands to scoop up bodies gently and bring them to the cabin to be healed. My mom sat beside them, coaxing water from the stream. Nathaniel only had a couple of cups, so the water floated in balls in front of those recovering. Jancarlo had used the communication rubies to call Boris back. Now Maria was en route to a holding cell to join the other Shadow. They put healing the Shadow on hold long enough to bring Sheila to heal our people in the mountains.

Eventually almost everyone had been healed. We ended up losing four more people. I hadn't known any of them, but it still hurt.

Soon everyone milled around Ross's body as we wondered what to do with it. Jancarlo made the decision to burn it, right there in the mountains.

All of our fire starters, about ten of them, stood shoulder to shoulder and Ross's body went up in flames. The light of the flame danced on the onlookers making everything else around us go black. I'd never seen something burn so swiftly. They incinerated it in a matter of seconds. A pile of ash lay where his body used to be. Then the plant manipulators stepped forward. When they were done, it looked like nothing had happened there at all. No flowers, no marker of any sort remained, just the same sparse grass that grew everywhere else in the small clearing.

Eventually, my mom turned her attention to me. Craning her neck up at me, she said, "This isn't exactly the reunion I envisioned. Do you know if you'll be able to get back into your own body?" I glanced at Liam who listened intently. All I could do was shrug my shoulders.

I turned to where I last remembered watching the fight. I couldn't see my body anywhere. Crap. I had put my cap on before I jumped into BamBam's body.

As I looked around the area bewildered, scratching my head, Liam stepped forward to help. I didn't dare move for fear I would squash myself. Liam eventually found my body in the area and removed the cap. Once we found it, I moved to sit by my body, not really knowing how to start.

Before I could try anything, Kin called out, "Wait! Do we know how that thing will act once she's out of him? I mean, do you think he'll attack us all over again?" They looked to me to see if I had any answers. I shrugged again. I had no idea what he would do.

"Well," Jancarlo said firmly, "He's made of rock and Ross used his rock moving powers on him. Hopefully, if he does attack, I'll be able to hold him off."

"I don't think he will." A familiar voice came from behind them. Vincent shouldered his way through the crowd to talk to us. "Eva has power to animate objects, but she can't always control them. They're suggestible. Like when BamBam stopped when Nathaniel ordered it."

Kin and Jancarlo began discussing what they would say to it, but Liam asked Vincent, "Do you know if Ella will be able to get out of him at all?"

He nodded again. "Yes. It's just an educated guess, mind you, but I think you should be able to get out." He hesitated then said quietly, "But it might be painful. A lot like when you had to come out of my mind. And," he motioned to Liam, "she'll probably need a healing stone applied as well."

I nodded slowly. With that bit of information, I knew what I had to do. But first I had a query for Vincent. I moved forward to kneel in front of him. I pointed to him then made the 'okay' sign with my fingers.

Vincent nodded, allowing the corners of his lips to curl up. His bottom lip quivered slightly as he said, "I'm fine, Ella. Better than fine." His chin trembled from silent joy. "It's all gone. Everything." He gave a short laugh then took a deep contented sigh.

I would've smiled, but I didn't have a mouth, so I settled for a nod. Then I situated myself back on the ground next to my body and steeled myself for what I had to do next. I pointed and Liam sat on the other side of my body with a healing stone. He applied the stone to my forehead and I focused on my mind.

Slowly I withdrew the millions of pieces my mind had been split into. Right again, Vincent. It was painful. Good thing I didn't have a mouth to scream with. Slowly, every inch excruciating pain, I pulled my mind together into a concentrated point. One foot of the giant started moving of its own accord, then the other. I pulled painfully out of the hands to watch them spring to life as well. I moved past the torso swiftly, but when it came to the head, I wasn't sure what to do. I finally resolved to push my mind back to the same spot it resided in my body. I concentrated, screaming internally, as I wrenched my consciousness into one small spot on the giant's forehead. I coiled my own consciousness out of the massive rock. In one stomach-turning strike, I pulled out of the giant completely, launching my mind in the general direction of my own body through the healing stone. Sure enough, everything went black again.

Chapter THIRTY-FOUR

I wondered for a moment if it had worked. Everything was dark. I couldn't be sure where I was, or whose body I was in, for that matter. I remembered everything that had happened and what I had been trying to accomplish. Then the pain hit me again. It stabbed my forehead. I screamed louder as the pain grew.

All at once, I could feel my body underneath me, but it felt like someone had a knife in my head, worming it around just for fun. I sat bolt upright, scratching and digging at my forehead while screaming in agony. I couldn't open my eyes or focus on anything but the pain in my head. I clawed at my head with my fingers, but there was nothing to grab onto at the source of the pain.

I remembered my powers, thinking if I could find something or someone, maybe, that would help it stop. My mind lashed out. Immediately the pain began to subside. I gasped for breath, panting as the pain decreased and ebbed away. I lay back down taking great gulps of air. My mind had been so tightly coiled up to itself that I was practically trying to read my own mind. Stretching away from me helped alleviate the pain.

I caught snippets of my mom's thoughts. I saw her funeral, but from a distant perspective. I saw numerous dark-skinned people surrounding her. I saw her holding a small child while she spoke with a woman. I saw her crying into her pillow at night. I tried to move past her mind and found Liam and others. The onslaught of information became too much for me, just as it had in the beginning, so I started bringing my mind back again. This time I didn't bring it in so snugly.

Eventually I could open my eyes to look around me. In a blur, I looked up at Liam's, Jancarlo's and my mother's faces. They all had their eyebrows smashed together in concern. I briefly wondered if things had gone bad again.

"Mom," I muttered.

With a sigh of relief, her shoulders dropped. Her face relaxed as she whispered, "I'm here. Are you okay?"

"I think so," I said. I pried my eyes open, forcing them to focus more. "Why do I always end up unconscious?" I asked rhetorically.

"You do have a proficiency for blacking out." Liam said. My mom snapped her eyes to his face, and he shied away. Jancarlo gave another sigh of relief then looked to Liam. Liam nodded, so Jancarlo got up to join Kin and Nathaniel who stood in front of the massive rock-man.

My mom fussed over me, even with her own wounds. A few people expressed their relief and gratitude for what I had done. I wasn't sure how to react but tried to be gracious. Soon, they formed a large group to transport back to the base.

Jancarlo told BamBam to stay in the mountains for the time being with Nathaniel to help him. Nathaniel only protested slightly then decided it would be nice to have company that he couldn't hurt.

When the large group had gone with Boris back to the base, it only left Jancarlo, Liam, myself, my mother, Kimi, Tony and Kin outside the little cabin with Nathaniel and BamBam. I sat on the grass recuperating and listening to my mother's story as the others talked around us.

"People were asking questions," she told me. "My boss was the worst of all. He sounded like he had proof that I manipulated the water at the facility. For the last month before I left, every day I went to work I expected someone to show up and haul me away." She squeezed her arm around me. "Someone named Adam came to me, and he could do the same thing that I did—"

"Move water?" I asked.

She nodded. "He told me I had to leave," she continued. "He said I could try to bring you with me, but if anyone found us, they would take you away from me anyway. We decided it was too dangerous for me to take you." She shook her head and tears leaked down her cheeks. "I didn't want to leave you, but I knew Daisy would take better care of you than I could. I couldn't take you on the run with me. What kind of life would that be for you?"

"It's okay, mom." I leaned my head on her shoulder. "You were right to leave." I didn't specify the part about leaving me behind. I still wasn't sure about that bit. "Where did you go?" I asked to change the subject.

Mom wiped her eyes with her other hand. "I've been in a little village in Africa. I still can't pronounce the name of it. It's an entire village of Storm People. Apparently, lightning strikes are so common out there, it's become a way of life. Even some children had powers. I helped bring in water and worked with people to control their powers. But I thought of you every minute. As soon as I heard you had been struck, I came right away."

"Unfortunately," Kimi said, planting herself on my other side, "communication is terrible between our people. No phones, so we rely on transporters to get messages."

"And move people?" I said. "No wonder Wiki felt so used."

Tony sat down next to Kimi, forming a little semi-circle, and Liam stood over everyone. "Maybe," Liam said, "that will improve with you around." He tapped the side of his head.

My mom squeezed me again, and we sat in silence. I watched where clouds broke apart and a myriad of stars could be glimpsed above. Being able to see better in the dark made the twinkling lights in the sky shine that much more brilliant. I couldn't help but wonder what it would look like without cloud cover. I had never been much of an outdoorsy person, but I thought it would be fun to spend a weekend in a little cabin just like this. Without the imminent threat of danger or a lightning strike, of course.

Nathaniel wandered over to Jancarlo who stood nearby to oversee everyone getting back to the base safely.

He produced the broken metal ring in his fist. "So," he asked Jancarlo, "Is this the product I've been waiting to hear about?"

Jancarlo nodded. "Don't worry," he said with a grin. "We have lots more at the base and we know how to use them now."

A curious calm crossed Nathaniel's face as he nodded and stared at the broken ring. Not wanting to intrude on his thoughts I turned to Liam who also heard the exchange. He knew my question without me voicing it. "We've been trying to figure out how to void Nathaniel's powers ever since he got struck. It took a few decades, but we finally figured out what kind of metal to make the rings out of a few years ago. It's an alloy only a metal mover and a fire starter can produce together. It wasn't until you figured out how to remove the rings that they were a viable option for Nathaniel."

Jancarlo told us Boris was ready to take us back. As we stood to leave, someone came out of the trees behind us. We turned to see Noah. I breathed a sigh of relief knowing he would indeed be going back to his family like he wanted. However, Kin gave him a questioning look. "I thought you already went back with the big group."

Noah shook his head, pointing a thumb back into the trees. "Just finishing up with some of the animals that helped out. I found this on the tree behind me." He held his other hand open to Kin. In his palm lay what looked to me like a diamond shaped mirror. I didn't really think much of the revelation until he continued, "It might sound crazy, but I think I saw Eva in it for a second."

We all sobered up at this. Kin grabbed the mirror from Noah to inspect it closely. The rest of us looked around into the forest while Kimi darted into the trees Noah had come from. The look in everyone's eyes confirmed no one knew where Eva had gone. She must have woken up during the fight then disappeared without anyone noticing.

Wondering if Eva had left some kind of clue there, I tried to find the final resting place of Devin Ross unsuccessfully. Our growers had done their job well. I searched the spot where I thought Eva had been a couple of hours ago, but there was nothing. I reached my mind out to the forest surrounding us but didn't find any minds other than Kimi's to touch. If Eva was out there, she was long gone.

We all came to the same conclusion. Eva had disappeared. Jancarlo stepped up to Kin, taking the small mirror in his own hand. He glanced at Kin who shook his head. Kimi stepped back out of the trees shaking her head slightly as well with her lips pressed thin. Jancarlo nodded slowly. He turned the mirror over in his palm then softly said, "She has nowhere to go."

Chapter THIRTY-FIVE

Three days later, I ducked a wicked right from Kimi. Then a left. Then a front kick.

"Stop ducking!" She barked as she danced around me. "Try fighting back for once!"

"Why would I do that?" I countered with a smirk. "I'm not crazy!"

Through narrowed eyes, she attacked me with a series of spinning kicks, but I dodged them just as easily as I had the last sequence. With a final yell, she threw her wrapped hands in the air. "I give up!" she exclaimed. "You've effectively worn me out!"

But she forgot, as usual, I could hear her plans. I shook my head at her. "Not falling for it. You're planning a surprise attack when my guard is down." I kept my hands up in a guarding stance. She hoped for a backhand then wrap around for a headlock. "You try it and I'll knock you out," I threatened. She knew I meant it.

"All right," she said, "But you know through my thoughts that I'm not about to let you leave here until you

FIGHT BACK!" she yelled the last part while she launched a new attack.

I knew she was right. She wouldn't let me leave until I proved that I could stand my own. I finally blocked her right hook and followed through with a punch to her body. She blocked me back and tried to follow through with a spinning hook kick but wasn't able to execute it. Halfway through her spin, I kicked the back of her knee, dropping her to the floor. I wrapped my arms around her neck in a would-be choke.

I could sense the spreading grin on her face. "Finally!" She patted my arm and I knew we were done.

Unwrapping my hands, I said, "I guess I can't put off seeing Jancarlo any longer."

"Uh huh." She lifted an eyebrow at me. "Is it really Jancarlo you're afraid of?"

Kimi was right. Jancarlo had been in serious discussions with my mother since morning. They were trying to figure out what the two of us would do for the future. The People of the Storm could manipulate a situation to get me back to my aunt and cousin, and I could continue my normal boring life with a few major differences. Or my mom and I could stay here, work on my schooling in a home-study environment and mom could help out where and when needed. I wanted to help too, but my mom would rather I focus on school. I got the distinct impression that she knew exactly what I wanted to do to help and she didn't like it.

I went back to my room and got cleaned up. Liam had offered a nice quiet dinner for tonight, inviting mom as well. Of course, mom hadn't given a direct answer when asked about it, and Liam hadn't been around enough for me to figure out what was going on. I had time to have a conversation with Jancarlo, then hunt down Liam.

Heading toward our newly installed front desk, I saw Kathryn coming down the hall. I called out to her, "Glad to see you're up." We had worked together again earlier in the morning making more communication devices. Although she didn't have as strong a reaction as the first time we worked together, it still unnerved me to watch. Thankfully, Gretchen had also been present to help her recover faster.

She grinned at me. "I think I'm getting a better handle on how to manipulate your powers," she said. "Tomorrow should be even better."

Kathryn and I had been set the task of creating an entire communication system for the base. Jancarlo claimed he needed something other than people running around to relay messages. I could see why. He had been all too reliant on Wiki in the past. Plus, we needed more reliable contact with the People of the Storm around the world. That way if another problem arose like the recent ones, we could get more help, quicker.

Walking into the lobby, I spotted Nathaniel sitting behind a large, granite desk. I waved. "How's your new position treating you?" I asked cheerfully. With the ring around his neck, he presented no danger anymore, so he had decided on a position with as little excitement as possible. He also enjoyed spending time with his grandfather.

"Nice and quiet." He smiled in return. He laced his fingers behind his head leaning back in his chair. "Just the way I like it."

"Glad you're enjoying it. Have you seen Liam?" After all, the point of having this desk was to make it easier to locate people.

Nathaniel looked down at the desk. A few gems glittered, embedded in the granite; the beginnings of the communications system. But Nathaniel wasn't looking at the gems. He glanced off to the sides checking the hallways then looked back up at me. He gave a quick jerk of his chin to the wall behind me, then spun his chair away from me.

It only took me a moment to realize what was going on. I turned to see Liam materialize behind me. Without a word, he crooked a finger at me and slid behind a corner. If I hadn't known Liam that well, I wouldn't have followed. Okay, maybe I would have.

I ducked around the corner to be wrapped up in his arms almost immediately. "Where've you been?" I asked accusingly.

"Here and there," he said, then nodded toward the opposite corner, "and there, and there, and there." He nodded at random spots around us while keeping his arms around my waist.

"Are you avoiding me?"

"You? Never."

"My mom?"

He scrunched up his face as if trying to hide the fact that he'd just bitten into a lemon.

"Are you at least coming with me to see Jancarlo?" I asked.

He sighed. "I think it's better if I don't."

"Well," I shrugged, "they won't have to see you."

Liam let his hands slide from my sides. He squeezed one of my hands and said, "Call me a coward, but there are some things even I'm not willing to face. Besides, I know you can take them." He winked at me.

"Fine," I said. "I'll do it myself." I spun around and marched away from him. Now, I just wanted to get this over with.

When I entered Jancarlo's office, he sat shuffling papers around his desk and peeking underneath them. "Looking for something, chief?" I asked casually.

"Haven't seen that mirror since yesterday," he said with concern on his face. I knew he looked into the mirror often, hoping to see Eva in it again. He wanted to find her, if for no other reason than to offer to heal her. "Maybe Kin's done something with it," he said more to himself than to me. "Sorry," he said, finally abandoning his search. "We have some business, don't we?" He motioned for me to take a seat. That's when I noticed my mother sitting in the other chair.

"Ella," Jancarlo started, "have you recovered completely from these past events?"

I nodded. I felt more like myself than I had in a couple years. I felt alive and excited for the future. However, I wasn't the one in charge of it.

"Good," Jancarlo continued. "After some deliberation, your mother and I have decided on a compromise for arrangements for your future."

My mother had never been exactly strict with me, but I'd never really had a boyfriend before. Especially one that was roughly three times my mother's age. I didn't say anything.

"We're going to stay here," my mom finally spoke. "I could do a lot of good in Africa, but I'd rather be here with you. I'm not going to make you go back to Daisy and Missy. They'll be better off not getting pulled into this world."

I nodded. At least my worst fear of her making me leave was gone. Now what?

"And?" I asked.

"And what?" my mom said. "You wanted to stay here, didn't you?"

"Yes," I said, "but what about me helping bring in new people? Did you decide if I could do that?" I had dug through Jancarlo's mind previously so I knew he wanted me to go see any younger people who were struck by lightning. Liam usually did it, and I wanted to help him. My mother wasn't so keen on the idea of us, how did she put it, "galivanting around the world" together.

"Well," Jancarlo spread his hands. "I have no problem asking for your help every once in a while."

"You'll have to keep up your schoolwork," my mom added quickly as my smile spread.

"And you'll have a chaperone."

When Jancarlo added that last bit, my grin faltered. "A chaperone?" I asked tentatively.

"You're only 16, Ella," my mom said.

"Liam's, like, 115 years old. That's not good enough?"

"You can't have it both ways, Ella," my mom said. "Either he's too old for you to date, or he's too young for you both to travel together. Which is it?"

She had a point. Liam's body and mind hadn't aged past 19 yet, so if I was going to date him, I had to allow everyone else to see him like that.

"Okay," I agreed. "Who did you have in mind?"

"Well," Jancarlo hemmed, "we would need someone who looks more of an adult than Liam—"

"Even though he's decades older than anyone here." I interjected.

"Yes, well," he continued. "Gretchen always played the adult role for him, so he's used to it. Plus, if you go see younger people, we thought it would also be good to have a motherly presence."

I couldn't help the smile spreading on my face. Even for all my bad acting, shifting both Jancarlo's and my mom's minds into position hadn't been difficult. It was so good to have my mom back, but I wasn't about to give up either of the people I cared for. When I met her eyes with a grin, she sunk against the back of her chair in defeat.

"This is what you wanted," she said. "Wasn't it?"

I smiled wider. "Welcome to the People of the Storm."

The action continues in…

People of the storm 2

Note to Readers!

I hope you are enjoying the adventures as I enjoy writing them! Although I love to write and create these stories, being an independent author is hard. I don't have teams of people ghost-writing, editing, formatting and marketing for me. I do it all on my own, so my only support comes from readers like you! Thank you for supporting me and my craft.

Another way you can support a lowly indie author like myself is to leave me a review. Feel free to use the link to let others know how much you enjoyed the story and you can pick up the next book at the same time! Enjoy the adventure!!

You can also sign up for my newsletter to be the first to hear about sales, signing events and new books! Sign up at avonoa.com, hrbcollotzi.com, or peopleofthestorm.com.

Or follow me on social media…
Facebook @hrbcollotzi
Instagram @hrbcolloti

People of the storm 2